The *Grandfather Rastin* Mysteries

The

Grandfather Rastin

Mysteries

LLOYD BIGGLE, JR.

Edited by

Kenneth Biggle

and Donna Biggle Emerson

Crippen & Landru Publishers
Norfolk, Virginia
2007

Cover painting by Barbara Mitchell

Lost Classics series design by Deborah Miller

Crippen & Landru logo by Eric D. Greene
Lost Classics logo by Eric D. Greene, adapted from a drawing
by Ike Morgan, ca. 1895

ISBN: 978-1-932009-56-6 (cloth edition)
ISBN: 978-1-932009-57-4 (trade softcover edition)

FIRST EDITION

Crippen & Landru Publishers
P.O. Box 9315
Norfolk, VA 23505
USA

e-mail: info@crippenlandru.com
web: www.crippenlandru.com

CONTENTS

INTRODUCTION

When we were kids, the fun part of the Grandfather Rastin stories were the mysteries themselves. They were the first Lloyd Biggle, Jr. stories we remember reading. In fact, we were the proofreaders of some of the galleys – a nickel for each mistake (we never collected). Years have allowed us a new appreciation: for the sense of place and for the characters created, especially that of Grandfather Rastin. As we completed the electronic text work on the stories, we thought readers might wonder about their source.

Ypsilanti, Michigan, where Lloyd Biggle, Jr. moved and lived with his family most of his adult life, is not Borgville. Henry Ford and World War II created the factory atmosphere that still permeates the town and the academics carved out their niches at Eastern Michigan University, and the University of Michigan.

However, our father comes from a farm background, with aunts and uncles running dairy and crop farms in rural Iowa and Wisconsin. He spent summers with these relatives and also, as an adult, enjoyed visiting them as well as friends in small towns around Michigan. Perhaps these memories came together to emerge as Borgville.

Lloyd Biggle, Jr. had the unique opportunity of knowing both his grandfather and great-grandfather. The Woodrings have a history of strong personalities. They also championed unpopular causes in a very forthright manner. Great-Grandfather Woodring began the Temperance Society in Waterloo, Iowa and relative Harry Hines Woodring was FDR's Secretary of War, adamantly opposed to the U.S. entry into World War II. Our memories of both of our grandparents, our father's parents, are of plainspoken people, verging on the cantankerous.

One must be cautious, however, in ascribing characters and events straight out to real-life influences in an author's past. Father was quite amused at a letter he received, from a reader of the Grandfather Rastin stories, who took him to task for Grandfather's stereotypical response to the local librarian in a story. Our father was quick to point out to the reader that the opinion expressed was Grandfather's and certainly not his own (especially with a daughter who had already chosen that particular career!).

Places and people. ... Lloyd Biggle, Jr. had an almost photographic memory of past events and personalities. He believed this to be only raw material. It is how an author blends and molds this material that makes writing an art form. The Grandfather Rastin stories afforded him a chance to revisit and rewrite memories and to create out of nostalgia, the strong sense of character and place that have become Borgville and Grandfather Rastin.

Kenneth Lloyd Biggle
Donna Biggle Emerson

A NOTE ON THE PREFACES

Lloyd Biggle, Jr. wrote prefaces to eight of the Grandfather Rastin stories before he died in September 2002. His purpose for the prefaces, in his words, was "... to provide background material on the setting and characters and also to lead into the stories they precede." They are printed as he wrote them and, as the preface contents are as unique as his stories, no attempt has been made to provide prefaces to the remaining stories.

THE KNAVE OF HEARTS

This is to introduce my Grandfather William Rastin, lifelong resident, first citizen, and the most prominent landmark of the village of Borgville, Michigan, population 812. Grandfather also is an octogenarian, but the only person I know who calls him that is Miss Emily Borg, our high school history teacher and Borgville's resident intellectual.

Because of this peculiar hobby Grandfather has, some people refer to him as a private detective, which is a very effective way to get him riled. Dr. Alford, who is Professor of Psychology at Wiston College, claims that Grandfather doesn't like being called a private detective because he isn't one – he's really a philosopher. I guess he is, and he's also a connoisseur, as Miss Borg would put it, of quirks of human nature and quaint facts about anything at all.

It's true that Grandfather hasn't much in common with the famous sleuths and private eyes and detectives and such that you read about. They solve one murder after another, and they can't go on a business trip or a vacation or even a Sunday drive without stumbling over a corpse. We don't often have a murder in Borgville, and when Grandfather wants to try his hand at that kind of crime he has to go somewhere else, usually to Wiston, which is the seat of Borg County's government and also its iniquity.

Some people think the greatest mystery of all is how we're able to have any mysteries in Borgville. There always are a dozen people who know more about your business than you do yourself, and Maggie Cross, who is an invalid, writes up the Borgville news for the Borg County Gazette *without ever leaving her bedroom. It even has been rumored that a representative of the U.S. Bureau of the Census did the 1970 Borgville census in five minutes while having a beer at Bailey's Bar. The government never officially confirmed that, but it hasn't denied it, either.*

When we do have a mystery, it's likely to be a lot more complicated than the murders you read about. As Grandfather says himself, at a given moment relatively few people want someone dead, but anyone at all might be tempted to steal, or perpetrate a swindle, or just do something stupid.

And in a real rip snorting humdinger of a Borgville mystery, you'll probably find various people doing all of that …

This mystery we had last August was so complicated that you have a hard time finding two people who'll agree as to what the mystery was. Sheriff Pilkins says it was the three burglaries and he solved them. Doc Beyers's wife thinks it was why Sally Carter decided to get married, and Grandfather Rastin says the reason a woman decides to do anything has got to be the ultimate mystery. By the time Harold Grant and that city slicker Charlie Griswold got mixed up in it, this turned out to be maybe the most complicated mystery Borgville ever had.

Though Grandfather is past eighty, he still likes to take a long evening walk, and sometimes I go along. We were headed out toward Borgville Park, Grandfather grumbling about some program he'd seen on TV and me not paying much attention because I was counting up the number of days left before school would start, and just as we turned onto Main Street we saw Harold Grant being tossed out of Bailey's Bar.

It was only seven o'clock, but Harold was already too drunk to walk, which should give you an idea of how fast he can drink. Around Borgville Harold is known as a serious drinker, and if that means what I think it does, it's a very good way to describe him. Mr. Bailey propped him up against a lamp post and went back inside, and Grandfather and I started past him, looking the other way.

Harold reached out and grabbed Grandfather's arm. "It don worry me none," he said. "This guy, he don worry me. She'll be my girl again. All I gotta do is whistle."

He whistled.

Grandfather stopped and looked at him, scratching his head. Before he could say anything, Sheriff Pilkins drove past. He stopped and got out of his patrol car to take a look at Harold.

"Where's your car?" he asked him.

Harold drew a circle in the air with one finger. "There," he said.

"Will you drive him home, Johnny?" the sheriff asked me.

"Glad to," I said. "But if I'm going to use his car, I'll need better directions than that."

"It'll be around here somewhere," the sheriff said.

We found Harold's convertible parked around the corner, and I took his keys and drove it back to Bailey's, and the three of us poured Harold into the back seat.

"What's the news about Sally Carter?" Grandfather asked the sheriff.

"I haven't heard any," Sheriff Pilkins said, "Why do you ask?"

"Something Harold said. Of course he's not what you'd call rational, but still – drive him home, Johnny. I'll wait for you here." As I drove off, I saw Grandfather going into Bailey's.

Harold Grant lives with his aunt, Mrs. Rollins, and her house is just three blocks from Bailey's, so it didn't take long to get him home. It didn't take long to get him into the house, either, because Mrs. Rollins handled him as if she'd had experience. I gave her the car keys and walked back to Bailey's. Grandfather was waiting for me. I asked him if he'd found out anything, and he said Sally Carter was a grown woman and what she did was her own business.

This may have been true when he said it, but by the next morning it was public property, mostly on account of things Harold Grant had said in Bailey's Bar. Our telephone started ringing early, with various women wanting to know what Mom knew about it, and that afternoon Doc Beyers's wife stopped by to see Grandfather. She was too excited to sit down. She stood in the middle of the parlor and waved her arms.

"Something has got to be done about this," she said.

"Have a chair," Grandfather said. He hates to see a stout woman standing. He says watching her hold all that weight up makes him feel tired.

"We can't let Sally make such a terrible mistake," Mrs. Beyers said.

"What mistake?" Grandfather asked.

"Haven't you heard? She's got herself involved with that book salesman that's been hanging around town. He's been going to see her almost every evening – and without a chaperone!"

"Have a chair," Grandfather said. "Sally Carter is a little past the age for chaperones."

"She won't be twenty-nine until next month," Mrs. Beyers said. "And no woman is *ever* past the age for chaperones."

"Have a chair," Grandfather said.

Mrs. Beyers sat down. "Look here," she said. "Sally Carter and Harold Grant were meant for each other. They had some bad breaks, but I know they'd be happy together if they'd just make up their minds to get married. And now this book peddler is going to ruin everything."

"I always figured Sally was derned lucky she didn't marry Harold," Grandfather said.

Mrs. Beyers looked shocked. "Bill Rastin! You know that isn't true. This is just one of those terrible mistakes life is always making. Harold started drinking because Sally wouldn't marry him, and then she wouldn't marry him because he was drinking. It's just a tragic misunderstanding."

"It all depends on how you look at it," Grandfather said.

I couldn't see that it made much difference how you looked at it. Sally Carter and Harold Grant were high school sweethearts, and when they graduated everyone thought their wedding day was as inevitable as Christmas. They decided to wait until Harold finished college, and he flunked out. Then they decided to wait until he got a steady job, and before that happened Sally's ma had a stroke and Sally had to nurse her night and day, and that went on for three years. Then Mrs. Carter died, and after the funeral Sally looked around and found Harold had lost his job – lost that one and six more like it – and he was a lot more serious about drinking than he was about Sally. The fact that Sally had been putting on weight could have had something to do with it. Either way it added up to a blighted romance.

"This book salesman may be a solid kind of fellow," Grandfather said. "Maybe he aims to marry Sally."

"I doubt it," Mrs. Beyers said. "And so do you. It's never safe to take up with a stranger, and with Sally pining away for Harold –"

Grandfather grinned. "Pining away?"

"I, guess you haven't seen her lately. She's lost a lot of weight, and that in spite of the fact that she's the best cook in Borgville. The trouble is, Harold won't take this peddler seriously."

"I'll think about it," Grandfather said.

"Do that," Mrs. Beyers said. She went to the kitchen to talk with Mom, and Grandfather scratched his head and looked at me.

"What do you know about this fellow Griswold?" he asked.

"Just about what you know," I said.

Charlie Griswold had come to Borgville a month before. He was selling sets of encyclopedias, and most of the families in town bought from him. When he finished with the town people he started calling on the farmers, and from what I heard he still was doing well. He'd rented a room from Ada Smith, over on Oak Street, and he'd got to know everyone in town, and most people liked him. He had a smile for everyone, and he enjoyed talking to folks, and if you didn't mind the way he mashed your fingers shaking hands, he was easy to get along with.

"Griswold seems to be a steady worker," Grandfather said, "and I notice he doesn't waste any time in Bailey's. How old would you say he is? Thirty-five?"

I hadn't any idea.

"I don't see that it's anything to get excited about," Grandfather said. "Just because Sally lives alone out on the edge of town, these women think there's something sneaky about Griswold calling on her. On the other hand, we don't know anything about Griswold, and he may not be up to any good. I'll have to think about it."

That night someone broke into Mr. Gregory's Star Restaurant and emptied the cash register. There wasn't much money in it – only six dollars and sixty-seven cents in change, and it was insured. But we don't often have a burglar working in Borgville, and it caused quite a stir.

Sheriff Pilkins came around to talk to Grandfather about it. "Hear about the Star Restaurant?" he asked.

Grandfather said testily, "Since I'm not deaf –"

"Got any ideas?"

"No," Grandfather said. "Should I have?"

"It could have been kids, I suppose. If it wasn't, I figure it was a stranger. Anyone from around here would know Gregory puts most of the restaurant money in the night deposit. There's only one stranger in Borgville. What do you think?"

"If you mean this fellow Griswold, I'd say he's been making too much money selling books to bother with burglaries at six bucks a crack."

"He didn't know there'd only be six bucks there," the sheriff said. "He eats at the restaurant when Sally Carter isn't feeding him, and Gregory says he was there three times yesterday. He had breakfast there, and in the afternoon and again late in the evening he stopped in for coffee. Could be he was casing the place."

"Could be," Grandfather agreed. "How are you going to prove it?"

"I don't know. Ada Smith says she didn't hear him go out during the night, but you know how deaf she is. If he fell down the stairs she'd never know it. Well, he didn't get much, and he'll know better than to try it again."

That night someone broke into Snubbs's Hardware Store and got eleven dollars from the cash register. And the next night Dimmit's Grocery was took for seventeen dollars. The sheriff moved into town with four deputies, and he even had a fellow in from the State Police Post at Wiston to look for fingerprints.

For the next few days no one talked about anything but the burglaries, and when Mrs. Beyers came over to see Grandfather on Friday he'd forgotten all about Sally Carter.

"Well, what are you going to do about it?" she asked

"That's Pilkins's job," Grandfather said, thinking she meant the burglaries.

"Pilkins, nothing," Mrs. Beyers said. "I asked him to help, and he said it was none of his business who courted Sally Carter. For two cents I'd run for sheriff myself. What are you going to do? You said you'd help."

"I didn't," Grandfather said. "I said I'd think about it. I'm still thinking."

She worked on him, but that's as much as he would say. After she left he went up to his room, and I heard his rocking chair start up. That's what he does when he has a problem – he rocks on it. He rocked most of the afternoon on that one, and I didn't see him again until supper time, when I started out to the kitchen to see what Mom was fixing.

"I won't be here for supper," I heard him say to Mom as I came down the hallway. I don't know what she said, or if she said anything at all, because Grandfather walked out of the kitchen and I nearly fainted. He had on his Sunday suit, and a white shirt, and the polka dot bow tie I gave him for Christmas. He nodded at me as he went by, and he was out the front door before I could get my mouth closed.

In the kitchen, I found Mom still shaking her head. "I guess it's a good thing he hasn't got any hair," she said. "He'd of curled it. Now what do you suppose he's up to?"

"I'd better have a look," I said. She called me back twice as I went out the door. If she'd meant it she would have called four times and come out on the porch after me, so I didn't even slow down. Grandfather was out of sight when I hit the sidewalk, but I didn't need any bloodhounds to tell me where he was headed. I took the alleys straight across town, circled around through Simmond's wood lot, and came out behind Sally Carter's house.

Mr. Griswold was sitting at the picnic table in the back yard. He was a big fellow with a hefty build, and he had curly hair and a neat little mustache. I thought he was pretty good looking. Probably it was the way he dressed that got Mrs. Beyers down on him so – he had on one of those funny-colored sport shirts that no Borgville man would dare to wear in public.

Sally Carter came out of the house a minute later, carrying a tray, and she went to work at the outdoor fireplace. She'd lost a lot of weight since I'd seen her last. I'd forgotten how pretty she was before she got fat. She had on a white dress and a little blue apron, and she really looked nice.

I was afraid there'd be fireworks when Grandfather came busting in on Mr. Griswold's date, but nothing much happened. Mr. Griswold shook hands with Grandfather, and the two of them talked while Sally worked on the food, and then they all sat down to eat.

Mr. Griswold took his eating seriously. Grandfather and Sally did some talking along the way, but he didn't say a thing except to ask them to pass the barbecued chicken again, or the hot rolls, or the potato salad, or the meat balls, and as a result he was running about two laps ahead when he got down to the dessert. I noticed that there were three kinds of pie on the table, and Mr. Griswold had a good sample of all three. Then he shook Grandfather's hand again, and said something to Sally, and left. That was as much as I could stand on an empty stomach. I ducked out and ran all the way home.

Mrs. Golden telephoned while I was eating supper. She said she'd seen Grandfather, all dressed up fit to kill, heading toward Sally Carter's house, and she wanted to know what he was doing. Mom told her to call back if she found out. Then Mrs. Pobloch called, and Maggie Cross, and Elizabeth Peterson, and when everyone in town seemed to be waiting in line for our number we stopped answering the phone.

Mom wanted to know if Sally and Mr. Griswold had acted romantic. I told her Mr. Griswold hadn't acted anything but hungry, and if that bothered Sally she'd kept it to herself.

Mom shook her head. "Sally just doesn't have any luck. I feel sorry for her."

When I finished eating, we went out on the porch to wait for Grandfather. He wasn't in sight, but Harold Grant had driven up in front of our house and parked, if you want to call it that, with one wheel right in the middle of Mom's big bed of moss roses. He stayed in his car, and Mom and I stayed on the porch, and about fifteen minutes later Grandfather came walking up the street.

Harold got out of his car and staggered up the sidewalk to meet him. He didn't say anything. He took a wild swing and missed Grandfather by two feet and fell flat on his face. Grandfather paid no attention to him.

Harold got up and came after Grandfather, but he couldn't make very good time, and Grandfather was turning in at our house when Harold caught up with him.

"You dirty so-and-so," Harold said, and swung again.

Grandfather grabbed Harold by the shoulders and shook him. As a young man he was the village blacksmith, and he still has the build for it. Harold kept trying to punch him, and missing, and Grandfather kept shaking him, and finally Grandfather let go and Harold sat down hard on the sidewalk.

"What were you doing at Sally's?" Harold demanded.

"I don't figure it's any of your business," Grandfather said, "but I'll tell you anyway. I always thought you were going to marry Sally, but being as you've given this book salesman a clear field, I've decided to marry her myself."

"You?" Harold exclaimed. "You've got grandchildren older than she is!"

"What does that have to do with it?" Grandfather asked him. He called to me, "Johnny, you'd better drive Harold home."

"I'll drive myself home," Harold said.

He ran over the curb three times in the first block, but finally he made it down to Main Street, and around the corner. Grandfather came up on the porch and sat down in his favorite glider.

"Was that necessary?" Mom asked.

"I don't know," Grandfather said. "Maybe not. Time will tell."

The next day, Saturday, Sheriff Pilkins was back to see Grandfather.

"This is the big day of the week for most of the stores," he said, "and if that burglar is going to work again it'll be tonight. Of course there won't be a dime left in any of the cash registers, but he won't know that. I'm looking for volunteers to watch for him."

"You aren't looking for me," Grandfather said. "I have a date tonight."

"I heard about that, but I didn't believe it. Just what have you got up your sleeve?"

"It isn't a burglar," Grandfather said. "What's Harold Grant doing this morning?"

"Getting drunk, I suppose. What's he got to do with it?"

"Like I said, I'm thinking about something else," Grandfather told him, "Go catch your own burglar."

"Why would Harold break into a place for a few bucks?" the sheriff asked. "His aunt gives him more spending money than most men earn. She even bought that convertible for him."

"Forget it," Grandfather said.

I told the sheriff I'd help him. "I know a lot of fellows who'd like to catch a burglar," I said.

"I don't need many," the sheriff said. "Just half a dozen, that haven't got hay fever and can keep their mouths shut. Think you can find them for me?"

"Sure. They'd have to tell their folks, though."

"Then pick six that have folks that can keep their mouths shut."

I went to work on it, and by noon we had everything arranged. The sheriff put one of his deputies in charge on each side of Main Street, and he'd found a few men who were willing to help out, and we went around picking places to watch from. Grandfather said it was a cinch Borgville would be better guarded that night than any time since World War II, when it had twelve air raid wardens in every block because there were that many men that wanted to do something for the war effort.

At supper time Grandfather dressed up again and went over to Sally Carter's. I was worried about him, because there was no telling what darned fool stunt Harold Grant might try to pull when he'd been drinking, and even though Mr. Griswold hadn't acted romantic the night before, that was no guarantee that he'd be hungry every night. When it started to get dark I took the lunch Mom had fixed for me and headed up town. I was wishing I'd kept my mouth shut and let the sheriff dig up his own night watchmen, because I figured that any action Borgville enjoyed at night would happen at Sally Carter's house, and wouldn't be a burglary.

I met Mrs. Beyers on Main Street, and she grabbed me and yelled, "Have you seen Harold?"

"No," I said, wondering if Grandfather had hung one on him.

"I saw him five minutes ago, and he's sober! This is the first Saturday night in years that he hasn't been drinking. Your Grandfather certainly is a dear. He straightened Harold out in a hurry."

"He didn't exactly straighten him out," I said. "He just shook him a little."

"Whatever it was, it was just what he needed," Mrs. Beyers said.

Main Street always is crowded on Saturday night, and from the talk I heard it was a tossup whether the people were more interested in the burglaries, or in Grandfather courting Sally Carter, or in Harold Grant being sober. I went down behind the bank and checked in with Steve Carling, Sheriff Pilkins's deputy, and he put me in a clump of bushes behind Jake Palmer's barber shop. By that time I was sure I'd made a mistake. Nobody with any sense would try to burgle a barber shop, and there I was, stuck for the night.

I finished all the food Mom gave me in the first twenty minutes, and then I sat there in the bushes and tried to swat mosquitoes without making any noise. Jake closed his barber shop at ten. He left a light on in one of his rear windows, which probably was Sheriff Pilkins's idea. A couple of the other stores had done the same thing. It didn't exactly floodlight the alley, but it helped.

By holding my watch just right I could see what time it was, and it read a little after midnight when Steve Carling came tiptoeing along. He said things were quiet everywhere except at Bailey's Bar, which was still open. "I figure Bailey's is where he'll hit," Steve said. "Places that close late sometimes are careless about their money."

"I'll bet Mr. Bailey won't be careless tonight," I said.

Steve grunted and handed me a sandwich and a bottle of pop, compliments of the sheriff. That was nice of Sheriff Pilkins, but I wasn't in a grateful mood by then. I asked Steve if he wanted a deposit on the bottle, and he said no, he'd pick it up on his next trip through, which would be maybe three AM., and I felt like hitting him with it.

One o'clock sneaked past, and at one twenty-seven – I'd just looked at my watch – I saw a shadow feeling its way along the buildings. I sat tight and waited, and the shadow kept coming. When it got even with me I yelled and jumped at it. The shadow let out a squawk and took off, but I caught it in about three long steps and brought it down with a tackle that was so pretty I was sorry there wasn't anyone around to see it. One of the men came running down the alley to help me and got kicked a good one in the shins, and I got half the skin scratched off one arm, and in case you've ever tangled with a bobcat in the dark you'll know how we felt.

In nothing flat there was a crowd there, and the shadow stopped struggling. Sheriff Pilkins came stumbling along with a flashlight, and all of us backed off and stared.

The shadow was Sally Carter.

"I'll be derned," the sheriff said.

Sally sat there on the ground with the light shining on her face, looking scared to death. She was wearing a man's overalls, which were not exactly form-fitting, but she was just as pretty as she'd been the day before all dressed up.

"So it was you," the sheriff said.

Sally started to cry. "I want to go home," she sobbed, and the sheriff couldn't get her to say another word.

Steve Carling wanted to haul her off to Wiston and lock her up, on the theory that she'd talk plenty after a night in jail. Mr. Crabtree, who is janitor for the First Baptist Church, said Sally hadn't done anything except walk down the alley in the dark, which wasn't exactly illegal, and if he was her he'd sue all of us for assault. Sheriff Pilkins told him he wasn't her and he should keep his mouth shut. "I'll drive her home," the sheriff said. "Maybe we can get this mess straightened out there."

An argument started, but I didn't have to hear the end of it to know how it would come out. Grandfather is the only one in Borgville who wins arguments with Sheriff Pilkins. I headed off down the alley, and Mr. Crabtree trotted beside me.

"I'm going after that fellow Griswold," he said. "The little lady needs someone to look after her."

I tore for home, got Grandfather out of bed, and told him what had happened. He was pulling his clothes on while I talked, and we both took off at a run for Sally Carter's house. We got there just as the sheriff arrived, with me panting from trying to keep up with him.

"What do you want?" the sheriff demanded.

"I've been courting this girl, haven't I?" Grandfather asked. "If she's in trouble, I aim to stand by her."

Sally, who was still crying and mopping her face with a handkerchief someone had given her, suddenly had a coughing fit. The sheriff said to me, "Don't tell me you've been courting her, too."

"No," I said, "but I'm the one that caught her."

"All right," Sheriff Pilkins said disgustedly. "Both of you have more business here than I have. You take over, and I'll go home to bed." But he let both of us stay, and he hadn't any more than closed the door when it jerked open again and Mr. Griswold came in. He was a sight.

He had on yellow pajamas with big red flowers on them. He rubbed his eyes and directed a yawn at everyone present.

"What's the trouble, Babe?" he asked Sally.

Sally buried her face in her hands and really started to howl.

Mr. Griswold turned on the sheriff. He had both fists doubled up, and he looked as if he knew how to use them.

"Get off her back," he said. "She hasn't done anything."

"That's what you think," Sheriff Pilkins said. "Three burglaries. Breaking and entering. And I'd just like to know why."

Sally didn't say anything. She couldn't, because she was bawling at the top of her voice.

"You did that?" Mr. Griswold asked her. "You must have had a reason. Tell him why, Babe, so we can all go back to bed."

I wanted to point out that some of us hadn't been to bed, but Mr. Griswold didn't look as though he'd welcome corrections. His build was something like Grandfather's, and he was a whole lot younger.

"Well, Sally?" the sheriff said.

"It's been hard," Sally said, between sobs. "There hasn't been much money since mother died, and I loved having someone to cook for, and I had to buy groceries somehow. Didn't I?"

All of us stared at her. Mr. Griswold managed a real eloquent, "Huh?" Sheriff Pilkins commenced scratching his head. "I'll be derned. You mean –"

"Charles was coming for supper every day, and sometimes for lunch, and I enjoyed it so, and there just wasn't any other way. Don't you see?"

The sheriff stepped forward to say something, and Mr. Griswold shoved him back out of the way. "Babe!" he exclaimed. "Do you mean you busted into those places just to get money to feed me?"

Sally started bawling again.

"That's a hot one," Mr. Griswold said. "A dame stealing to feed Charlie Griswold. I never thought I'd live to see that." He turned to the sheriff. "What's the damage, Pal?"

"Well, now," Sheriff Pilkins said. "I suppose if the money was returned and the damage taken care of – and it wouldn't amount to much – none of the merchants would want to prosecute. Forty-five dollars ought to cover it."

Mr. Griswold pulled up his pajama top and went to work on a money belt.

"Here's fifty," he said, handing a bill to the sheriff. "Anything left over, give it to the Boy Scouts, or something. And tell me, Pal. What's the quickest way for a couple to get spliced in this burg?"

Sally let out a squeal. "Charles!"

"Yep. I always figured I'd be a bachelor all my life. I like to travel and I like the selling game. But if a gal wants to cook for me that badly, I say she's got herself a job. Hey, Babe – do you suppose you could cook in one of those trailers the way you do in that kitchen?"

"Try me!" Sally yelled. She jumped into his arms, and Sheriff Pilkins herded Grandfather and me toward the door.

"The meeting," he announced, "is adjourned."

We took our time walking home. Grandfather kept shaking his head. "Now what do you make of that?" he asked me finally.

I didn't know what to make of it.

"I'll tell you this much," Grandfather said. "It doesn't make sense."

I didn't see Sheriff Pilkins again for a week. By then Sally Carter and her new husband were on their way to Niagara Falls, but a few of Grandfather's friends were still joshing him about losing his girl. Harold Grant, after dropping completely out of sight for a few days, was back in town. His car was parked in front of Bailey's Bar.

Grandfather was sitting on the bench in front of Jake Palmer's barber shop reading Mr. Snubbs's morning paper when the sheriff drove up. He got out and came over and sat down beside Grandfather, who nodded at him without looking up from the paper.

"I'd like to know something," Sheriff Pilkins said.

Grandfather turned a page without saying anything.

"Sally Carter," the sheriff said. "Griswold, I mean. I been doing some checking. Her pa had money, and even though it cost something with her ma being sick so long, she had plenty left over. She's run two, three hundred through her checking account every month, and that's plenty of money for a single woman in Borgville, especially when she owns her house. Now why did she have to break into those places for a few dollars?"

"She didn't," Grandfather said.

"She didn't? But she said – now look here!"

"I've been doing some checking, too," Grandfather said, "and I say your burglar wasn't Sally Carter."

"Then who was it?"

"A couple of weeks ago," Grandfather said, "you had Johnny drive

Harold Grant home from Bailey's. Remember? Well, I had a talk with Sue Rollins. She thought it was the last straw when she saw a high school boy bringing her no-good nephew home, and she told Harold she'd never give him another cent. But Harold couldn't do without his liquor, and he stole the money so he could go on drinking. Then he got wind of the trap you were setting, and that scared him enough to sober him up for a few days."

"He was sober for a couple of days," the sheriff admitted. "I thought he was trying to reform, to get Sally back."

"Sally heard from his aunt what had happened," Grandfather went on. "She knew Harold was the burglar, and she was afraid he'd try it again and get caught. So that Saturday night she went up town to stop him before he got himself in trouble, and she got caught. Then Sue Rollins decided she'd rather have Harold drunk than in jail, and she gave him some money and chased him out of town until the trouble blew over."

There was a mild commotion across the street at Bailey's. Mr. Bailey escorted Harold Grant out the door and leaned him against a lamp post.

"I figured he'd stopped reforming because Sally got married," the sheriff said. "Johnny, why don't you drive Harold home?"

"Nope," I said. "That's what started all the trouble."

The sheriff sat there for awhile, looking across the street at Harold Grant. "Look here," he said finally. "Do you mean to say that Sally Carter was so worried about Harold she went chasing around town in the dead of night to keep him out of trouble, and she took the blame for stealing that money when it was Harold that did it, and then when this Griswold guy asked her to marry him she jumped at it?"

"That's just what I mean to say," Grandfather said.

"I don't believe it."

"Don't, then," Grandfather said.

The sheriff looked at Harold Grant again. "Women," he said, "are fickle."

"I suppose so," Grandfather said, "but so is everyone else."

THE PHANTOM THIEF

I've never heard Grandfather Rastin claim to be infallible, but once in a while he hints that the last time he made a mistake was in 1913, when he turned down the first automobile dealership in Borg County because he knew people wouldn't be foolish enough to accept a contraption so much noisier, smellier, and less dependable than a horse. He hasn't changed his opinion of the automobile, but he says the experience taught him not to place boundaries on human foolishness.

*He is the only Democrat in Borgville that admits it, and he has a few other strong prejudices (*against *Borg County's Republican Sheriff Ed Pilkins, riding in cars with open windows, riding in the back seat of anything, and – in their less rational moments – women;* for *foot power over wheel power, women in their more rational moments, and uncommon common sense.)*

He also is strongly prejudiced in favor of Borgville, Michigan. Borgville has been called a one-horse town, and Grandfather says that's a pernicious falsehood, because Borgville doesn't have any horses. It has two churches, and the best volunteer fire department in the state, and very efficient municipal sewage and water departments, and a nice business section with a gasoline station, a bank, a restaurant, a drugstore, a grocery store, a hardware store, a barber shop, and several other establishments. It has streets lined with big old maples and oaks and poplars, and well kept houses that were built to last and did. It has no police department at all, because it's never needed one.

It also has a very good school system of consolidated districts, with students bussed in from miles around, and to a lot of the adults (but not to Grandfather Rastin) Borgville High School is the source of some highly perplexing mysteries …

The Borgville High School crime wave happened on a Tuesday during fourth period, which is right after lunch, and it couldn't have lasted more than a few minutes. During that time someone stole a new bunsen burner from the chem. room, a ceramic brooch from the art room, a cheap slide rule from Mr. Grace's room, an expensive book from the library, and sixty-eight dollars from Miss Elson's purse.

Things don't often get stolen in Borgville High, so just one missing item would have caused a flap. Even so, the brooch and the bunsen burner and the book and the slide rule didn't exactly add up to grand larceny, and Mr. Obermeyer, our principal, probably would have handled the matter himself and kept it out of the papers if it hadn't been for the sixty-eight dollars.

The instant he heard about the missing money he called Sheriff Pilkins. He admitted afterward that this was a mistake, which shows you how serious a mistake it was. Teachers rarely admit that they're wrong, and principals never do.

Sheriff Pilkins didn't see anything very complicated about the problem. He thought all he had to do was search 217 students. Mr. Obermeyer suggested diplomatically that the sheriff might lose a few votes if he and his deputies started searching high school girls, so he turned that job over to Miss Frailing, the girls' physical education teacher, and he told his deputy, Steve Carling, to search the boys. Steve is not the brightest deputy sheriff in the world, or even in Borg County, but after he'd searched ten or twelve of us it occurred to him that it wasn't really necessary to undress a student to find out whether he had that big book, or a bunsen burner, or even a slide rule concealed about his person. He mentioned this to Sheriff Pilkins, and the sheriff decided to send everyone back to class and search lockers instead.

He encountered a momentary obstacle in Jim Douglas, who is president of the Borgville High School Civics Club. Jim announced that the sheriff already had committed one felony by searching students without due process, and opening lockers without a search warrant would be another, and anyway, it was a pretty poor excuse for a law officer who couldn't catch one guilty student without humiliating two hundred and sixteen innocent ones.

"All right, smart aleck," the sheriff said. "Where were you during the fourth period?"

"I refuse to answer questions without the benefit of legal counsel,"

Jim answered.

Two more deputies had arrived by then, and the sheriff told them to take Jim to the principal's office and put him through the ringer.

The lockers got searched. Mr. Obermeyer has all the combinations on file, and he was too shook up about Miss Elson's sixty-eight dollars to tolerate any nonsense about search warrants, even from the president of the Civics Club. The sheriff and his deputies searched lockers for the rest of the afternoon, and they said afterward that they wouldn't have believed the amount of junk that a student can cram into a narrow space if they hadn't seen it themselves. They found dirty clothes and leftovers from last fall's lunches, and enough waste paper for a Salvation Army drive, but – contrary to reports that circulated later – no marijuana and no pornography unless you include Betty Bronson's paperback copy of *Peyton Place* that she'd talked Miss Burkart into approving as optional outside reading.

They didn't turn up any stolen goods, and no money except the dime that Tracy Corning had dropped in her locker six weeks before and hadn't been able to find.

It was an hour after dismissal time when the sheriff finally turned us loose, and then we had to march past a gamut of deputies as we left the building and let them search our notebooks and briefcases. We were almost two hours late getting home, which worried our parents. The bus drivers had to be paid overtime, which worried the School Board. Parents started telephoning the school to find out what had happened, which worried Mr. Obermeyer. It also worried the sheriff, because all of those parents were voters. All things considered it was a very worrisome day, and the most worried of all was Miss Elson, because the sixty-eight dollars was from a social security check she'd cashed for her next-door neighbor.

The sheriff and his deputies stayed there until midnight, searching the school, and they returned the next morning for another go at the students. By noon Sheriff Pilkins was threatening to suppress the school paper and arrest the entire senior class, and it was then that Mr. Obermeyer did what he should have done in the first place. He telephoned my Grandfather Rastin.

I first heard about it when Mr. Obermeyer came up to the cafeteria during lunch period and asked me if I'd mind going after Grandfather.

"Did he stop laughing long enough to say he'd come?" I asked him.

"What do you mean?"

"I told him last night what the sheriff had been doing, and he was still laughing at breakfast, and I thought maybe –"

"It isn't funny," Mr. Obermeyer snapped. I ate the rest of my sandwich very quietly, and then I got my jalopy and went.

Lunch period wasn't quite over when Grandfather and I pulled into the school parking lot. Mr. Lewton, the chemistry teacher, was just driving away in his Cadillac convertible, and I told Grandfather, "That's what I want for Christmas."

"The Texas Company would declare a dividend every time you started it," he said.

Mr. Lewton wheeled onto Mud Lake Road, and at the same time Mr. Jaffrey, the band director, putt-putted into view on his motor bike. This is a sight you don't believe even when you see it, because Mr. Jaffrey weighs maybe three hundred pounds and it's a small motor bike. He looks like a big dog trying to ride on a flea.

As he and Mr. Lewton approached each other, Mr. Jaffrey swerved into the left hand lane, and Mr. Lewton mashed his accelerator, and they ran head on at each other until Mr. Jaffrey zipped back into the right lane at the last instant.

Grandfather glowered. "What kind of imbecility is that?"

"They do that all the time," I said. "They're bachelors, and when school started they leased a house in Wiston. They hadn't lived together for more than a day and a half before they commenced hating each other, but they're stuck with the lease through next summer."

Mr. Jaffrey putt-putted up beside my jalopy and climbed off. "Hi, Johnny," he said. "Who's the antique Yul Brynner?"

He shouldn't have said that. Grandfather has been bald for a long time – he claims he lost his hair as a result of driving around in an open car back in the winter of '25 – but he still can be sensitive about it.

"This is my Grandfather Rastin," I told him. "Mr. Obermeyer asked him to solve the thefts."

"Oh," Mr. Jaffrey said. "I thought maybe one of the kids had come up with an anti-Beatle haircut."

He waddled toward the main entrance, which is in the old building, and Grandfather and I headed for the new wing where Mr. Obermeyer's office is. Mr. Obermeyer shook hands with Grandfather and told me I was excused from classes and I should take Grandfather anywhere he wanted to go and tell him what he wanted to know if I could. We waited until the corridors cleared and the second bell rang for fourth period, and then we started out.

Borgville High is shaped like a lopsided T. The old building is two stories high, and at one end, forming the top of the T, are two new one-story annexes. The shorter one, which is on the right, has the principal's and superintendent's offices, the counselor's office, and teachers' lounge, and a couple of small classrooms. The longer annex, on the left, has the homemaking room, the chemistry room, the music office and practice rooms, and the gymnasium, which is also the auditorium and the band practice room. The architect who put the homemaking and chemistry and music departments together in that new annex knew what he was doing – students who produce anti-social sounds and smells are off by themselves where they won't bother anyone but each other.

A corridor runs straight through from one annex to the other and intersects the first floor corridor in the old building. At that intersection, right by the stairs, there's a monitor who sits in a chair placed where he can see the length of both corridors. On the second floor by the stairs at the other end of the old building there's another monitor.

Howie Orlich, the smartest kid in the senior class, had been fourth period monitor the day before, but he'd lost his job after all those thefts happened right under his nose without him seeing a thing. Mort Palmer had taken his place, and as we came down the corridor from Mr. Obermeyer's office, Mort, who had been taking part in a lunch period basketball game, trotted along from the other direction shaking water from his hair. He looked me over very carefully and asked, "Where's your pass?"

"I have Mr. Obermeyer's permission," I said.

He leered at me. "No pass, no passie."

So I went back to the office, and Mr. Obermeyer apologized and made out a pink slip for me.

"I gave strict orders," he said. "I wanted to see if Mort was on his toes."

He wrote, "All afternoon," on the pass, and I took it back and showed it to Mort.

"What's this?" Grandfather asked.

"It's a general pass," I said. "I can go anywhere in the school during the time written on it."

"Except the girls' rooms," Mort said, leering at me again.

"There's also a white slip," I told Grandfather. "It's a destination pass. A student going to the library from the study hall would have a white slip. He'd also sign out when he left the study hall, and Miss Burkart would sign his pass at the library, and he'd sign in and surrender the pass when he got back to the study hall. At the end of the day all the passes and the sign-out sheets are sent to the office, and Mr. Obermeyer's secretary files them."

"It's just like a prison," Mort said.

"Do you mean to say there's a record of where every student was during fourth period yesterday?" Grandfather asked.

I nodded. "Where every student was, and what students left their rooms and at what time and for what purpose and where they went. That's what has everyone so confused. The thefts happened between one o'clock and one-twenty, and no one signed out of anywhere before one-twenty-five. And Howie was sitting right here and didn't see anyone, and yet all those things were stolen."

"That's very interesting," Grandfather said.

"Interesting isn't the word Sheriff Pilkins used," I said. "There's only one possible explanation. Borgville High has a phantom thief."

Grandfather chuckled. "No wonder Pilkins is in a flap. He has trouble enough with real thieves."

We went first to the chemistry room, which isn't used during fourth period.

"Mr. Lewton teaches a seventh grade science class over at the elementary school," I said. "Before he left he set up an experiment he wanted to show his fifth period chemistry class, and when he came back the bunsen burner was gone."

Grandfather walked over and looked at a conglomeration of tubes and flasks on Mr. Lewton's desk. "Is this where it was?"

I nodded. "It's the same experiment. Because of the excitement about the thefts he didn't get to do it yesterday. You'll notice, though, that he didn't leave a bunsen burner out today. At first he thought maybe he'd forgot to hook one up, but after he heard about the thefts he checked and it'd been stolen. He's irked, because it was the only new burner he had."

"All right. Show me the other rooms."

We went back to the old building. The first room on the right after you turn the corner is Miss Elson's. She was there alone – fourth is her free period – and she looked even more worried than she had the day before.

"Where was your purse?" Grandfather asked her.

"On my desk." She sniffed into her handkerchief. She's a real nice old lady, and she's been teaching in Borgville almost long enough to remember when Grandfather had hair. We all felt sorry for her.

"I thought I'd only be gone a minute," she said. "I went up to the cafeteria to ask Mrs. Derry about having coffee for Open House next week – the homemaking girls will make the cookies – and we got to talking, and it was one-twenty when I got back."

"When did you miss the money?"

"Right away. I looked in my purse for a pencil. I'd had the bills folded and tucked in this inside pocket. I didn't put them in my billfold because I didn't want them mixed up with my money."

"How much money was in your billfold?"

"Four dollars and sixty-three cents. The sheriff made me count it. As far as I could tell, nothing was touched except the sixty-eight dollars."

"The thief saw that when he opened your purse," Grandfather said. "Obviously he grabbed it and ran."

"Mrs. Wagner – that's my neighbor – she's been too sick to go to the bank, and she needed the money to buy medicine, and I had to cash the check for her during the lunch period because the bank is closed after school." She sniffed again. "I just didn't think to take my purse with me. Nothing like this has ever happened. Not in Borgville High. I know they're always having trouble in Wiston, but you know those big city children. Our Borgville children are *good*. They don't take things. At least, they never have."

Grandfather told her about the one bad apple, but his version is that while a bad apple may spoil the barrel, it can make a much more interesting cider.

"Do you have insurance?" he asked.

She said she had life insurance and medical insurance and car insurance, but she didn't think any of those policies covered her purse.

We crossed the corridor to the art room. All the posters and drawings were still on display, but the ceramics projects had been locked up. Miss Rogers, the art teacher, also had fourth period free, and she wasn't in the room.

"Where was the brooch?" Grandfather asked.

"On the table nearest the door," I said. "There was a mess of stuff on display there – brooches, ear rings, bracelets, ash trays, paper weights –"

"Anyone have any theories as to why the thief took only one?"

I shook my head. "Sally Winks thinks it's because that brooch was the best one, but that's because she made it."

"Next room," Grandfather said.

Mr. Sandler was teaching a biology class next door to Miss Elson's room, and on the other side of that room was Mr. Grace's mathematics classroom.

"Mr. Grace has a free period, too," I said. "He's probably down in the teachers' lounge with Miss Rogers. That's where they were yesterday. They're engaged, and they're holding long discussions to try to figure out whether two married teachers can get along on two single teachers' salaries."

"Where was the slide rule?"

"On his desk. It was a battered old thing worth maybe two cents at a rummage sale."

We moved on to the library, which is on the other side of the corridor and just beyond the entrance. Grandfather asked Miss Burkart, the librarian, about the missing book.

"Miss Rogers came after it just before fourth period started," she said. "Someone had put it on the wrong shelf, and I couldn't find it, and she said she'd come for it later. Of course I found it two minutes after she left. I put it on the checkout desk there by the door. When I looked again it was gone, and I thought she'd taken it and forgot to sign the card."

"Where were you?" Grandfather asked.

"Working on the shelves at the back of the room." She waved her hands disgustedly. "A disorganized library is no library at all, and if I don't check shelves once a week I can't find anything. I'm only here afternoons – in the morning I teach English – and the shelves didn't get checked last week because I was cataloging new books."

Grandfather sat down at one of the tables and looked the room over, scowling. Just then Sue Walton and Mary Fasuli came in from the study hall, and they picked out books, and Miss Burkart checked out the books and stamped their pass slips.

"I spend most of my time running from one end of the room to the other," she complained.

"The first question," Grandfather said to me, "is whether there's any significance in *what* was stolen, and if there is I can't see it. Those things don't add up no matter how you arrange them."

"There are two theories about that," I said. "One theory says it was a boy, on account of the bunsen burner and the slide rule, and because there were about fifty boys taking gym yesterday during fourth period and everyone knows a teacher can't keep track of that many boys in a gymnasium. The other theory says it was a girl because of the brooch and the book and because some girls were practicing in the music room and only a girl could have found the money that fast in a woman's purse."

"What do you think?" Grandfather asked.

"I think it was a boy. He could have wanted the brooch to give to someone, and as for the book – it was a big art book, *The Works of Michelangelo*, with a lot of pictures of statues and paintings and things. Some of the art books that size are kept locked up because they have reproductions of nude paintings. I think it was a boy, and he thought it was one of those books."

Grandfather called to Miss Burkart, "Were there any nude pictures in the Michelangelo book?"

Miss Burkart tilted her nose. "I wouldn't know, I'm sure. Ask Miss Rogers – that's *her* speciality."

Grandfather pushed back his chair and motioned to me, and we climbed the stairs to the second floor, where Joe Bratchner was monitor. I waved my pink slip at Joe, and Grandfather looked in at the cafeteria, which is the study hall except during lunch period, and then he went the whole length of the corridor looking into every room. We used the stairs at the other end of the building, and at the bottom I tried to give my pink slip to Mort Palmer again, and he was studying geometry and told me to cut the nonsense.

Grandfather sat down on the steps and asked, "What's this between Miss Burkard and Miss Rogers?"

I grinned at him. "Last year it was Miss Burkart and Mr. Grace who were trying to add up salaries, and they couldn't quite make it work out. This fall Miss Rogers came here, and she is maybe better at arithmetic, or at least at figures. So Miss Burkart takes digs at Miss Rogers whenever she can, and Miss Rogers isn't above digging back now and then."

Mr. Grace came by and pretended to have a stroke when he saw Mort studying geometry. Mr. Jaffrey waddled down to the teachers' lounge and came back carrying a paper cup of coffee, which is against the rules, and he stopped and pretended he was going to baptize Mort with it. Mort told him to get lost.

"Johnny," Grandfather said suddenly, "pretend you're the thief. Start at the chemistry room and steal those things. I want to time you."

So I went to the chemistry room and stole a non-existent bunsen burner, and then I went to Miss Elson's room and told her we were doing an experiment and took a non-existent sixty-eight dollars from her purse. I went through the motions of swiping the brooch from the art room and the slide rule from Mr. Grace's room and the book from the library, and then I went on up the stairs as far as the study hall, which is the route I'd figured out for the thief. When I came back down the stairs, Grandfather called to me to do it again going the other way, so I worked back from the library to the chemistry room, Miss Elson looked at me rather strangely when I popped into her room for another go at her purse, and I was feeling silly about it myself.

"Two and a half minutes," Grandfather said when I got back. "And you dawdled. The thief wouldn't have dawdled. It could have been done in a minute and a half, easily. I don't suppose this school has such a thing as a rocking chair."

"I've never seen one here," I said.

"Educators ought to know that rocking chairs stimulate thought," Grandfather grumbled. He scowled at me. "It's the *order* that doesn't make sense. I'm assuming that the thief worked straight down the corridor in one direction or the other – if he'd wandered back and forth he'd have been asking to be caught. On the other hand, no matter where he started, Miss Elson's room should have been his last stop."

"Why?" I asked.

"Sixty-eight dollars is a lot of money. To a student, it's a fortune. He wouldn't take the risk of stealing more claptrap with that in his pocket. He'd head for wherever he was supposed to be and stay there. So he stole the bunsen burner and the money – and stopped – or he stole the book and the slide rule and the brooch and the money – and stopped. The money had to be taken last, but it wasn't, not unless the thief paraded up and down the corridor like an imbecile, and imbeciles aren't supposed to be in high school. It doesn't make sense. I'd better have a look at those records."

We went to the office, and Mr. Obermeyer's secretary, Mrs. Fletcher, showed Grandfather the records. During the last half of fourth period forty students had signed out of their regular classes. Grandfather pushed the list aside and said it might as well be the entire student roster.

He marched into Mr. Obermeyer's office with me on his heels, closed the door firmly, and asked, "Has it occurred to anyone that the thief could have been a teacher?"

Mr. Obermeyer winced. "I'd hate to think so, but I also hate to think it was a student."

"How many people knew that Miss Elson cashed that check?"

"Quite a few, I'm afraid. We're a small school, and there aren't many secrets."

"Teachers?"

"Teachers and students."

"Johnny?"

"Some girls asked Miss Elson if they could make up a quiz during lunch period," I said. "She told them she was going to the bank. I don't know how many students knew she was going to cash a check."

"Did you?"

"No. But Betsy Morgan heard her tell Miss Rogers."

"Make another list," Grandfather said. "Teachers who have fourth period free, teachers like Miss Burkart and Mr. Jaffrey, who can wander around when they feel like it, any teacher who left his class for any reason during the critical time, and also people like the janitors and your secretary."

"I don't believe it," Mr. Obermeyer said, shaking his head.

"Put yourself on it, too," Grandfather said. "Then the others can't complain when the sheriff lights into them. There's just one kind of person in this school that a monitor might overlook completely: an adult. A student he'd look carefully at, because that's his job. He's there to make certain that students are where they're supposed to be. Teachers and janitors and secretaries are none of his business. A teacher would have a lot better chance to dispose of the stolen property, too. Did Pilkins search the teachers' briefcases?"

"No. All right. I'll have the list made for you."

"Not for me," Grandfather said. "Give it to Pilkins. He's good with lists, and his mind works best when it has a track to run on."

We went back to the old building, and Grandfather sat down on the stairs again. Five minutes later Sheriff Pilkins came along waving Mr. Obermeyer's new list:

"You" he bellowed.

Grandfather didn't say anything.

"What's he doing here?" the sheriff asked me.

"Mr. Obermeyer invited him."

"He would. Look here – this is MY investigation!"

"Then why aren't you investigating?" Grandfather asked.

The sheriff sat down on the other side of the stairway and found an itch in the little bald spot on top of his head.

"You think it's one of these?" he asked pointing to the list.

"It could have been."

"Got any ideas which one?"

Grandfather shook his head.

"Got an ideas at all?"

"A few," Grandfather said.

"Did you check with the bank?"

"Now see here. You don't think for one minute Miss Elson didn't cash that check!"

"Of course not," Grandfather said. "But I don't *know*, either, and there are one or two other questions you might ask the bank. And I've been wondering what anyone would want with a bunsen burner, since they run on gas and Borgville doesn't have gas." The sheriff stared at him.

"Of course quite a few homes have bottled gas," Grandfather went on, "and I suppose it's possible that –"

The sheriff scrambled to his feet and legged it down the corridor toward Mr. Obermeyer's office. As well as I could remember, it was the shortest interview he'd ever had with Grandfather.

Miss Elson went to the teachers' lounge, nodding at Mort as if she was glad to see that one monitor was awake. Miss Rogers came along, and when she saw me standing there she stopped to ask Mort if they were now putting monitors on the monitors.

The bell rang. Mort got up, yawned, said, "Back to the mines," and fell in step with Susan Long, who came out of biology. I backed up against the wall to avoid being stepped on, but Grandfather stayed where he was, scowling, and let the traffic move around him.

The corridors cleared except for some girls with gym excuses, who straggled past heading for the study hail. The fifth period bell rang. Jeff Osman came hurrying down the corridor to take over as monitor, and right on his heels, swinging a briefcase, came Mr. Lewton, returning from his elementary science class. I showed my pink slip to Jeff, and Grandfather got up to interview Mr. Lewton.

We called him "the mouse that roars," because he was a little man, smaller than most of his students, but when he wanted to turn it on he had a voice that could be used for public address announcements in Yankee Stadium. He was one of Borgville High's best teachers, and he taught the elementary science class during his free period because he didn't think his high school students had the right kind of preparation in science.

"You were gone all fourth period yesterday?" Grandfather asked him.

He nodded. "I have one class at the elementary building, and I have to hop to make connections. Anything I need for my fifth period class I set up during lunch period, before I leave."

"Can you think of any reason why a student would take a bunsen burner?" Mr. Lewton shook his head. "The students who might have a use for it." "Where's your pass?"

Ed Edwards, who'd come ambling along with his fat, innocent face hanging out, jumped three feet in the air when Mr. Lewton boomed at him. He handed over his white slip. Mr. Lewton glanced at it and handed it back to him.

"It's only good for fifth period," Mr. Lewton told him. "At that rate you may not make it."

Ed rocketed away, and Mr. Lewton said, "Some teachers – whom I won't name – are rather careless with passes. What was I saying? Yes. The good students who might have a use for a burner are the ones who'd be least likely to take it. The only thing I can think of is that the thief was grabbing anything he could take conveniently, and the rest of the apparatus was clamped in place. To take the burner all he had to do was jerk the hose loose. I'm late. If you'll excuse me –"

Grandfather walked with him as far as the chemistry room and then went on to the music office. The office was empty and only one of the practice rooms was in use – Edna Beck was practicing her trombone. She winked at me through the window and didn't miss a note. She is a very accomplished winker. There is a joke around school about her and Sally Winks, that being Sally's name. Sally Winks, the saying goes, but Edna winks better.

Grandfather opened the middle drawer of Mr. Jaffrey's desk. In one corner was a neat pile of destination passes.

"How many of the students know these things are here?" Grandfather asked.

"Everybody," I said. "All the teachers have them."

"In unlocked desks?"

"I guess they're supposed to lock them up when they leave the room."

"This pass system suddenly looks a little less than air tight." He sat down at the desk and went through the other drawers, picking out a sheet of Plank paper and a pair of scissors.

"What are you doing?" I asked.

"Just indulging my curiosity."

He took a pass and cut a piece of paper the same size. Then he opened the practice room door and said to Edna, "Would you like to take part in a scientific experiment?"

"Sure," she said. "What is it?"

He explained it to her, and she laid down her trombone and took the blank piece of paper. We followed her down the corridor. She waved the paper at Jeff Osman and winked at him. He returned the wink. She went on to the library, with us following. Miss Burkart was at the back of the room. Edna grabbed a book from the nearest shelf and called, "Shall I check myself out, Miss Burkart?"

"Go right ahead," Miss Burkart said.

Edna signed the card, stamped it and her blank pass, and walked away. She winked again when she passed Jeff, but he had his nose in a physics book and didn't even look up.

We caught up with her at the music room. "How'd I do?" she asked.

"Perfect," Grandfather said. "The office records don't mean a thing. Any student in this school could have been loose during those critical twenty minutes, with a stolen pass or no pass at all."

"The records wouldn't mean anything anyway," I said. "Howie Orlich was on monitor duty – remember? And during those twenty minutes *nobody* passed him. It was a phantom thief – unless you're right about monitors not paying any attention to teachers."

"Probably I'm not. I've been watching, and I have yet to see a teacher pass a monitor without being noticed. Usually they speak."

"So what good was that list?"

"It'll give Pilkins something to do."

Mr. Obermeyer came in then, looking for Grandfather, and Grandfather told him about the passes in Mr. Jaffrey's unlocked desk and how Edna had gone from the music room to the library and back with a blank piece of paper, and Mr. Obermeyer turned pink like my general pass, and then white like a destination pass, and went charging off. When we returned to the old building five minutes later there was a new monitor on duty, Steve Culver, and he took my pink pass and read it through very suspiciously. And down at the end of the corridor, Mr. Obermeyer was conversing with Mr. Jaffrey, but not in conversational tones.

Grandfather sat down on the steps again. A moment later Mr. Jaffrey waddled by and hissed at me, "You keep baldy out of my desk – see?"

"Have you any way of knowing how many of your students were loose in the corridors during fourth period yesterday?" Grandfather asked him.

"Passes – bah!" Mr. Jaffrey said. "If the teachers spend all their time keeping books on the students, how can they do any teaching? I have students coming and going all day long. They come for music lessons, they come to practice, they run errands. There are maybe a dozen kids in this school who can't be trusted, and those we keep an eye on. They don't bother me because I won't have them in band. The rest are good kids. We've never had trouble before."

"Don't your students use passes?"

"Sure. But it's just a formality to keep the office happy. A kid needs a pass, I tell him to make it out himself. I have better things to do."

"Obermeyer doesn't seem to think it's a formality," Grandfather said.

Mr. Jaffrey waved away whatever it was Mr. Obermeyer thought. "The whole system is a bunch of nonsense. Look. Who are the monitors? The best students, because they can get along without a study period. That's the theory. The way it works out, all it means is that they do their studying in the corridor instead of in the study hall. They're able to concentrate, which is why they're good students. Some of them concentrate so well that they don't even see an elephant like me passing unless I step on them. The monitors should be the dumb students, who don't study anyway and can't concentrate. Then the monitors would do some monitoring. Me, I couldn't care less. I'm leaving at the end of the year anyway. I have a job at a school where there's less bookkeeping and they serve real food in the cafeteria."

He waddled away.

"Do you have a nickname for Mr. Jaffrey?" Grandfather asked.

I nodded. "Blubber Boy. He's very particular about what he eats. He goes up town and has lunch at the Star Restaurant."

"That so?"

"That's one of the things that caused trouble between him and Mr. Lewton. They started housekeeping together and sharing the expenses. Mr. Jaffrey not only eats a lot – he likes expensive food. Mr. Lewton said it was bad enough trying to feed his car, which is a gas hog, without having to feed Mr. Jaffrey, who is a porterhouse steak hog. They stopped sharing expenses after the first day."

"Is that where Jaffrey was coming from on his motor bike? The Star Restaurant?"

"Yes."

There was a ruckus at the other end of the building, and Deputy Steve Carling marched down the stairs hauling Howie Orlich along by the arm, Steve looking mad and Howie looking white and very scared. They swept past us, headed toward the office, and a moment later Sheriff Pilkins came hurrying after them.

He stopped when he saw Grandfather and announced, "I'm a nitwit!"

It was an opening if I ever saw one, but Grandfather just arched his eyebrows.

"Since yesterday I've been trying to see how a thief could operate with a monitor sitting there," the sheriff said. "It wasn't until three minutes ago that I figured it out. The monitor was the thief!" He was trying to act disgusted with himself when he was bursting with pride. "You can go home, now. Everything is under control."

He hurried away.

"Maybe," Grandfather said softly, "but I think not. It'd be logical if it was just the money, but I can't see him wandering off in both directions to steal things when the first teacher that looked into the corridor would be wanting to know why the monitor's chair was empty. I'd also like to know what he's supposed to have done with the stuff."

For a time he sat there on the stairs, scowling and muttering to himself, and when I got tired waiting I sat down beside him. Steve Culver was reading his geography book but looking up and down the corridors every few seconds. Mr. Armbruster, one of the janitors, started bringing folding chairs down from the second floor, and Mr. Sadler, who is assistant principal when he isn't teaching biology, came from the office and caught him at it. They argued for a moment and went off in different directions to check.

Mr. Jaffrey walked past and did some muttering of his own when he saw Grandfather. At the other end of the corridor a bunch of kids came down the stairs from the study hall to use the library. A few students went by running errands, and Steve stopped them and checked their passes. Mr. Frazier, the French and Latin teacher, who had a free period, went to the teachers' lounge, and Miss Borg, the history teacher, who didn't, went to the office. I pointed out to Grandfather that the whole tenth grade history class now was free to wander off in all directions stealing things, and he grunted. Mr. Armbruster returned and started carrying the chairs back to the second floor.

The bell rang. Steve snapped his book shut and took off, and I moved away from the stairs and waited for the traffic to clear. Grandfather stayed where he was, scowling and muttering. The sixth period bell rang.

Grandfather got up slowly. "Now I see how it was done."

"Tell me," I said. "I'd like to be a phantom – not to steal things, just to get out of school on hot afternoons. Where are you going?"

"To call the bank."

"Didn't Sheriff Pilkins call the bank?"

"Probably, but he wouldn't ask the right question."

I started after him, and Pete Walton, who was taking over as sixth period monitor, called me back and made me show my pass. Before I could catch up with Grandfather, he'd chased Mr. Obermeyer out of his office and closed the door. He came out a couple of minutes later and said, "I'd like to have some people down here. Right now."

"Who?" Mr. Obermeyer asked.

"The boy that was on monitor duty when it happened."

"Howie Orlich. The sheriff just took him to Wiston."

"Call the sheriff's office," Grandfather told Mrs. Fletcher. "They can reach the sheriff by radio. Tell him I want that boy back here, and fast."

"Who else?" Mr. Obermeyer asked.

"The teachers who had things stolen."

"Miss Elson, Miss Rogers, Miss Burkart, Mr. Lewton, and Mr. Grace. Anyone else?"

"Mr. Jaffrey."

Mr. Obermeyer hurried away and Grandfather and I went to the teachers' lounge and waited.

The teachers arrived one at a time, because Mr. Olmstead had to make arrangements about their sixth period classes. Then he had to find Mr. Jaffrey, which took longer. In the meantime, Sheriff Pilkins stormed in spouting questions, and when Grandfather wouldn't answer them he sat down in The corner and sulked. Howie Orlich sat on the sofa with me, still looking scared. Finally Mr. Obermeyer and Mr. Jaffrey came.

"Its your show," Mr. Obermeyer told Grandfather.

Grandfather nodded. "I'll make this as brief as possible. The reason the monitor didn't see the thief yesterday was because there wasn't any monitor."

Everyone looked at him blankly. "This afternoon I saw monitors take their places at the beginning of every period," he went on, "but it wasn't until sixth period bell rang with no monitor on duty that I realized that *all three of them had been late*. Only two or three minutes late, but late. Earlier this afternoon, Johnny and I proved that the thief needed at least two minutes, and the reason the monitor didn't see him was because the thefts occurred at the beginning of the period before the monitor arrived. Howie?"

Howie jumped.

"How late were you yesterday?"

Howie gulped, thought a moment, and said apologetically, "I went in during lunch period to talk to Mr. Grace about a trig problem – I found a way to solve it that wasn't in the book. It took longer than I thought it would, and –"

Mr. Grace interrupted. "He was still there when the second bell rang."

"Then I went up to my locker to get my lit book," Howie said. "I wanted to do some reading during fourth period. But gee, it didn't take me more than –"

"Two or three minutes?" Grandfather suggested.

Howie nodded.

"Where were you right at the beginning of fourth period?" Grandfather asked Mr. Grace.

"I came here as soon as Howie left."

"Miss Rogers?"

"I was here when the period started."

"What about the rest of you?"

Miss Burkart had been working at the back of the library. Miss Elson was on her way to the cafeteria when the second bell rang, and Mr. Lewton was on his way to the elementary school. Mr. Jaffrey said, very politely, that his whereabouts were none of Grandfather's business, and when Mr. Obermeyer started to snap at him, Grandfather waved for silence.

Sheriff Pilkins said thoughtfully, "Now all I have to do is find out what students were late to their fourth period classes."

"Don't you have enough lists now?" Grandfather demanded. "What good is a name when you have no witness and no evidence? Or have you maybe located the stolen property since I last saw you?"

The sheriff didn't say anything.

"Before you compile another list," Grandfather said, "I'd like to take a careful look at two people who could have been in the corridor about that time. Mr. Jaffrey?"

Mr. Jaffrey grinned at him. "You'd better start wearing a hat. Your brain is suffering from a lack of insulation."

"Returning from your sumptuous repast at the Star Restaurant, you entered the old building at the entrance by the library and walked to the music office, passing all the rooms where things were stolen. Did you take Miss Elson's sixty-eight dollars, Mr. Jaffrey?"

"It's none of your business," Mr. Jaffrey said, "but just to show you what an ignoramus you are – I'm over at the elementary school two afternoons, Tuesday and Thursday. I go there directly from lunch. I wasn't in this building at all yesterday afternoon. Sorry to disappoint you."

"The contrary. You wouldn't be a suspect anyway, *because you would have* been headed in the wrong direction. In concentrating on the unseeing monitor, a more important problem was overlooked – the disappearing stolen goods. I think we're entitled to ask a question or two of the one person known to have left the building about that time. Did you take Miss Elson's sixty-eight dollars, Mr. Lewton?"

"I did not," Mr. Lewton said quietly.

"Let's see how it would have worked out. You ate lunch and returned to your room to set up an experiment you intended to perform for your fifth period class. It was a complicated experiment, or perhaps you'd dawdled over your lunch because you had other things on your mind. In any case, you were later than usual. You grabbed your briefcase and started out just as the second bell rang. Naturally you'd use the door by the library, because it's closest to the parking lot. On your way there you glanced into Miss Elson's room. Her purse was on her desk, and you knew she'd gone to the bank during lunch period to cash a check. You looked around – there was no monitor on duty and no one in the corridor. If the money hadn't been in plain sight when you opened her purse perhaps you would have thought about the consequences. It was in plain sight, and you took it and rushed from the room."

"But then you started to think. The theft would cause a commotion. Another theft, of something no teacher would be suspected of taking, would divert suspicion. There still was no one in the corridor and no monitor. You dashed into the art room to take something, anything, and dashed out again, Still no one in sight. Mr. Grace's room, nothing there but a cheap slide rule, so you took that. These were trivial things, and you needed something big and valuable, but there was no time. Passing the library, you looked in. On the desk by the door was a large book. One quick movement, the book was in your briefcase, and you were on your way. The phantom thief's career was brief but highly effective," He looked at me. "If I hadn't started out reasoning that the money was taken last, I could have finished this a lot sooner."

"For once Jaffrey was right," Mr. Lewton said. "You should start wearing a hat."

Mr. Jaffrey squared himself around and said apologetically, "I made an ass of myself. I beg your pardon. Borgville High could use a man like you. Can you teach chemistry?"

Grandfather turned to the sheriff. "What are you waiting for? You have a case."

"Case, nothing. Things don't happen just because you say they do. Where's the evidence?"

"Try Bryce Creek at the Mud Lake Road bridge. He crossed it on his way to the elementary school. You called the bank, didn't you?"

"What's that got to do with it? She cashed the check just like she said she did."

"Did you ask if anyone connected with this school had made a deposit- or a payment?"

The sheriff didn't answer.

"Teachers shouldn't buy expensive cars," Grandfather said. "Not teachers with Borgville salaries. Lewton was behind in his payments, and the bank was about to take his car. He telephoned yesterday morning and asked if he could have more time, or if the bank would accept a two-thirds payment, and the bank told him no. He left his elementary class early yesterday, stopped at the bank on his way back here, and made a full payment – a hundred and ninety-eight dollars. Would you like to explain how you managed to get ahold of one third of that sum so quickly, Mr. Lewton?"

Mr. Lewton didn't say anything. No one said anything.

Grandfather said softly, "It's a shame, Everyone says he's a fine teacher."

The sheriff got up and walked over to Mr. Lewton. Suddenly Howie Orlich exclaimed, "Oh! *Mr. Lewton!*"

We all turned and looked at him.

"Sure," he said. "I saw *Mr. Lewton* in the corridor yesterday. Just after I sat down I saw him come out of Mr. Grace's room. But nobody *asked* me about *teachers*."

"Did you see him go in the library?" Grandfather asked.

"Well – no."

"Howie," Grandfather said, "they tell me you're a first-rate student and that you want to study engineering. Is that right?"

"Yes, sir. I'd like to be an engineer."

"Do that, Howie," Grandfather said. "Don't ever let anyone talk you into trying to be a policeman."

THE MOTHER GOOSE MURDER

The county seat of Borg County, Michigan, is the city of Wiston, which in addition to the county building has such cultural advantages as Wiston College and a state police post commanded by Grandfather's friend Sergeant Reichel. Wiston also has a large business section surrounded by acres of parking problems.

This is the one of the multitude of differences between Wiston and Borgville that can hurt the most. In Borgville, if you park your car illegally – and it's in someone's way, you'll be asked to move it. If it isn't in anyone's way, no one will care. If you park beside a fire hydrant, and there's a fire, the volunteer fire department will use another hydrant, because Borgville is a progressive community and has several. If you do any of those things in Wiston, the District Court will extort money from you. If you park legally, the city has a parking meter on the spot to extort money from you. If you overstay your time, the court steps in to take you for anything the parking meter missed.

Another important difference is Wiston's crime rate, which is so bad that in Borgville the Wiston newspaper is something we don't leave lying around for children to read. This may be why Sheriff Pilkins is so bad-tempered when he comes to Borgville – some silly little complaint is interfering with all that work he has to do in Wiston, and in the process of looking into it he's likely to collide with Grandfather. Grandfather usually is content to let the sheriff have his Wiston crimes to himself; but sometimes someone invites Grandfather, and sometimes he admits to a perverse curiosity …

Mr. Obermeyer, our high school principal, claims that feeding time at the zoo is a quiet and peaceful occasion compared with lunch time in the high school cafeteria. He says he could shoot a cannon off, and it wouldn't be noticed if no one smelled the smoke. He may be right, because once when Mrs. Patousel slipped behind the counter and broke her leg, no one heard her yelling for help until half the students had left for class. It only goes to show that discovering a murder isn't anything like breaking a leg. Everyone in the cafeteria heard Sue Byers scream.

What happened was that Dianne Storrow was excavating in her purse for a letter she wanted to pass around, and something came to the top that she'd forgot she had. She said, "Oh, that old bone," and tossed it onto the table. No one paid any attention.

Two minutes later Sue Byers, who was sitting across the table, looked up and saw the bone.

You should know this about Sue Byers. She lives with her uncle, who is Borgville's only doctor, and her ambition is to be a doctor herself. She spends all of her spare time studying her uncle's medical books, and she already knows so much about anatomy that the boys are afraid to go out with her.

Sue took one good look at that bone and screamed, and one second later the cafeteria was so quiet that Fatts Fasuli later claimed he was able to hear the ice cream melting on his pie a la mode.

Sue stood up and motioned to Mr. Sadler, the assistant principal and biology teacher. He came and looked at the bone, and then he looked at Sue, and finally he said, "I think so."

"I know so," Sue said.

"Where did it come from?" Mr. Sadler asked.

"That old bone?" Diane said. "I've had it in my purse since last summer. You see, I had this job –" Then she understood, and she screamed.

A lot of lunches didn't get finished that day. Mr. Sadler picked up the bone and whisked both girls off to Mr. Obermeyer's office, and everyone else left off eating and tried to figure out what had happened. It wasn't until after school that we finally found out: Since the middle of the summer, Diane had been carrying a human finger bone around in her purse.

My Grandfather Rastin already knew about it when I got home. Doc Beyers had told him. Doc was plenty irked at Sheriff Pilkins, because the sheriff thought a doctor should be able to take one look at that little hunk of bone and tell him the initials of the person who'd owned it. All Doc was willing to say was that it was human and it'd probably belonged to an adult with small fingers.

"Male or female?" the sheriff wanted to know.

"Adult," Doc said.

"Small stature, you say?"

"Small fingers," Doc said.

"Well, if the fingers were small, then the hands must have been small, and if the hands were small –"

"I seen smaller fingers than that on hands that were bigger than yours," Doc said.

"Women have small fingers. Could it have been a woman?"

"There's no way I know of to determine sex from one finger bone," Doc said. And walked out, slamming the door.

Grandfather said meditatively, "Women's purses being what they are, I suppose something like this was bound to happen sooner or later."

"Dianne's purse isn't exactly a purse," I told him. "It's more like an oversized feed bag with draw strings. It wouldn't surprise me if she had a skull or two rattling around at the bottom."

"It'd surprise me," Grandfather said. "The word I got was that she gave the whole shebang to the custodian to burn, even including what was left of this week's allowance."

"Has anyone admitted to losing a finger bone?" I asked.

Grandfather didn't answer.

"For that matter, where did Dianne get it?" I asked.

Grandfather sighed. "I guess we'd better go over to Wiston."

I got out my jalopy, and we went.

Along the way, Grandfather told me what had happened. "Fellow named Daille," he said, "Jim Daille. I knew his grandfather. He has some kind of construction job, and from early spring until late fall he travels around the state working on highways and bridges. He's a widower, and he hires a housekeeper to look after his daughter Betsy, who is three.

"Last summer his housekeeper had to quit suddenly, and she persuaded Dianne Storrow to take the job until Daille could find a replacement. Dianne's parents weren't enthused about the situation, but the pay was good, and Daille wasn't at home – he didn't come home all the time she was there – and after a couple of weeks he sent a woman down from the Upper Peninsula to take over."

"How does the bone come into it?" I asked.

"The child had it. Every night Betsy picked out a bedtime story she wanted to hear, and one night it was the one about the wee little woman who found a wee little bone. Remember it? She put the bone in her wee little cupboard, and then she crept into her wee little bed and blew out her wee little candle, and suddenly, in the dark, she heard a wee little voice say, 'Give me my bone!' "

"I remember," I said.

"And the voice kept asking until the wee little woman sat up in bed and said, 'TAKE IT!' It almost frightened Betsy into convulsions. She jumped out of bed and got the bone from her toy box and gave it to Dianne, and then she hid under the covers and cried herself to sleep. Dianne put the bone in her purse, meaning to dispose of it when the child wasn't around, and of course she forgot about it."

"Then the main question is where the kid got it."

"Right," Grandfather said. "And if Sheriff Pilkins doesn't handle it just right, Betsy will be too scared to tell him anything." He thought for a moment and added, "As long as I've known Pilkins, he's never handled anything right."

We turned onto Shady Lane, which was a little dirt street leading off Highway 29 on the outskirts of Wiston. There was plenty of shade but only four houses, set far apart on the north side of the street, and just beyond the fourth house the street dead-ended up against an eight-foot woven wire fence topped with four strands of barbed wire and plastered with NO TRESPASSING signs. That is, it was supposed to dead-end there, but some idiot had mistaken Shady Lane for the Indianapolis Speedway and crashed through the fence and into the pine forest on the other side.

We drove the length of the street, pursued by two barking mongrels, and we found five sheriff and state police cars parked near the last house. I managed to pull in between two of them without picking up any fresh scratches. Grandfather was looking at the hole in the fence.

"That's very interesting."

"What's in there?" I asked.

"That's the old Forsythe estate."

"You've got to be kidding!"

He didn't answer. He thinks slang is vulgar if anyone but him uses it. Sheriff Pilkins came to meet us with the dogs frisking at his heels. He said, "You heard what happened?" Grandfather nodded.

"Daille's wife disappeared over a year ago. First Daille said she was visiting relatives, and then he said she took sick suddenly and died."

"That shouldn't be hard to prove one way or the other," Grandfather observed.

"Yeah – once we get our hands on Daille. No one knows where he's working, not even his housekeeper. Or so she says. If she tips him off that we're looking for him, we may have a long look."

Grandfather jerked a thumb at the hole in the fence. "Looking in there?"

"Later, maybe. That happened last spring, which was a long time after Daille's wife disappeared. With all the wide-open spaces available around here, I can't see him climbing a fence to dispose of a body."

"There are worse places to hide a body than a thick pine forest surrounded by a fence and no trespassing signs."

The sheriff shrugged. "For that matter, one of these dratted dogs could have brought the bone from miles away and buried it in the kid's sand box. But this is where it turned up, and this is where there's a person missing, and that's reason enough to start looking here."

The sheriff walked away, but the dogs stayed and started frisking around Grandfather. I asked him if any of Old Man Forsythe's wives were missing, and he said there wasn't any point in an outsider trying to keep track of them when Forsythe hadn't been able to.

For years we kids had been calling the house on the Forsythe estate Bluebeard's Castle, but I never could figure out why. It was just a big old house, Old Man Forsythe's beard wasn't blue at all but a kind of dirty red that turned white as he got older, and he didn't have nearly as many wives as Bluebeard had. He'd been dead for a long time, but the surviving wives were still fighting over his estate, which probably was why the hole in the fence hadn't been fixed.

"Isn't Forsythe buried in there somewhere?" I asked Grandfather.

He stared at me. "I'd forgotten that. He established a private cemetery. That's why the wives were contesting his will. He's buried in the central plot, surrounded by graves of his favorite dogs, and the wives don't inherit anything unless they agree to be buried with the dogs." He chased after the sheriff and said something to him, and the sheriff raised both hands forlornly and headed for his patrol car.

"Is he going to check the grave?" I asked. Grandfather nodded.

"Forsythe had small hands."

"How far is it to the Wiston Memorial Gardens?"

"About a mile and a half, no fences or pine forest to negotiate, and if anyone makes inquiries of a cemetery about stray finger bones he gets sued for libel."

We walked around a bit, dodging the dogs. In the distance some deputies and state troopers were moving in a line between the Forsythe fence and Highway 29. Otherwise, except for the shade trees along the street and the muddy ruts by the houses where the people parked their cars, as far as the eye could see it saw weeds. As far as my eye could see. Grandfather sees a lot more then I do, in spite of his being past eighty. He says my trouble is that I don't know the difference between looking and seeing.

We circled behind the houses and walked to the highway and back again, and along the way Grandfather picked up one of those little shovels that kids play with in the sand, and a doll's leg, and a marigold blooming so deep in the weeds that I was surprised it bothered, and a ham bone the dogs had been gnawing on.

He pocketed the shovel and the doll's leg. The marigold he sniffed, making a face, and threw away. The ham bone he scowled at and gave to one of the dogs, which ran off closely chased by the other. After he showed me where to look I helped him by finding a petunia and two moss roses near where he'd found the marigold. These were the only signs of cultivation in sight and might have been helpful if we'd been looking for a sloppy horticulturist instead of a murderer.

We went back to the Daille house, and Grandfather knocked on the door. Daille's housekeeper was a girl who couldn't have been long out of high school. She wasn't dressed for company, her hair was a mess, and behind her smudged glasses her eyes were very, very scared.

"I'm an old friend of Jim's family," Grandfather said. "I thought perhaps I could help."

"Oh," she said. "Won't you come in?"

She already had a roomful of company, but that was only because the living room was small and one of the three women present was large enough to make a gymnasium look crowded. As we walked in, the women looked us over as though we were some kind of rare insect showing up out of season. Something crashed in the next room, and the housekeeper excused herself over her shoulder as she dashed out.

"I'm Bill Rastin," Grandfather said. "This is my grandson, Johnny."

"We're Betsy's neighbors," the fat woman said. "I'm Tru Wyler, and this is Ruth Loken and Joyce Dockett."

Grandfather wanted to know who lived where, and the Wyler woman, with the tone of her voice making it very clear that it was none of his business, explained that Ruth Loken lived next door, and Joyce Dockett lived nearest the highway, and she lived between them. The other two could have done a Mutt and Jeff act. Even when sitting down the Dockett woman looked tall enough to play for the Boston Celtics, and Ruth Loken was tiny. Both of them looked positively undernourished beside Tru Wyler. Wyler's head fascinated me, it was so perfectly balanced: several layers of platinum blond hair piled up on top, and several layers of chin piled up underneath. She caught me staring at her and stared right back, and there's no telling where that might have ended if Daille's daughter hadn't started crying in the next room.

"Men!" Tru Wyler said, turning toward the doorway. "That poor kid came down here to look after Betsy because she thinks Daille's going to marry her. A pretty sneaky way of getting a housekeeper to work for nothing, I'd say."

Then Betsy ran into the room. She was a cute little kid with blonde hair tied in pigtails, and she went straight to Tru Wyler, who gathered her up and cooed, "Hello, honey baby." Betsy cooed back and performed a smacking kiss. Tru Wyler commenced making faces at her, and since she had so much material to work with she was able to put on quite a show. Betsy laughed herself into a fit of coughing, and Tru Wyler got that stopped and began whispering baby talk. Grandfather, who thinks children are people, gave her a look of absolute disgust. Fortunately she didn't notice.

Sheriff Pilkins came stomping up the steps. I opened the door for him, and he looked in, glared at Tru Wyler – who glared right back at him – and jerked his thumb at Grandfather. Grandfather excused the two of us, and we went outside.

"Forsythe's grave hasn't been touched," the sheriff said.

"Since when?" Grandfather wanted to know.

"Since it was sodded, right after he was buried. There's a full-time caretaker."

"I didn't say it was a good idea." Grandfather gestured at the horizon, beyond which the police search had disappeared. "If Daille wouldn't climb a fence with the body, what makes you think he'd tote it for miles?"

"I don't. I've called them back." The sheriff pointed at the fence. "We'll have a look in there."

"What are you looking for?"

"The body that bone came from," the sheriff snapped. He stomped away, and Grandfather and I went back into the house.

Tru Wyler was still cooing over Betsy. The housekeeper was sitting across the room. Grandfather took the only other chair, and I stood by the door.

"Is this the book?" Grandfather asked, picking one up from an end table.

The housekeeper nodded. "The sheriff was looking at it."

It was a typical Mother Goose book for children, with stories and nursery rhymes, and most of the colored pictures had been touched up, but not improved, with crayon scribbles. Grandfather turned the pages slowly. Betsy and Tru Wyler continued to coo, and Ruth Loken and Joyce Dockett watched them and tried not to look jealous. The housekeeper looked as if she'd rather the whole parcel of us cleared out.

A car drove up outside, and a moment later a young man came charging up the front steps. He took one step into the room, pointed at Tru Wyler, and shouted, "Out!"

Wyler's face turned a sort of mottled crimson, which did not go at all well with her platinum hair. She wrapped her arms protectively around Betsy and hissed, "Wife-killer!"

He stepped across the room. They faced each other, her in the chair and him standing over her, and both of them breathing heavily and hating. He'd come directly from work, probably driving a long way, and his shirt was crusted with salt where perspiration had dried, and his curly hair was a tangle, and he looked calm and deadly. She looked hot and flustered even though she had on a light summer dress and didn't have one platinum hair out of place.

Suddenly he snatched at Betsy. The kid started to howl, and Wyler held on, and for a moment I thought they were going to play tug of war with her. Then Daille drew his fist back, and Wyler seemed to know that any notions he might have about chivalry wouldn't apply to her. She let go, and he handed Betsy, still howling, to his housekeeper and chased her out of the room with a glance.

He pointed at the door, which the other two women were already using. It was something to see Tru Wyler struggle out of that chair. Her chins moved one at a time, she pushed with both hands, and it wouldn't have surprised me if she'd popped like a cork coming out of a bottle. Finally she got to her feet and started to move. I expected her to shake the house when she walked, but she took delicate little steps and managed to look about as dignified as one can when being ordered out of a house.

At the door she turned. "Wife-killer," she hissed again. "The poor baby – her own mother's finger –"

He took a step toward her, and she went through the door sideways and disappeared. Daille turned to us, still pointing at the door.

Grandfather said, "Are you Jim Daille? I'm Bill Rastin, a friend of your grandfather's. This is my grandson, Johnny."

"Oh," Daille said. He closed the door and slumped back against it with his hands over his face.

"The witches!" he muttered. "The filthy witches!" His whole body was trembling with rage. Suddenly he straightened up and looked at Grandfather. "What's going on here?"

Grandfather told him, speaking very slowly and keeping his eyes on Daille's face.

"Bone?" Daille repeated. "A human bone?" Grandfather nodded.

"So that's what the old witch meant!"

"You didn't know anything about this?"

He shook his head. "Shirley telephoned my landlady that there was big trouble here and I was needed, and I started as soon as I got the message. This filthy neighborhood! I should have left years ago, but I've had so darned many bills, and what with my work being seasonal –"

In the next room Betsy started to howl again. Daille said bitterly, "It wasn't enough that they poisoned my wife's mind. Now they're working on my daughter and I suppose on Shirley, too. The witches! I've put up with this long enough. Shirley!"

The housekeeper stuck her head around the corner, looking scared to death.

"Start packing," Daille said. "We're getting out of here right now. Permanently."

"This might not be the best time for you to leave," Grandfather said.

"The best time would have been a long time ago. But I hated to farm Betsy out like an orphan, wanted her brought up in her own home, and with all the bills I've had I just couldn't manage another place."

"What sort of trouble have you been having with your neighbors?"

Daille snorted. "Those foul-minded witches! Couldn't keep men of their own to bedevil – all three of them are divorced – so they take their spite out on any man they can get their claws into. If you'll excuse me – I want to pack some clothes. Then I'm going to walk away and leave this house and every lousy thing in it to rot."

He went to the bedroom, and Grandfather sat down in a chair and crossed his legs and screwed up his face. He was thinking so hard that he didn't even look up when the sheriff came to the door.

"Is Daille here?" the sheriff asked.

I nodded.

The sheriff hesitated, did some thinking of his own, went out and came back with four deputies. As it turned out, this was one situation he handled correctly. It started out real friendly-like, the sheriff saying, "Where's your wife, son," and Daille answering politely.

"None of your damned business", and the sheriff saying, less friendly but just as politely, "I think it is and I have a warrant for your arrest."

By the time it ended the sheriff needed all four of his deputies, and it was just as well that Daille wasn't planning on taking the furnishing with him because two chairs, the coffee table, a floor lamp, and the television set weren't in condition to furnish anything but a junk yard.

Grandfather and I ducked outside when it started and waited until they'd persuaded Daille to come quietly. The sheriff had one eye that was going to get worse before it got any better, and Daille's shirt was ripped, but otherwise the furniture took most of the punishment.

We helped the housekeeper clean up the mess. She was being brave about it and trying not to cry. Grandfather sat down in the kitchen to talk with her, and I spent the next half hour baby sitting. I read aloud from the Mother Goose book, and Betsy pulled herself onto the sofa and sat watching me very seriously. I gave her the latest scoop on the three little pigs, and Goldilocks and the three bears, and then – intentionally skipping the history of Tom Thumb – I acted out Jack and the three beanstalks in a new and improved version of my own.

When Grandfather finished, we went outside. Steve Carling, one of Sheriff Pilkins's deputies, was standing by the hole in the fence looking forlorn. "Those dratted trees are thick," he complained. "You need a machete to hack your way through."

"Cheer up," Grandfather said. "Maybe Daille will confess."

"Not him. He isn't stupid. He'll know we haven't got much of a case with one finger bone."

State Police Sergeant Reichel drove up and wanted to know where his men were, and when Steve pointed at the woods the sergeant shook his head and commenced wondering if he should start sending out search parties.

"This fellow Daille seems to be a very unusual sort of murderer," he said.

"Have you bought it?" Grandfather asked.

"I think so. Haven't you?"

"I came over here ready to buy it, but since I got here I've turned up something that has me wondering."

"What's that?"

"Nothing that says he didn't do it. Just something that makes me wonder if he did. Pilkins should have done some checking before he arrested him."

The sergeant had a big bag of hamburgers, which he invited us to share. The two mongrel dogs showed up as soon as we started eating and hung around until the Dockett woman, in the house nearest the highway, called them and put out a pan of food.

Sergeant Reichel told us that Daille had spoken only four words after his arrest, "I want a lawyer," but that Sheriff Pilkins had his man and seemed pretty confident about finding a body to go with the finger bone.

By that time it was getting dark. Sheriff Pilkins drove up and hallooed everyone out of the woods, but they were coming anyway. They stood around eating Sergeant Reichel's hamburgers and arguing.

The sheriff said disgustedly, "Those dratted women can't even agree on when they last saw Daille's wife. Mrs. Wyler is positive he took her and the kid on a trip and came back without her."

"That's interesting," Grandfather said. "He brought back just a finger bone?"

The sheriff shrugged. "Wyler lives two houses away and anyway is gone half the time visiting her sister. Ruth Loken lives next door and should know, but she has a cottage on Mud Lake and spends half her time there in warm weather. Anyway, she's positive she saw Mrs. Daille a number of times after that trip. Wyler didn't see her. Mrs. Dockett is still trying to remember. The only proposition that gets no argument is that Daille is a heel. All three of them hate his guts."

"Why?" Grandfather wanted to know.

"At a guess, because he hired housekeepers instead of letting one of them look after Betsy."

The sheriff announced that he was going to have another try at getting the kid to talk. Grandfather walked off with Sergeant Reichel and Steve Carling. I went with the sheriff, because he'd heard about my reading stories to Betsy and wanted to find out if I could coax anything out of her.

The moment she saw him she started to howl. I quieted that by standing on my head, which made her giggle, but every time I stopped she began howling again, and I am not good at asking questions while standing on my head. All the sheriff did was sit in the corner and scratch at his bald spot, and when we finally gave up his head must have been as sore as mine.

Then the three witches – excuse me, Mrs. Wyler, Mrs. Loken, and Mrs. Dockett – came in from the rear of the house, and about the same time Grandfather entered from the front. I gave the sheriff my resignation, telling him that a performance before such a large audience would jeopardize my amateur standing.

Chairs were moved in from the kitchen to replace the broken ones, and everyone sat down. Betsy was already cooing at Mrs. Wyler, and that gave the sheriff the bright idea that Mrs. Wyler should ask the questions.

"Nothing doing," she announced flatly.

"Look," Sheriff Pilkins said. "You used an hour of my time this afternoon telling me what a rat Daille is. Don't you want him convicted?"

"You bet your fat head I do!"

"This is all I need to wrap up the case."

She was torn. She thought the little innocent shouldn't be tricked into giving evidence that would convict her own father, but at the same time she had a happy vision of Daille behind bars, and obviously she wanted to keep him there, "All right," she said finally.

She cooed at Betsy, "Look, honey babe. Remember the little bone?"

Betsy cooed right back at her, "Noooooooooo." And that was how it went.

Grandfather listened disgustedly for a few minutes, and then he picked up Betsy's story book. During the next lull in the cooing, he announced "Old Mrs. McShuttle lived in a coal-scuttle, along with her dog and cat."

The sheriff and the women glared at him. Betsy giggled.

Grandfather went on, "What they ate I can't tell, but 'tis known very well, that none of the party were fat."

"The bone, honey babe," Mrs. Wyler said icily.

"Noooooooooo," Betsy said.

Grandfather spoke again. "Old Mother Hubbard went to the cupboard, to get her poor dog –"

"Shut up!" the sheriff snapped.

"The little bone you were playing with, honey baby. You must remember where you found it."

"Noooooooooooo."

"They all ran after the farmer's wife, who cut off their tails with a carving knife."

"For God's sake!" the sheriff exclaimed.

"She whipped them all soundly and put them to bed. Doesn't it frighten you the way the children of America are brought up on such unvarnished tales of violence?"

"The little bone, Betsy –"

"Noooooooooo."

"Be he live or be he dead, I'll grind his bones to make my bread."

All of the women blanched, and when Tru Wyler tried again to say, "The little bone –" she choked on it.

"And crime," Grandfather went on, seeming not to notice. "The Knave of Hearts he stole some tarts. Tom Tom the Piper's son stole a pig and away he run." He paused. "I don't think so much of the grammar, either."

The housekeeper, whose eyes were now very red behind her glasses, came in to announce that it was Betsy's bedtime. No one paid any attention.

"The little bone," Mrs. Wyler cooed. "Where did you get the little bone, honey babe?"

"Noooooooooooo."

"Mistress Mary, quite contrary how does your garden grow? With silver bells and cockle shells and little bones all in a row."

That produced a commotion all around the room, but I didn't pay any attention to it because I was watching Betsy. She giggled. "Little bones."

"Little bones," Grandfather said. "Little bones among the flowers, you sit and play with them for hours."

Mrs. Wyler's chins were making like an accordion. Mrs. Loken had opened her mouth and forgot to close it. Mrs. Dockett was leaning forward, and I noticed for the first time that she wore a hearing aid.

Everyone seemed absolutely fascinated except Betsy, who climbed onto Mrs. Wyler's lap, held up her hands pattycake style, and said, "Play."

Mrs. Dockett, who was sitting by the window, suddenly exclaimed, "There's a light out there behind your house, Ruth."

Mrs. Loken looked out. "Something funny's going on out there."

The sheriff started for the door, and everyone chased after him except the housekeeper, who finally was able to claim Betsy, and Mrs. Wyler. When I left the room Mrs. Wyler, was struggling to get out of her chair, but the only things moving were her chins.

She was the last one to find out that the light was behind her house.

Steve Carling and another deputy were digging a hole while a state trooper held a flashlight for them.

"What's going on here?" the sheriff roared.

Steve leaned on his shovel. "It's Rastin's idea. Sergeant Reichel is on his way with a search warrant, but in the meantime you were keeping the old dame occupied, and we thought –"

"Who are you working for – me, or Rastin, or Reichel?" He was about to explode, but he postponed it to ask one more question. "What have you found?"

"Nothing, yet."

"Nothing, yet. Of all the idiotic, lamebrained, imbecile things to do! Walk onto private property in the middle of the night and start digging a hole. I ought to dump you into it and fill it in. If you're hard up for exercise –"

He stopped, because Tru Wyler came up behind him very quietly and stuck a shotgun into his back. "Get out," she purred. "All of you – get out."

Steve turned quickly and fell into the hole. It was only six inches deep, so he climbed out fast and headed for the property line. Grandfather stood his ground. The rest of us backed off, all except the sheriff, who had been caught facing the wrong way. He marched straight ahead.

Mrs. Wyler made one small miscalculation. She had the shotgun, but the state trooper held the flashlight. He suddenly thought to turn it off, and when he turned it on again Grandfather had the gun. He handed it to the sheriff, who checked it and announced that it wasn't loaded.

"They're digging," Grandfather told Mrs. Wyler, "because this is where Daille buried his wife."

"Here? In my yard?"

Grandfather nodded.

"I don't believe it." She stared at him for a moment, very coldly, and he stared right back. "Go ahead and dig," she said finally, "but I don't believe it."

She went back to her house, taking those dignified little steps, and then she spoiled the effect by slamming the door. Just then Sergeant Reichel arrived with his search warrant and seemed pleased to find that it wasn't needed. I meant to ask him how far down a search warrant covers but forgot.

The deputies started to dig again, with Grandfather standing by to examine every shovelful. Things went easily enough for the first couple of feet and then progressively harder until they struck clay that obviously hadn't been disturbed for years. The sheriff said to Grandfather, "Well?"

"It was just an idea," Grandfather said.

"Sure. You didn't say it was a good idea. Why'd you have them digging here? You been using a devining rod, or something?"

"Something like that," Grandfather said.

"The next time you have an idea –"

A cool voice said sarcastically, "If you've finished playing games, you can fill in the hole."

The three women were standing there in the dark, watching. "Fill it in," the sheriff said disgustedly.

"Fill it in neatly," Tru Wyler said.

She stood by giving orders and enjoying every minute of it, with the other women giggling and offering gratuitous suggestions of their own, and they raised such a fuss about leaving the yard in the precise condition we'd found it that the sheriff promised to send someone out in the morning to replant the weeds.

Sergeant Reichel had gone over to use the radio on his police car, and he came back and said to Grandfather, "They found it."

"Congratulations," Grandfather said. "I can't remember a more efficient investigation."

"Congratulations to you. It was right where you said it would be."

"Yes. Well – people tend to repeat themselves."

"I don't want to sound inquisitive," Sheriff Pilkins complained, "but if it's this murder case of mine that you two are talking about, I'd like to know what's going on."

"Where can we talk?" Grandfather asked. "Mrs. Wyler's house?"

"Certainly not!" she snapped.

"I thought maybe you'd want to know why we were digging up your yard," Grandfather said. "We've bothered Daille's housekeeper enough for one day, but I suppose we can go back there."

Mrs. Wyler decided that maybe we could use her house, but she wouldn't let us in until she'd spread newspapers all over her living room floor. There weren't enough chairs for everyone, so I stood in the corner behind Grandfather. Mrs. Wyler had her own oversized chair on the other side of the room, Ruth Loken and Joyce Dockett took the sofa, and the deputies and state troopers played Alphonso and Gaston with the chairs that were left.

"The first question," Grandfather said, keeping his eyes on Tru Wyler, "was where the bone came from. The only place for some distance around here where any dirt has ever been turned over is the flower bed in your back yard."

"I didn't see any flower bed," the sheriff objected.

"I had bad luck with it this year," Mrs. Wyler said. "Nothing came up but weeds."

"I saw it because I was looking for it," Grandfather told the sheriff. "Once I'd found it there wasn't much of a problem in figuring out what happened. Look at it from Daille's point of view. He had a body to dispose of, and in Mrs. Wyler's yard was a flower bed maybe just spaded for the season and the right size for burying a body. What could be simpler than to go out on a night when no one was home, bury the body, carry away any surplus dirt, and leave the bed all ready for planting?"

Mrs. Wyler said, "You mean all this time – in my flower bed –"

Grandfather nodded. "For almost a year. But this spring Mrs. Dockett adopted a couple of stray dogs, and Daille looked out one day and saw them digging in the flower bed. Of course that wouldn't do, so he picked another time when his neighbors were away, dug up the body, and hid it somewhere else. His timing was a little off, though. The flowers already had been planted. After he turned the dirt over they didn't do well."

Sheriff Pilkins leaned forward. "The bone?"

"Working at night, he easily could have overlooked one bone. Or maybe one of the dogs did dig up something, and Betsy found it."

"So that's what you were getting at with that Mother Goose stuff about bones in flower beds!" Tru Wyler exclaimed.

Grandfather grinned. "Not exactly, but that's why we dug up your yard. I figured we wouldn't find anything, but we had to check. There was always the chance that more than one bone had been overlooked."

She nodded, working the accordion under her chin. "I see. He dug up the body –" She paused. "My flowers were planted toward the end of April, so if he dug there shortly after that – for a moment you had me fooled, Mr. Rastin. I thought you were an exceptional man, meaning that you might possibly possess normal intelligence. I was wrong. This year Daille was gone all spring. If the dogs were digging in my flower bed he wouldn't have seen them, and he couldn't have done any digging there himself."

"He could have returned at night. With you and Mrs. Loken gone –"

"No," She shook her head. "It's no use, Mr. Rastin. You can't think that body into my flower bed. It was early summer last year when Mrs. Daille disappeared, and my flowers had a nice start by then. He couldn't have buried her there without ruining them, and last year they were beautiful."

The sheriff said dryly, "I can't see Daille burying his wife so shallow that a dog could disturb the body."

"Frankly, neither can I," Grandfather agreed. "And if he wouldn't do it that way, and if the flower bed wasn't disturbed when she disappeared, and if he wasn't home this spring to dig her up, that brings us to the next question: Whose body was it? Because there was a body in your flower bed, Mrs. Wyler. That was where the bone came from. Unfortunately Sheriff Pilkins has a talent for jumping at conclusions. Daille's daughter had the bone, Daille's wife was missing, so he jumped. The fact is that on this short street there are four missing persons."

"Four?" the sheriff exclaimed.

"One wife," Grandfather said, "and three husbands. Do you have anything to say about that, Mrs. Wyler?"

"Only that you get more ridiculous every time you open your mouth. All three of us are divorced."

Grandfather nodded. "So I heard. And ever since I heard it I've been wondering if maybe one of your husbands didn't leave soon enough. But first, tell me how it is that you happen to have a flower bed, Mrs. Wyler. I don't mean to be discourteous, I'm just looking at the situation objectively. You don't impress me as the gardening type. Did you plant the flowers yourself?" She didn't answer.

"And spade the ground? And weed it? A flower bed entirely surrounded by weeds would require a lot of weeding."

Mrs. Wyler set very still. She was looking a little like that Egyptian Sphinx would look if it had a lot of chins. Then, very slowly, she turned to Mrs. Loken.

"Ruth – Ruth always spaded it. Spaded it and planted it and weeded it. She said she was glad to do it for me. The whole thing was her idea. I was away, and when I came home she said, 'You always talked about having a few flowers. Well, I've made a flower bed for you.' That must have been ten years ago."

"Eleven," Grandfather said. "Enough time to account for the fact that there wasn't any tissue left on the bone. And this year she stopped weeding it?"

Mrs. Wyler did her accordion nod.

"And the first year she planted it was the year her husband 'divorced' her?"

Mrs. Wyler hesitated. "I think – yes –"

"We had four missing persons on this street," Grandfather said. "Thanks to some remarkably quick and efficient investigating by Sergeant Reichel, three of them are accounted for. Daille's wife died down in Indiana, as he said, and is buried there. Mr. Wyler divorced his wife twenty years ego, and he died – legitimately – five years later and is buried in Hollyhock Cemetery in Wiston. Mr. Dockett is living in Cincinnati. He remarried and has seven children. Mr. Loken disappeared eleven years ego and hasn't been seen since-not until this evening, anyway, except for one finger bone. Would you like to tell us about him, Mrs. Loken?"

Now Ruth Loken was the Sphinx, minus chins, staring straight ahead and not moving a muscle.

Grandfather turned to Mrs. Wyler. "Let's start over again. Instead of a husky man, we have a rather small woman with a heavy husband to dispose of. That's the description the sergeant turned up – a small man, with small hands, but very obese. Daille's house hadn't been built eleven years ago, and the only neighbors were yourself and Mrs. Dockett. Information is that you've been paying your sister these overnight visits for more than eleven years, and eleven years ago Mrs. Dockett already was hard of hearing. Mrs. Loken maybe had the idea of dragging the body away somewhere and hiding it, but she quickly found out that she couldn't do it. She made a flower bed instead."

"So that's why she was so good about tending my flowers," Mrs. Wyler said through clenched teeth.

"Until this year," Grandfather said. "This year her husband was no longer buried there, and she lost interest. Why did you move him, Mrs. Loken? The dogs? Betsy digging with her little shovel?"

Mrs. Loken had gone ghostly white, and she wasn't saying a thing.

"That's all very well," the sheriff said, "but one finger bone still doesn't make much of a corpus delicti."

"Oh, we have the rest of him," Sergeant Reichel said. "He was buried right where Rastin told us to look – at her lake cottage under a flower bed."

"You told me to do it!" Mrs. Loken shrieked, jumping at Mrs. Wyler. "You said a man like him deserved to be dead!"

They hauled her away, still screaming.

After that the gathering broke up fast, and we were left alone with Mrs. Wyler. She'd aged in those few minutes until she looked as old as she actually was, which is a horrible condition for any woman to be in. She said, "I didn't know. I always talk, but I never thought of anyone doing a thing like that."

"People react to talk in different ways," Grandfather said. "Do you know what happened to Mrs. Daille?"

"No."

"She'd had a nervous breakdown before they moved here. Her doctor thought a quiet place in the country might be good for her. Because Daille was gone so much he didn't realize what you were doing to her until it was too late. He put her in a private mental hospital down in Indiana – it was expensive, he's still paying for it – and while she was there she succeeded in committing suicide. He's trying to keep it a secret, for Betsy's sake."

"Men –" she croaked.

We left her.

"She's as much a murderess as Mrs. Loken is," I said, as we were getting into my jalopy. Grandfather agreed. "But the law can't touch her," he said. "We'll have to leave it to her conscience – and hope she has one."

"You already had everything figured out. Why all that fa de la with the Mother Goose rhymes?"

"Reichel hadn't found the body yet, and I wanted to make certain I was right. Did you see Mrs. Loken's face when I first mentioned bones in a flower bed?"

"No. I was watching Betsy."

"You and Pilkins both. Put him in the room with a murderess and he looks the other way."

"If you'd told me to watch a murderess, I'd have picked Mrs. Wyler. She looks like one. It was her back yard, too."

Grandfather shook his head. "I can't see her going out at night with a shovel to bury a body and then digging it up again and burying it somewhere else. Anyway, I knew she wasn't directly involved in this particular murder because she told the truth about Daille's wife. She said Daille took his wife on a trip and came back without her. She wouldn't have said that if she hadn't thought it was true, or if she'd been worried that the police might decide it wasn't Daille's wife there were looking for. She hated Daille's guts, and she really thought he'd killed his wife, but where he did it wasn't important to her. It was very important to Mrs. Loken. From her point of view Mrs. Daille had to be killed here, to account for the bone. So she lied and said she'd seen Mrs. Daille at home after the trip, and the lie gave her away."

"I still think something should be done about Mrs. Wyler," I said. "She's the only woman I ever met who could play a witch without being made up. Isn't there some way to punish her?"

"I think maybe there is," Grandfather said. "It wouldn't be much, but I suppose I'm bound to do what I can."

What he did was persuade Jim Daille to sell his house to three crusty old bachelors. It'd be nice to report that Mrs. Wyler mended her ways, dieted off a hundred pounds, and married one of them, but she didn't. She put up with them for all of two weeks, and then she moved away.

A MATTER OF FRIENDSHIP

Borg County, Michigan, is an old-fashioned kind of place. It's still possible to find a blacksmith there, just in case you have a horse to keep in footwear, but his business comes from city slickers who board riding horses on Borg County farms. Borg County railroad crossings are still mostly guarded by those X-shaped STOP, LOOK, LISTEN signs. (Grandfather Rastin maintains that the most important word was left out – THINK! There's no other way to explain the people who come to a full stop, wait, and then drive in front of a train.)

Towns and villages in the county still have Ladies' Literary Societies, and thus far no men's lib group has been interested enough, or foolish enough, to try to join one. A lot of people still go to town on Saturday night, and meet their friends, and do their shopping. In the summer, high school bands give Saturday night concerts in village bandstands. Fourth of July is the biggest day of the year, with parades and community picnics, and fireworks, and it's a rare Borg County politician that doesn't have a rousing, patriotic Fourth of July speech ready to deliver at the drop of a Roman candle.

There aren't any special Senior Citizens' Days or Old-Timers' Days, because senior citizens and old timers are considered people like everyone else. They're a part of everything that happens, and in Borg County we don't need special days to remind us that they're still with us. Not many of the old timers are Grandfather's age, but there are plenty of men and women ten or fifteen years younger. Grandfather has known these youngsters for forty or fifty years or longer, and he mostly regards them with tolerance and amusement while waiting for them to attain the age of wisdom and responsibility. And when, now and then, one of them commits some kind of foolishness and gets criticized for living so long without learning anything, Grandfather always objects. "He learned plenty," he will say, "but he had so many years to forget what he'd learned."

The most unusual house in Michigan stands half a mile west of Borgville, on Dry Creek Road. It's built of stones and cement and bottles and tin cans, and there are bottle necks sticking out all over the thing. The owner is a queer old geezer named Mike Fitzharris, who built the place himself, and Mike claims that on a windy day he has the prettiest-sounding house in the whole state.

In case you have some idea of driving over on a Sunday afternoon to enjoy the music – don't. It takes a personal invitation from Mike to get you close enough to that house to hear the bottles, and Mike isn't generous with his invitations. The People-Who-Have-Heard-Mike's-House make up what is probably the most exclusive society in Borgville, where we have a lot of exclusive societies.

I didn't have music on my mind when I drove out Dry Creek Road that Saturday morning. All I was thinking about was eggs, which Mom had suddenly discovered she was without. She'd promised to bake a cake for the church social that night, and since she does not consider an egg to be fresh unless it can be traced pretty directly to the chicken, I was on my way to the Carter farm for what Grandfather Rastin likes to call hen fruit.

As I passed Mike's place, his daughter, who is the Miss Azalea Fitzharris who teaches fifth grade at the Borgville elementary school, stepped into the road and flagged me down.

"I'm afraid something's happened to dad," she said.

I went up to Mike's house with her – that is, we went as far as the six-foot board fence that is topped with three feet of barbed wire. On the other side of the fence Mike's dog walked slowly back and forth and snarled whenever we touched the fence.

Mike's dog isn't easy to describe. I once asked Grandfather what kind it was, and he said it was a 'cross between a Shetland pony and a mountain lion. I can tell you this much about it: whenever anyone fusses with the latch on Mike's gate, that dog acts a lot more like a lion than a pony. I've heard people call it a man-eating dog, which isn't true, but only because no man has been foolish enough to give it a chance.

I threw some rocks at the door, and the dog started an awful uproar and tried to knock the fence down to get at me.

"I'd better get Mr. Carter," I said.

I ran across the road to the Carter farm, and Mr. Carter, who'd had some personal experience with Mike's dog, said he never liked getting bit that early in the morning. He called Sheriff Pilkins, and then we went back to Mike's place and waited.

It was nearly ten o'clock when Sheriff Pilkins got there. He wasn't in much of a hurry to get bit himself, and he said Mike probably had gone to town, or fishing, or something, so why not just wait until he got back? Miss Fitzharris said Mike always was home on Saturday, because that was the day she did his cleaning, and fixed food for him for the next week, and drove him if he wanted to go anywhere. So she knew he was in the house waiting for her, and if he didn't come out it was because he'd had a stroke or something.

"I guess I'll have to shoot the dog," Sheriff Pilkins said.

Mr. Carter said Mike wouldn't like that – he was powerfully fond of that dog. We stood there talking it over, while the dog made lunges at the fence, and finally Mr. Carter went for a rope and a ladder, and lassoed the dog with a lucky toss, and tied it up. We found the inside of Mike's house looking as if a tornado had passed through, and Mike was on the floor unconscious with his head bashed.

Doc Beyers came in a hurry, and the sheriff radioed to Wiston for an ambulance. Mike came to just before the ambulance got there, but the only thing he could tell us was that someone had knocked on his door sometime during the night, and when he opened the door they let him have it. He didn't even get a glimpse of them. He'd come to a couple of times before help got there, but he was too weak to get off the floor.

"Was the dog tied?" Sheriff Pilkins asked.

"Never tie him at night," Mike said.

"Then how could anyone walk up and knock on your door?"

"I dunno," Mike said. "He never barked or nothing. Never made a sound, or I'd of heard it. I'm a light sleeper."

"What about your money?" the sheriff asked.

Mike laughed. "That's safe enough."

"Tell me where you keep it, and I'll see if it's still there."

Mike laughed again, and Doc Beyers told the sheriff to stop making Mike laugh because it wasn't good for his head. The ambulance took him to the hospital in Wiston, and I turned my jalopy around and headed home to tell Grandfather what had happened.

Grandfather was rocking on the front porch, and he grinned at me as I came up the steps and asked, "Were the chickens on strike?"

"My gosh!" I said. "I forgot all about the eggs."

"Never mind. Your mother waited for an hour and a half with the egg beater in her hand, and then she borrowed some from Mrs. Peterson. If I were you I'd stay clear of the kitchen until lunch time."

I told him about Mike Fitzharris, and Grandfather stepped up his rocking a notch or two.

"There's something mighty peculiar about this."

"Even Sheriff Pilkins could see that," I said.

Grandfather rocked a little faster. "Maybe I should go out there. Is the dog still tied up?"

"It was when I left. Do you want to go now?"

"After lunch," Grandfather said. "I want to get that rent money to the bank before it closes."

I walked over to the bank with him. In the meantime Sheriff Pilkins had been doing some heavy thinking, which is more of a strain on him than he likes to admit. He thought the problem through forward and backward, and then he and his deputy, Steve Carling, drove to Borgville and made a few inquiries, and at ten minutes to twelve they walked into the Borgville Bank and arrested Grandfather Rastin.

The sheriff has been threatening to do that for years, but no one ever took him seriously, least of all Grandfather. I'd say Grandfather was the most shocked man in forty-eleven counties when the sheriff stepped up to him, yanked the deposit slip out of his hand, and told Steve Carling to use his handcuffs.

The bank is always crowded and noisy on Saturday morning, but ten seconds after the sheriff walked in you could have heard a penny drop, if anyone present had wanted to invest a penny in a scientific experiment. Everyone turned and stared. Mae Robinson, who was working the teller window because her pa was laid up with rheumatism, opened the grill and leaned out to watch.

The sheriff might have got away with it if it hadn't been for Mrs. Pobloch. She was making out a withdrawal slip at the back of the lobby, and at first she didn't see what was happening. Just as she looked around, Grandfather decided to make a joke of the whole business. He raised both hands high over his head. Mrs. Pobloch didn't see the sheriff, and she thought to herself, "My God! It's a holdup!"

She turned around and ran out the back door into the alley and circled around to Main Street. The sheriff's car was parked at the curb, and when Mrs. Pobloch saw it she got in and waited for him so she could tell him about the holdup.

I expected an argument between the sheriff and Grandfather that would crack the ceiling and break the bank's plate glass window, but Grandfather didn't say a thing. First he put his hands up, and then he started to laugh.

You will understand that I have never had any experience, but I think it must be terribly difficult to arrest a man who is laughing. Sheriff Pilkins stood there with a foolish look on his face, and Steve Carling stood beside him holding the handcuffs and not knowing what to do with them. Finally the sheriff grabbed Grandfather's arm.

"Come along," he said.

Grandfather went, still laughing, and Steve followed behind them still trying to decide what he should do with the handcuffs. The sheriff steered Grandfather out of the bank and down the sidewalk toward his car. I hurried after them, meaning to ask Grandfather if I should tell Lawyer Arnell about it, but before I could say anything Steve Carling stepped ahead and opened the rear door of the patrol car. Mrs. Pobloch, who was hiding on the floor of the back seat, rolled out onto the sidewalk.

"The bank's being robbed!" she screamed. What happened next is called a reflex action in the psychology section of our high school science text. Suddenly the sheriff and Steve Carling were disappearing back into the bank, and Grandfather was headed along Main Street, walking away fast.

I caught up with him and asked him what he was going to do.

"I feel the need of a shave," he said.

He went into Jake Palmer's barber shop and spoke to Jake, and Jake tilted him back in a chair and slapped a towel over his face. I ducked into an alley, and when the sheriff came out of the bank maybe one second later, both of us had disappeared.

It'd be hard to describe what happened there on Main Street for the next thirty minutes, except to say that Borgville hadn't seen anything like it since the day Marty Barnett's monkey got loose. The sheriff and Steve charged up and down, stopping people and asking questions and getting madder by the second. The only one who could have helped them was Nat Barlow, who was sitting on the bench in front of the barber shop, and Nat has his own reasons for not liking Sheriff Pilkins.

Nat told the sheriff he'd seen Grandfather ride by in Bill Sorenson's pickup truck, and the sheriff put out an alert for Bill, and the State Police arrested him over by Wiston. By the time things were straightened out, Bill had wasted two hours and the sheriff had lost forty votes, because there are a lot of Sorensons in Borg County.

After threatening half the population of Borgville with arrest, the sheriff finally gave up and drove away.

I found Grandfather in Walt Pobloch's apartment above the barber shop, talking with Walt and Jake Palmer.

"What's got into Pilkins?" Grandfather wanted to know.

"Mike Fitzharris was hit over the head and robbed last night," Walt said.

"What's that got to do with me?" Grandfather asked.

"Pilkins thinks you went to the bank to deposit Mike's money."

"Horse feathers!"

"It's the truth," Walt said. "He was around earlier asking who Mike's friends are. He thinks it had to be someone that visited Mike regularly, on account of the dog."

"That's the way Pilkins's mind would work," Grandfather said disgustedly. "No one but a real close friend would hit a man over the head and rob him."

"What are you going to do now?" Jake asked.

"I've been meaning to take a look at that new county jail," Grandfather said, "but I'd rather do it on visitor's day. I think I'll stay out of sight until Pilkins simmers down."

"You can stay here," Walt said. "If Pilkins comes looking for you, we'll stuff you into the attic."

"Thanks," Grandfather said. He turned to me. "Johnny, see what you can find out about this mess."

When I left he was looking around for a rocking chair, but the Poblochs didn't have one.

My first thought was to tell Mom what had happened, and when I got home Sheriff Pilkins and Steve Carling were waiting on the porch.

"Where's your Grandfather?" the sheriff asked.

"I thought you arrested him," I said.

The sheriff roared something about arresting me, too, and that brought Mom to the door.

"What this county needs," she said, "is a woman sheriff."

The sheriff didn't have any answer to that. He sat down in the porch swing, and Steve sat on the railing and played with his handcuffs.

"Where was your Grandfather last night?" the sheriff asked suddenly.

"Asleep in bed," I said.

"Yeah? Where'd he get that money he was putting in the bank?"

"That was the rent money from the house he owns in Jackson," I said. "I drove him up there yesterday to collect it."

"Your Grandfather's a pretty good friend of Mike Fitzharris, isn't he?"

"As far as I know," I said.

"Your Grandfather and who else?"

"Nat Barlow," I said. "Mr. Gregory. Fred Wallace. Probably some others."

"Tell your Grandfather he's a fugitive from justice, and I'm getting a warrant. Come on, Steve."

They drove off. Mom had lunch ready, and while I was eating I told her about Grandfather being arrested. If it worried her she didn't stop laughing long enough to show it.

After lunch I went back up town. People were talking mainly about two things that afternoon – how Grandfather made a monkey out of the sheriff, and what happened to Mike Fitzharris. Of course the one thing everyone wanted to know was whether the crook had found Mike's money. For years there'd been rumors about the fortune Mike had hid in his house, and that tall fence and a vicious dog of one kind or another running loose inside hadn't done anything to quiet them. People thought there had to be something there that was worth guarding.

They also thought it was just as safe as it would have been in the bank, if not safer, because the Borgville Bank was held up once, back in 1937, and if anyone had figured out a way to get past one of Mike's dogs he hadn't had the nerve to try it out.

Not until now, that is. The sheriff soft-pedaled the way the crook had torn Mike's house apart, but keeping something like that quiet in Borgville is a little like trying to plug a volcano.

I wandered around listening to people, and in twenty minutes I knew as much as the sheriff did and maybe a little more. Then I sneaked down the alley and climbed the outside stairway to the Pobloch's apartment.

The door was locked, and I heard Mrs. Pobloch squeal when I knocked. Walt asked through the door who it was, and then he let me in. Grandfather was sitting in a big easy chair looking through the curtains at Main Street.

"There goes Pilkins again," he said. "A chicken with its head cut off has more brains."

I sat down and told him what I'd found out, which wasn't a lot more than we already knew. What bothered the sheriff was the fact that Mike's dog let the crook walk right up to the door and knock. The sheriff even got our local veterinarian, Doc Williby, to check the dog over and see if it'd been drugged. Doc never finished his examination, but he got a few licks in before the dog bit him, and he said there wasn't anything wrong with it that a shotgun wouldn't cure.

"Maybe the crook tossed it a steak," I said.

"That wouldn't keep it from taking the hide off anyone that stepped through that gate."

"Anyway, that's why the sheriff tried to arrest you," I said. "That, plus the fact that he found you in the bank. He figures the crook has to be a close friend of Mike's, because no one else could have got past the dog. It had to be someone the dog was used to. Maybe he has the right idea, at that."

Grandfather shook his head. "Neither of us will live long enough to see Pilkins get a right idea. He can't see beyond his nose, and he has a short nose. For one thing, any friend of Mike's knows that dog well enough to stay out of the yard when Mike isn't standing by. The dog seems to like me, but you'd never catch me sneaking through that gate in the dark. I'd throw rocks at the door until I got Mike out of bed so he could keep a hand on the dog. For another thing, no friend of Mike's would try to rob him, because Mike hasn't got any money. He lives from one pension check to the next, and his checks aren't large.

"How many of his friends know that?" I asked.

"All of them."

"Lots of people believe those rumors about him being rich. Sheriff Pilkins wanted Mike to tell him where the money was hid, and Mike laughed at him."

"He would," Grandfather said. "He thinks those rumors are a joke. What's Pilkins doing now?"

"He's still investigating Mike's friends. One of the deputies took Nat Barlow somewhere for questioning. I don't think Nat minded, because he got to ride in the sheriff's patrol car. Sheriff Pilkins cornered Mr. Gregory and asked to see his restaurant books, and then he claimed Mr. Gregory robbed Mike because his business was bad. Mr. Gregory said the restaurant business always has been bad in Borgville, and he'd of robbed Mike years ago if he thought it would help. Now the sheriff is looking for Fred Wallace."

"It wasn't any of them," Grandfather said. "They know Mike hasn't any money, and even if they didn't they'd be afraid of the dog."

He thought for a moment. "Walt – where was it that Mike got that dog?"

"Can't say that I ever heard," Mr. Pobloch said.

"See if you can find out," Grandfather said to me.

I went down the alley and circled around to Main Street, and in front of the barber shop I met Mr. Snubbs, who runs the Snubbs Hardware store.

"Ah, it's you, Johnny," he said. "What's this I hear about your Grandfather being in trouble?"

"He's not in trouble," I said. "Sheriff Pilkins just thinks he is. Do you know where Mike Fitzharris got that dog of his?"

A voice right behind me cut in, "So that's it. I figured your Grandfather would be up to something."

It was Sheriff Pilkins, looking more harassed than I'd ever seen him.

"You can tell your Grandfather that I'm able to handle the law enforcement in this county," he said. "What's more, I'm already seven jumps ahead of him. That dog was the first thing I checked. It belonged to Bert Cowler, over in Wiston. Bert couldn't get along with it, and it kept biting him, and finally he gave it to Mike. You tell your Grandfather that Bert retired two years ago and moved to Florida, and last March he had a heart attack and died, and any police school I've ever been to taught that being dead is a pretty good alibi. You can also tell your Grandfather to mind his own business. When you have a moment, Snubbs, I'd like to talk to you about Mike Fitzharris."

Steve Carling was eying me from a parked patrol car, so I crossed the street to the Borgville Pharmacy and telephoned Pobloch's.

"Bert Cowler?" Grandfather repeated. "I remember, now. Anything else?"

"The sheriff didn't say so this time, but I suppose you're still a fugitive from justice."

"What justice?" Grandfather wanted to know. "If I only had a chair I could think in, or if I could get out to Mike's place – but I can't. You'll have to do it. Talk to Ed Carter. See if anyone knows anything."

I went home, and told Mom I was a working detective, and took my jalopy.

There wasn't anything I could do at Mike's place except drive past. Sheriff Pilkins had left a deputy on guard, but the house didn't need much guarding. The deputy was asleep in his car, and Mike's dog was loose in the yard again, looking big, and mean, and hungry.

At the Carter farm I found Ed out in his north pasture watching a crew of surveyors work. Ed had the idea of damming up his creek to make a lake, and he'd hired the surveyors to make a contour map of the farm. They had a little table on a tripod, and they were drawing the map right there in the field. They were young fellows, but they seemed to know what they were doing, and Mr. Carter was too interested in that map to be answering questions about Mike Fitzharris. He said he'd already told the sheriff all about it, and he didn't know anything anyway, and what did my Grandfather have to do with it?

On the way back to my jalopy I met the youngest Carter boy, Billy. He's a bright kid, about eight, and I came right to the point with him.

"Did you hear anything last night?" I asked.

"Sure," he said.

"That screech owl that's been hanging around here?"

" 'Tweren't no owl. It was somebody whistlin' "

"You sure it wasn't your pa snoring?"

"T'was a funny kind of whistle," Billy said. "Over by Mike's place."

"What time was that?"

"I dunno. I hadda go to the bathroom, an' when I got back up to my room I opened the window a little, 'cause it was hot up there, an' then I heard the whistlin'."

"Did you tell the sheriff?"

"Naw. He just wanted to talk to pa, an' pa didn't know nothin'."

I asked to use the Carter's phone, and I called Grandfather and told him what Billy had heard.

"What do I do now?" I asked.

"Ask Billy what the whistle sounded like." I did, but Billy couldn't describe it.

"Ask him if he can make a whistle like the one he heard," Grandfather said.

Billy said he couldn't, but he thought he'd recognize it if he heard it again.

"All right," Grandfather said. "Come on home."

The only alternative would have been to take Billy out looking for whistlers, and even in Borg County there are lots of people who can whistle. So I went home.

The first thing I heard when I walked in the door was Grandfather's rocking chair.

"He just came in five minutes ago," Mom said. "He said he was expecting a telephone call, and he went upstairs to rock while he waits for it."

"Is Sheriff Pilkins still looking for him?" I asked.

"I don't know. Mr. Pobloch drove him home."

The telephone rang. It was Maggie Cross, who writes for the Borg County Gazette, wanting to interview Grandfather about his arrest. I told her he wasn't available. When I hung up, Grandfather was hanging over the balustrade.

"Was that the telephone?"

I told him it was Maggie Cross. He snorted and went back to his rocking. He still was going at a reckless clip an hour later, practically tearing up the rug, when a call came for him from Sergeant Reichel, who commands the State Police Post at Wiston. He slammed on the brakes and came barreling down the stairway, and then all he did was listen and grunt a few times.

"What happened?" I asked, when he'd hung up.

"Nothing – yet."

"Do you suppose they'll ever find out who did it?"

"We know who did it," Grandfather said. "The problem is proving it."

At ten o'clock that night Grandfather and I were sitting on Carter's big front porch. The night was overcast and gloomy, and there wasn't any moon. We sat there in the dark and looked in the direction of Mike's place, which we couldn't see, and waited for something to happen.

After a while Sergeant Reichel came up from his car, which was parked behind the barn, and said, "No sign of him yet."

"I didn't give you a guarantee," Grandfather said.

A car drove by slowly, and Mr. Carter, who was standing in the door, said, "The Wades, coming home from town." Across the road, Mike's dog growled and barked a couple of times.

"I hope the boys don't get him riled up," Sergeant Reichel said. "Well – if the guy comes, we'll get him. If he doesn't come we'll get him anyway, but there won't be much evidence."

"I was afraid Pilkins would leave that deputy here all night," Grandfather said.

"He decided that the dog was guard enough."

"It wasn't last night."

Sergeant Reichel went back to his car. Grandfather rocked in the rocking chair Mrs. Carter had brought out for him, and I listened to night noises and finally dozed off. The next thing I knew it was after midnight, and Sergeant Reichel was saying, "He's on his way."

"Are you ready for him?" Grandfather asked.

"A lot readier than he'll like," the sergeant said grimly.

"Then let him come."

We waited. Grandfather asked me what time it was three times in five minutes. He was rocking on a floorboard that creaked, and that bothered me, even though I knew that the noise didn't amount to anything. Then we saw headlights far up the road. They came closer, swerved, and went off. The sound of the motor reached us faintly.

"Turning around," Sergeant Reichel said. "That's where he left the car last night."

The motor cut off. Grandfather stopped rocking, and we strained our ears for footsteps. He must have been wearing soft shoes, because I didn't hear a thing until he whistled. The whistle came from the road right in front of us. It was an odd, fluttery whistle, soft, but it carried perfectly. It came again from the direction of Mike's place, and then I heard the dog whine. A flashlight went on and off. I think he said something to the dog as he opened the gate.

Then we heard the hinges creak as the door to the house opened and closed.

"We've got him!" Sergeant Reichel said. He waved his flashlight, and flashlights came on all over the place. Ed Carter turned on the porch light. A police car started up behind the Carter barn and drove over to put a spotlight on Mike's house. Mike's dog went crazy, tearing around the yard and snarling and barking.

Grandfather stood up. "Come on, Johnny. Let's go home."

"We'll take him as soon as we can get the dog tied up," Sergeant Reichel said. "Don't you want to wait?"

Grandfather shook his head. "Don't tell Pilkins," he said.

"I won't," Sergeant Reichel promised. "He can read it in the papers like everyone else."

Mom shook me awake at nine thirty the next morning to ask if I was ready for breakfast. I told her she ought to know by now that I'm always ready for breakfast.

"I'll bring it up," she said. "Your Grandfather is having his in his room."

"What's the matter with him?" I asked.

"Sheriff Pilkins is downstairs. He's been waiting for an hour."

"Gosh!" I said. "Is Grandfather still asleep?"

"No, but he won't go downstairs. He says it's time the sheriff acquired a little patience."

I dressed and had breakfast with Grandfather in his room, and then Mom brought up the Sunday paper, and we divided it up and read it.

"If you make him wait much longer, we'll miss church," I said finally.

Grandfather nodded. "I suppose I'll have to go down," he said reluctantly.

Sheriff Pilkins was sitting in the living room, fussing with his hat. Grandfather nodded at him and sat down on the sofa. The sheriff's face got very red, which usually happens only when he's mad about something, but he didn't look mad.

"Something on your mind?" Grandfather asked:

"Mike's off the critical list," the sheriff said. "Doc says he'll be all right."

"I heard," Grandfather said.

The sheriff went back to fussing with his hat.

Grandfather stood up. "Well, we'll have to be getting ready for church."

"Just tell me one thing," the sheriff blurted. "How'd you do it?"

"By seeing beyond my nose."

The sheriff scratched his and didn't say anything.

"That rumor about Mike's money has been kind of a joke for years.

Suddenly someone swallowed it and acted on it. Seemed to me it was likely to be a stranger hearing the rumor for the first time, and right across the road from Mike's place were three strangers making that map for Ed Carter. "I asked Ed for their names, and one of them was named Cowler. Heard enough?"

"Go on," the sheriff said.

"Sergeant Reichel did some checking for me. Mike's dog hadn't belonged to Bert Cowler – it belonged to his son, Jim, and when Jim went to college to study engineering, Bert had to look after the dog. The dog didn't like Bert, and vice versa, and when Mike took a fancy to it, Bert gave it to him. Bert told his son the dog had run away, and Jim never knew what happened to it. Heard enough?"

"Go on."

"Well, Jim Cowler took this summer job surveying, and while he was working on Ed Carter's map he heard the rumor about an old man with a fortune hidden in his house and a man-eating dog to guard it. Out of curiosity he aimed a surveying transit at the dog, and derned if it didn't look like his own pet. The temptation was too much for him. He told the other surveyors he had a date with a girl, and he sneaked up to Mike's place and gave the dog the special whistle he always used on it. The dog came wagging its tail. So it wasn't any trouble for him to walk up and knock on the door and slug Mike. Of course he didn't find the money, because there wasn't any."

The sheriff's head jerked back. "Are you sure?"

"Positive. It might have been a hard crime to prove if Jim Cowler hadn't decided to have another look for the money. The State Police were most cooperative."

The sheriff's face got redder. "That's right. Rub it in."

Grandfather grinned, but he didn't say anything.

"Anyway," Sheriff Pilkins said, "you have to admit I was on the right track. I said it had to be someone the dog was used to."

"You were as wrong as a man can be," Grandfather said. "You pestered a lot of innocent people and stirred this whole town up trying to pin that crime on one of Mike's friends. And all the time you should have been looking for a friend of the dog's."

THE FABULOUS FIDDLE

Most of Borgville's houses were built at a time when builders still gave generous measure and before they'd even thought of using substitutes. Our houses have genuine basements, and rooms that are a pleasure to move around in, and ceilings you have to look up to see, and attics. A Borgville attic isn't a place reached through a hole in the ceiling where nothing taller than a cat can stand up. Borgville attics have oak stairs leading up to them, and windows, and dormers, and if the ceilings aren't high enough for basketball, at least they let you stand erect. There'll never be a housing shortage in Borgville, because there are so many attics that can be remodeled into very nice apartments.

Borgville's houses were built before the lumber industry started experimenting to see how thin two-inch timbers could be made before buildings start collapsing, and the floor joists are big, and thick, and solid. This is a good thing, because most Borgville houses are top-heavy with the hundred years of so of discards that are stored in the attics. Occasionally someone will find a genuine antique there, and make a little money and also inspire a round of community attic cleaning. This means that everything in everyone's attic gets sifted over every ten years or so, and one would think that by this time there'd be very few treasures, or even usable junk, left. But as Grandfather says, a treasure depends on the eye of the beholder, and one man's priceless antique is another man's eyesore. And of course there is always the bureau drawer – or the strangely shaped box – that no one bothers to look into …

It was a sight Borgville had never seen before and most likely would never see again, and I almost missed it.

It'd been raining hard all morning, and for the want of anything else to do I was down in the basement getting in some target practice with my air rifle. I had a couple of windows open, and when I heard something that sounded like a stampede moving along our sidewalk, naturally I went to look. It was Doc Beyers's wife, and she was running!

Mrs. Beyers prides herself on being the most sedate woman in Borgville – though as Grandfather says, she really hasn't much choice. There's so much of her to move around that it's only a question of doing it sedately or staying put. She even holds her laughs down to chuckles because of what she'd have to move if she cut loose. If I'd known she was going to be running in front of our house, I'd have set up some chairs and charged admission.

I watched her until she started up our walk, and then I headed for the stairs. I got to the front hall just as she came stumbling across the porch. Grandfather had seen her coming, and he was waiting at the front door. He helped her out of her raincoat, and she gasped, "Elizabeth ..." and collapsed onto the sofa.

"Take it easy," Grandfather said.

"Elizabeth ..."

"Elizabeth will keep for a couple of minutes. She's standing out on her porch now, looking over this way, so she can't be in very bad shape. Wait 'til you get your breath back."

For the next ten minutes Mrs. Beyers panted on the sofa and was hushed by Grandfather every time she opened her mouth. I came close to dying of curiosity, but Grandfather sat down and rocked as if it was an ordinary social call. He's always said the first lesson a man has to learn from life is patience, and in eighty years he's learned it pretty well.

Finally Mrs. Beyers got a grip on her breathing, and Grandfather let her talk.

"Elizabeth found a violin in her attic!" she said.

Grandfather nodded. "You don't say. That'd be –"

"It's a Strad – Strad –"

"Stradivarius? You don't say. That'd be –"

"It's worth a fortune!"

"You don't say. That'd be Old Eric's fiddle. I heard him play it many times, when I was a boy. I often wondered what'd happened to it."

"It's a godsend, what with Elizabeth needing money for Ellie's wedding. She wants you to come and see it."

"I've seen it," Grandfather said. "Many times. Old Eric was quite a fiddler in his day."

"He lived to be a hundred and two," Mrs. Beyers said.

"A hundred and three. And he loved to tell about the time –"

"Will you come and see it?"

"I suppose."

We got our raincoats and went back to Elizabeth Peterson's house with Mrs. Beyers, all three of us walking very sedately.

Elizabeth Peterson has been a widow for more years than I was old, and in a friendly way half the women in Borgville hate her. She was the example everyone holds up to them. She has no income at all, and has to work at anything offered to her at Borgville wages, which aren't much, but somehow she manages wonderfully well.

Lately, though, she'd been worried. Her daughter Ellie, the prettiest girl in Borgville, was graduating from high school and getting married. Her fiancé was Mark Hanson, whose father is our Village President, and President of the Borgville Bank, and the richest man in town. Naturally Mrs. Peterson wanted her daughter to have the prettiest wedding and the biggest and best reception in the history of Borgville, if not the whole state of Michigan, but she didn't have any money.

So I wasn't surprised to find her hardly touching the floor as she paced up and down on her porch while she waited for us. Even I had a vague notion that a genuine Stradivarius violin might be worth a lot of money.

"Do you think it really is?" she asked Grandfather, all out of breath, as if she, rather than Mrs. Beyers, had been doing the running.

"Of all the things I'm not an expert in," Grandfather said, "I am probably the most inexpert on the subject of violins. But I'll take a look. How'd you happen to find it?"

"It was more a matter of remembering it than finding it. It's been up there in the corner of the attic for years, and I guess I just forgot it was there. The funny thing is, I knew all the time it was valuable. It's a Peterson family tradition. My husband told me once that when he was a little boy playing in the attic his mother would tell him not to go near Grandpa Eric's fiddle, because it was a valuable instrument. It never occurred to me that the value could be measured in money."

"That's the usual way of doing it," Grandfather said.

"Anyway, yesterday at the church social Miss Borg gave a talk about people finding fortunes in their attics, in old stamps and old books and things like that, so afterward I asked her – just as a joke – about old violins, and she came by today, and – come in and see it."

Miss Borg was still there, standing by the big round dining room table. She's a little old lady with white hair, and in her more relaxed moments she looks nothing like the terror she is teaching history at

Borgville High School. The violin was on the table, and she was gazing at it as though it was the Holy Grail in Tennyson's *Idylls of the King*, which is one of a murderous assortment of items the students at Borgville High have stuffed into them.

The violin looked like something that might possibly raise nine cents at a rummage sale. The case was a battered old thing of wood. The hinges were missing, and it'd been held together with a couple pieces of rope. The one string left on the violin had snapped, and the whole contraption was falling apart. There were loose pieces in the bottom of the case, and on the violin there was a big crack along one side, which meant that whatever else it might do, it would never hold water. There was loose hair all over the place, except on the bow where it belonged.

Miss Borg said when she was a little girl she heard the Peterson family legend about Old Eric's valuable violin, but she doubted that anyone, including Old Eric, ever realized just how valuable it was. She shined a flashlight down into the violin, and said, "Look!"

Grandfather looked, and then I looked. Pasted inside the violin was a piece of paper, brown with age, and on the paper were some letters. The ink was badly faded, and some of it was illegible, but with Miss Borg's help I was able to make out, "... *adivarius Cremon*."

"That's his label," Miss Borg whispered. "See – it says so right here." She had a thick book called *Biographical Dictionary of Musicians* and under "Stradivari, Antonio," it said, "His label reads, 'Antonius Stradivarius Cremonensis. Fecit Anno ...' "

Grandfather gave his bald head a vigorous scratching. "I guess it might say that. The only way to tell whether or not it's genuine is to take it to an expert. If it's really valuable I suppose it could be fixed."

"A violin maker would take it completely apart and put it together again," Miss Borg said. "It would be as good as new. Better. An old instrument is always better than a new one."

"Maybe," Grandfather said. "My advice would be to not get excited about it until an expert sees it."

Mrs. Peterson wasn't listening. "What do you think it's worth?"

"I've heard that Stradivarius violins bring as much as fifty thousand dollars," Miss Borg said. "Or more. Of course some are worth more than others. Even if it isn't one of the best ones it should bring quite a lot. Five or ten thousand dollars, at least."

"Five or ten thousand!" Mrs. Peterson said.

"Since it's Saturday, you won't be able to do anything with it before the first of the week," Grandfather said. "If I was you, the first thing Monday morning –"

"Five or ten thousand!" Mrs. Peterson said again. Most likely she'd just moved the wedding reception from the church basement to the big room above the Star Restaurant.

"Maybe there's someone in Jackson who'd know about it," Grandfather said. "Monday morning, why don't you –"

Mrs. Peterson still wasn't listening. She looked again at the violin-looked at it as if she was seeing it for the first time – and then she sat down and started to cry. Grandfather dragged me out of there, and on the front porch we met Hazel Morgan, and Dorothy Ashley, and Ruth Wood, all coming to see the violin. Half a dozen others were on their way, from various directions. It was then I noticed that Mrs. Beyers hadn't come in the house with us. She was out spreading the Good Word.

Grandfather had nothing at all to say on the way home, or even after we got there. As soon as it stopped raining he went over to Main Street to borrow the Detroit paper from Mr. Snubbs, who runs the Snubbs Hardware Store, and the rest of the day, whenever I mentioned the violin, he hushed me up.

"Whether or not a violin was made by Stradivarius is just not the kind of question I can settle," he said. "I refuse to waste energy even thinking about it."

"Miss Borg shouldn't have spouted off about all those dollars before they find out," I said.

"Emily Borg should be spanked," Grandfather said.

The Saturday night talk all up and down Main Street was about Elizabeth Peterson's violin. Suddenly everyone in town remembered hearing a grandfather, or an uncle, or some elderly person next door, tell about what a remarkable fiddler Old Eric Peterson was, and what a valuable violin he had. The queer thing was that my Grandfather Rastin, who usually remembers such things better than anyone else, was acting skeptical about the whole business.

He and some other old timers were sitting on the benches in front of Jake Palmer's barber shop, and when Grandfather suggested that it might be better to get an expert's opinion before sticking a price tag on the violin, Nat Barlow got pretty hot about it.

"Everyone knows it's valuable," he said. "My father heard Old Eric say so himself. Anyway, Old Eric played dances all over this part of the state, even some in Detroit, and everyone said he was the best fiddler they'd ever heard. Why wouldn't he have a valuable violin?"

"Is Sam Cowell in town tonight?" Grandfather asked.

"Haven't seen him," Nat said.

"How much would you say his car is worth?" Everyone laughed.

"That pile of junk?" Nat asked.

"There isn't a better driver in Borg County than Sam Cowell," Grandfather said. "Seeing as he's such a good driver, why wouldn't he have a valuable car?"

That shut Nat up for the next hour.

"I've been trying to remember a few things about Old Eric," Grandfather said. "He loved to talk about the time he played for Ole Bull, and Ole Bull –"

"Who – or what – is Ole Bull?" someone asked.

"Another fiddler," Grandfather said dryly. "He was a famous Norwegian violinist, one of the greatest. He was touring this country giving concerts, and Old Eric went off to Cincinnati, or Chicago, or somewhere to hear him. He took his fiddle along, on the chance of picking up some money along the way, and after the concert he got to meet Ole Bull. He introduced himself as another Norwegian fiddler, and Ole Bull asked him to play. Old Eric –"

The crowd wasn't much interested in Ole Bull. "They tell me a Wiston reporter was over to see Elizabeth this evening," Bob Ashley said. "There'll be a piece about the violin in the Wiston paper."

"Got your oats in yet, Bob?" Grandfather asked.

"I don't suppose a Stradivarius violin turns up every day," Bob said.

That was when Grandfather headed for home, looking disgusted. I caught up with him and asked him for his version of the Peterson family legend.

"I never heard of any legend," he said. "Old Eric may have told his family *something* about that violin, and whatever he told them was so, because Old Eric was no fool. If it was a Stradivarius violin he'd have known it, and so would everyone else in Borgville, which makes it seem odd that I never heard anything about it. On the other hand, I do remember something about Old Eric's fiddle, but I haven't been able to remember what it is."

After Sunday dinner the next day, we sat on our front porch and watched the procession to Elizabeth Peterson's house. Those who hadn't seen the violin yet wanted to see it, and a lot of those who'd seen it wanted to see it again, and traffic on our street was heavy. Then Mark Hanson came by. He was home from the University for the weekend, and on his way to an afternoon date with Ellie. Mrs. Beyers met him in front of our house, and made some crack about him marrying an heiress, and he shrugged his shoulders and came up on the porch to talk to Grandfather.

"Family tradition or not, I don't think that violin is worth anything," he said. "It couldn't possibly be a Stradivarius. It has a very odd shape-too short and too wide. Did you notice?"

"One violin looks just about like another one to me," Grandfather said.

"I talked to Mr. Gardner – he's the orchestra director at Wiston High School. He says thousands of violins have a Stradivarius label, but all it means is that the violin maker *copied* a Stradivarius violin, or tried to. This one isn't even a good copy."

"What does Ellie think about all this?" Grandfather asked.

"She agrees with me, but we're both worried about her mother. The truth will be a terrible blow to her, and there doesn't seem to be a thing we can do about it. Mr. Gardner is coming over this evening to see the violin. Most likely one look is all he'll need."

"If it's the wrong shape, as you say, then anyone who knows violins would see that right away. When is he coming?"

"He didn't know for sure. Some time after eight."

"I'll be over," Grandfather said. "I'd like to hear what he has to say."

"Glad to have you," Mark said. "But please don't tell anyone else he's coming. What he has to say may not be pleasant, and I don't want a big audience there."

Mark went after Ellie, and the two of them walked back up the street hand in hand, Ellie looking lovely in a new spring dress and Mark admiring her as a fiancé should. By that time I'd got tired watching the procession so I went off to play baseball, but I made a point of being on hand when Grandfather went over to Peterson's that evening.

News has a way of getting around in Borgville, and there was a small crowd there – enough to fill the parlor. Mrs. Peterson bustled about, happy and excited, trying to feed people. The Peterson family legend got another kicking around, and every now and then someone would go into the dining room for another look at the violin.

It was nearly nine o'clock when Mr. Gardner came up the street, driving slowly and looking for house numbers, which very few Borgville houses have. He had to be introduced to everyone, and he went through the motions of this in a very abrupt way, as if he wanted to get on with the business at hand. I noticed when I shook hands with him that his hands were white and soft, and sometimes he would bow to a lady and show the bald spot at the back of his head.

"It's in here," Mark said finally, and led him into the dining room. Miss Borg, and Mrs. Peterson, and Ellie went along. The rest of us crowded up to the big arch that separates the dining room from the parlor, and watched.

Miss Borg tried to give Mr. Gardner the flashlight, so he could read the label, but he waved it away. "I don't care what's written inside," he said. He picked up the violin, and it came out of the case trailing loose parts. He looked at it, turned it over for a glance at the bottom, and put it back. There wasn't a sound in the house. In the parlor everyone stopped breathing.

I will say this for him – he didn't prolong the suspense.

"Junk," he said.

Mrs. Peterson's face suddenly was very white. "You mean – it isn't worth anything."

"Worth anything?" Mr. Gardner snorted. Grandfather snorts sometimes, when he's disgusted, but this was different. It was a nasty snort. "It's worth something, I suppose. If you had it fixed, which would cost – oh, maybe forty dollars, plus a new case – then you might be able to sell it for twenty-five. My recommendation is that you burn it. There are enough bad violins around. One less would make the world a much better place for violin teachers."

He left without waiting to be thanked, though Mrs. Peterson was in no condition to thank him anyway. Everyone else left right after him, except Miss Borg, who was indignant, and Grandfather, who seemed very thoughtful.

"The idea!" Miss Borg said. "Why, he didn't even look at the label!"

"If you don't mind –" Mrs. Peterson said. Then she started to cry, and it wasn't at all like the crying she'd done when she thought the violin was worth a lot of money.

"Don't burn it just yet," Grandfather told Ellie. "I want another look at it myself."

Ellie nodded, and Mark showed us to the front door.

"I guess the reception is back in the church basement," I said to Grandfather, as we crossed the street.

He didn't seem to hear me. "I finally remembered something," he said.

"Something about the violin?"

"It was such a long time ago. I was only a boy, you know, when Old Eric died. But it seems to me –"

He went straight up to the rocking chair in his bedroom, where he usually takes his problems, and he was still rocking when I went to bed.

I fell asleep wondering how rocking could possibly turn Mrs. Peterson's piece of junk into a valuable violin.

I never found out what Grandfather thought about that, because in the morning it seemed as though all of his rocking had been wasted. Sheriff Pilkins dropped in while we were at breakfast to ask Grandfather if he'd heard anything about a burglary the night before.

"Not yet, I haven't," Grandfather said. "News doesn't travel very fast this early in the morning. Where was it?"

"Elizabeth Peterson's house," the sheriff said. "Someone stole a violin."

We yelled together. "Violin!"

"Yep. She had this violin on her dining room table, and when she came down this morning it was gone. Naturally she can't remember the last time she bothered to lock her doors. Funny thing, though – the burglar wasn't really stealing it. He was buying it. He left her an envelope full of money."

"How much money?" Grandfather asked.

"A thousand dollars."

Grandfather whistled, and I dropped my toast into my cereal. "Last night Mr. Gardner said that violin might be worth twenty-five dollars if she spent forty dollars fixing it up," I said.

"So I heard," the sheriff said. "There are some funny angles to this thing. How many people knew she had what might be a valuable violin?"

"Half of Borg County," Grandfather said.

"Right. And how many people knew this Mr. Gardner said the violin was practically worthless?"

"Those that were there last night, and whoever they managed to tell before they went to bed. Say a fourth of Borg County."

"That leaves a lot of people who didn't know."

"You won't have any trouble narrowing your list of suspects," Grandfather said. "There aren't many people around here who'd have a ready thousand dollars for a violin speculation."

"Tell me something I don't know."

"How is Elizabeth taking it?"

"Not very well. She's pretty blamed mad about the whole thing. She's sure, now, that the violin is worth a fortune, and someone is trying to do her out of it."

"It's just possible that taking a thousand dollars for that violin is more of a crime than stealing it," Grandfather said.

"That's what I think myself. But Elizabeth is certain the thief wouldn't have left the thousand if he hadn't known the violin was worth more. She wants her violin back, and hang the money. Which is why I'm here. You didn't chance to notice any suspicious-looking characters hanging around last night, did you?"

"Borgville doesn't have any suspicious-looking characters," Grandfather said.

"They're all suspicious-looking to me. Look – I know you can come up with information I can't touch. Let me know if you find out anything."

Grandfather nodded. "I'll go have a talk with Elizabeth and look around."

So Grandfather went to Peterson's, and I went to school. Miss Borg stopped me in the hallway and asked me if I'd heard the news. She seemed excited about it – in fact, until I could get to a dictionary I thought she was excited to the point of being sick, because she said she felt vindicated.

I didn't go home for lunch, so I don't know how Grandfather spent the day. Sheriff Pilkins passed the time working hard with his usual lack of success, and when he came to see Grandfather that evening he was looking glum.

"I have a list of suspects," he announced.

"Good," Grandfather said. "You're further along than I am." Normally that would please the sheriff, but this time it seemed to make him mad. "Emily Borg," he said, "was indignant about what Gardner said about the violin. She could have taken it with the idea of getting another expert opinion about it."

"She could have done that without stealing it," Grandfather pointed out. "Somehow I can't see Emily burgling a house. And where would she suddenly get a thousand dollars on a Sunday evening?"

"Then there's this Gardner," the sheriff went on. "He could have lied about the violin and then stolen it so he could sell it himself.

Elizabeth favors that one. Problem is, he wouldn't have the thousand, either – he supports a large family on a school teacher's salary. And even if he had the money, why would he give it to Elizabeth? Why not just steal the violin? I've never seen a crime like this."

"Who else?" Grandfather asked.

"Pete Wilks. He took an unusual interest in the violin, and he lives right behind Elizabeth, on Maple street."

"He has an old violin of his own," Grandfather said. "He wanted to find out if his might be valuable. There's also the question of where he would get the thousand dollars. The money complicates things."

"It sure does. My favorite would be Mark Hanson. It's common knowledge that the Hansons tried to give Elizabeth money for the wedding, and she wouldn't take it. Mark could have used this as a back-handed way of making her take the money, and the Hansons could have come up with the thousand dollars. Trouble is, they didn't do it. Mark was with Ellie until nearly midnight, and then his folks drove him back to Ann Arbor and stayed there over night. The one thing I've been able to prove is that the violin was still on Elizabeth's table when they left Borgville."

"So where does that leave you?" Grandfather asked.

"Nowhere."

"I have an idea or two. Let's go see Elizabeth."

Mrs. Peterson met us at the door, and she didn't waste any time in letting the sheriff know what was on her mind. "Did you get it back?" she asked him.

Sheriff Pilkins sputtered all over the place. Law officers don't like blunt demands for results. They'd rather talk about all the progress they're making, which they can do without getting any results at all.

"Did you think over what we talked about this morning?" Grandfather asked.

"I certainly did," Mrs. Peterson said. "I want the violin."

"Give me the money, then, and I'll try to get it back for you."

The sheriff stared at Grandfather. "Where are you going to get it?"

"The law isn't involved in this," Grandfather said. "Party unknown bought Elizabeth's violin for a thousand dollars. The transaction isn't satisfactory to her, so she's going to buy the violin back for the same amount. If I can arrange it, that is."

"Baloney!"

"I don't see that there's much you can do about it."

The sheriff didn't seem to, either, and he stood there glaring at Grandfather. I'm not much interested in art, but I never get tired of watching the way his face changes color when he and Grandfather meet head-on. Finally he stomped down off the porch muttering about accessories, and withholding information, and interfering with legal processes. Mrs. Peterson came back with an envelope, which she handed to Grandfather.

"You understand that if Gardner turns out to be right about the violin, you've made a bad deal for yourself," Grandfather said.

"We went through all that this morning," she said. "I want the violin."

"I'll get it for you if I can."

Grandfather stuffed the envelope into his shirt pocket, and the two of us went home.

I'd like to tell you all about Grandfather's system for tracking down a violin thief, but I can't. I expected him to make a mysterious telephone call as soon as it got dark, and then head for a rendezvous by way of the alley. Instead, he sat down and read all evening, and he was still reading when I went to bed.

In the morning, when I went down to breakfast, the violin was lying on our dining room table.

"Where'd you get it?" I asked.

"You're as bad as Pilkins. What difference does it make? Elizabeth will be satisfied, the person that took it isn't complaining, and beyond that what happened is nobody's business."

After breakfast he took the violin over to Elizabeth Peterson, who was very happy to have it back. That is, she was happy until later that day, when Mr. Hanson drove her to Jackson to see a violin repair man there. This man told her even more emphatically than Mr. Gardner had that the violin was junk, and he didn't think it would be worth twenty-five dollars even if it was fixed.

The violin went back to the Peterson attic, and Mrs. Peterson started all over again to try to figure out how to pay for a big wedding and reception without any money, and Sheriff Pilkins stopped by three times a day the rest of the week in hope of prying the name of the violin thief out of Grandfather.

Other than that, nothing happened. That is, I thought nothing happened, but on Friday Jimmy Edwards, whose mother works in the telephone office at Wiston, asked me how come Grandfather was getting all those long distance telephone calls.

"What long distance calls?" I asked.

"How would I know if you don't?" Jimmy said. "All I know is that Mom said your Grandfather has been getting calls from all over – New York, Los Angeles, Chicago –"

"I don't know anything about it," I said, "but I'm sure going to find out."

But I didn't. All Grandfather would do when I asked him was grunt and shrug his shoulders, All Friday evening he grunted and shrugged, and all Saturday morning, until about ten o'clock. Then a big limousine such as had never been seen in Borgville drove up in front of our house. A chauffeur in a fancy uniform popped out and opened the rear door, and a tall, gray-headed man got out and walked up to our house. Grandfather met him on the porch.

"You're Mr. Rastin?" the man asked.

Grandfather nodded and shook hands with him. "Where is it?" the man asked.

"Across the street," Grandfather said.

They headed for Elizabeth's house, with me tagging along, and Grandfather introduced the man to Elizabeth as Mr. Edmund Van something or other and chased Ellie up to the attic after the violin. We sat down in the parlor and waited. "Has it been in your family for a long time?" Mr. Van asked.

"It belonged to my husband's great-great grandfather," Mrs. Peterson said.

"You don't say. Treasures often are preserved in this way. My first Stradivarius violin –"

Ellie bounced in, all out of breath, and plunked the violin down on a coffee table beside Mr. Van. She untied the knots and took off the top of the case, and then she scooted back out of the way, as if she expected Mr. Van to throw the violin at someone the moment he saw it.

He did look at the violin. He looked at it once, with an expression of disgust such as I never hope to see again. Then he picked up the loose lid of the case and held it on his lap looking at the violin bow that was hooked onto it. "Francois Tourte!" he exclaimed.

"The label is under that little do-hickey that screws in and out," Grandfather said.

"Under the frog. Yes. It really has a label?"

He unscrewed something or other, fished a magnifying glass out of his pocket, and said, speaking very softly, "This bow was made by Francois Tourte in 1822, aged seventy-five years. Splendid! Tourte never branded his bows and rarely labeled them."

"Is it genuine?" Grandfather asked.

"Unquestionably genuine."

"I had no way of knowing. A label, of course, can be stuck onto anything."

"Unfortunately true. Even such a violin as that one –" He made a face. "Even that violin could have a Stradivarius label. But craftsmanship cannot, as you say, be stuck on. One looks at the shape of the head – Tourte. It still has the original frog – Tourte. The thickness of the shaft, and narrow ferrule, all Tourte. It's in remarkably fine condition. The grip is a little worn. The slide, too, but not badly. The man who owned this bow knew its value. I stand by my offer. I'll pay four thousand dollars for it."

He looked at Mrs. Peterson, and for a long moment she couldn't find her voice. Then she stammered, "You want to buy the violin?"

Mr. Van winced. "Not the violin. The bow. This bow, Ma'am, was made by Francois Tourte, who was to the violin bow what Stradivarius was to the violin. And more. There were great violin makers before Stradivarius, but Tourte created the modern bow – its design, its materials, to some extent its mechanics. Without the Tourte bow, string instrument technique as we know it would be impossible, and the work of the great instrument makers would to a considerable extent be wasted. Will you sell the bow for four thousand dollars, Ma'am?"

"It's a very good offer," Grandfather said.

Mrs. Peterson still didn't seem to understand. "The violin –"

Mr. Van clapped his hand to his forehead. "The violin I do not want, but I'll buy it if I must. What is it worth? Five dollars? Ten? I'll give you four thousand and ten dollars for violin and bow."

"Oh," Mrs. Peterson said. "You just want the bow. I'll sell that, and keep the violin for a – a memento."

"Splendid!" Mr. Van whipped out a check book and scribbled. He presented the check, shook hands with everyone present, and walked back to his car carrying the case lid with the bow still hooked onto it. He carried it the way I've seen couples carry their first baby when they bring it home from the hospital.

Mrs. Peterson sat down and looked at the check for a long time. "I don't know how to thank you," she said. Then she started to cry, and

Ellie looked as if she wanted to cry, too, and it was as good a time as any for Grandfather and I to get out of there, which we did.

"Sheriff Pilkins will have a fit," I said, when we got back to our porch.

"It'll do him good," Grandfather said.

"He'll say anyone who stole something worth four thousand dollars belongs behind bars, and he'll threaten to put you there if you don't tell him who it was."

"Let him threaten," Grandfather said. "That's one crime that will stay unsolved permanently."

"How'd you know the thing was valuable?" I asked.

"Something I remembered Old Eric saying. He played for Ole Bull, and he had a bow that was better than anything Ole Bull had. Ole Bull tried to buy it from him. I figured if the bow was good enough back in the eighteen sixties, or whenever it was, for a great violinist to want it, it might still be valuable. But none of these local experts thought to look at the bow. The violin was unbelievably bad, and it distracted their attention. So when I got the chance I looked it over, and I found that label. I told Professor Mueller, at Wiston College, and he said a Tourte bow might be worth a fair amount of money, and the person who'd pay the most for it would be a collector of old instruments."

"Why not a violinist?" I asked.

"A bow can be made today that plays just as well as that one. Maybe a little better, for all I know. It's the same with postage stamps. An old stamp may be worth hundreds of dollars, but you can buy one at the post office for a few cents that will do just as good a job of getting a letter through the mails. Professor Mueller got the word around to some collectors, and this man made the best offer, so I told him to come and see the bow."

"Then Old Eric knew the bow was valuable, rather than the violin, but after he died the family legend got it twisted."

"I suppose."

"That still doesn't explain who stole the violin."

"Like I said, that's one crime I don't intend to explain."

"You don't have to," I said. "I can figure that one out myself. Someone thought the violin – or maybe the bow – just might be valuable in spite of what Mr. Gardner said. So he went to Mr. Hanson and said, 'Look – we should get this violin to a genuine expert, but of course there's a good chance that it really isn't worth anything, so why not do it this way. You put up a thousand dollars, and I'll steal the violin and leave the money. If it turns out to be worth more than that, we can give Mrs Peterson the difference. If it turns out to be junk, she'll still have the thousand dollars for the wedding. She wouldn't accept the money as a gift, and now that Mr. Gardner has said the violin is junk she wouldn't sell it to us for a thousand dollars, because she'd figure that would be the same thing as a gift. But if we steal it, and leave the money, she'll think the thief didn't know it was junk and it serves him right to lose the money.' The trouble was, Mrs Peterson didn't think that way at all. She thought the theft proved the violin was worth a lot more than a thousand dollars, and she called in the sheriff and messed up everything."

"Not bad," Grandfather said. "It only goes to show that you can't figure out in advance how a woman will react to anything."

"And of course there was only one person who had any reason to think the violin – or the bow – might be valuable after Mr. Gardner said it was junk."

Grandfather grinned. "Right again. I stole the thing myself."

THE GENTLE SWINDLER

The local people like to call Borgville a real friendly town. Grandfather Rastin disagrees. He says people come in the same sizes everywhere – friendly, unfriendly, and indifferent – and small towns only seem friendlier because it's easier to get to know people there. And the more people you know, the more friends you'll make, no matter what size town you live in.

He adds that small towns only seem friendlier to the people who live there. A total stranger in a small town feels stranger than he would anywhere else, because he's in a place where everyone knows everyone and he doesn't know anyone. Fortunately for strangers, in Borgville not many of them remain strangers very long.

There are two exceptions. A stranger who is selling something has to have a very special talent for friendliness to make friends in Borgville. And no matter how remarkable his talents are, he's unlikely to make any friends at all if he's trying to give something away. …

I first saw this Mr. Allen one afternoon last August when Grandfather and I came back from Main Street and found a snappy convertible parked in front of our house and a stranger on the front porch. He'd made himself comfortable in Grandfather's favorite glider, and he was sitting there as if he owned the place.

He smiled and said, "Howdy."

Grandfather didn't answer. He tore back through the house to the kitchen, where Mom was talking with Mrs. Pobloch.

"Who in tarnation is that?" he demanded.

"Hush!" Mom said. "That's Mr. Allen. I met him in Dimmit's Grocery Store. He was looking for a place to stay, so I rented him the front bedroom."

"Damnation!" Grandfather exclaimed.

"Hush!" Mom said. "It's only for a week, and he's paying me ten dollars. He won't be any trouble."

Grandfather glared at Mrs. Pobloch, as if she maybe had something to do with it. "No trouble? He looks like a confidence man!"

He stomped up to his room, and I heard his rocking chair start up. You can always tell how Grandfather feels by the way he rocks, and that day I thought he'd tear holes in the rug.

Of course Mrs. Pobloch told at least twenty people what Grandfather had said, and each of those twenty told another twenty, and by evening it was all over town. Right after supper, Sheriff Pilkins showed up.

"I heard," the sheriff said to Grandfather, "that you have a confidence man staying with you."

I think right at that moment Grandfather changed his mind about Mr. Allen. Those two rarely agree about anything, and in the twenty-five years the sheriff has been running for office, Grandfather is maybe the only adult in Borgville who has never voted for him, and the sheriff knows it.

"I suppose you've got nothing better to do than listen to gossip," Grandfather said. "You'll catch a lot of criminals that way."

The sheriff walked over to the front window. Mr. Allen had walked over to Main Street to have supper at the Star Restaurant, and he was just getting back.

"Good-looking fellow," the sheriff said. "He'll give those single girls something to think about."

"He won't give them anything new to think about," Grandfather said.

"Walks kind of funny, doesn't he?"

"The way a man walks is none of the law's business."

"Borgville isn't exactly a health resort," the sheriff said. "A man wouldn't plunk himself down here for a week for the fun of it. I better have a talk with him."

The sheriff went out on the porch and introduced himself. "What's your business?" he asked.

"Manufacturer's agent," Mr. Allen said. "But the grind gets me down, every now and then, and I like to take a few days off. This is a fine little town. Quiet. It seems good to breathe fresh air, for a change."

"That so?" the sheriff said. He wasn't believing a word of it. They talked a little about the weather, and then the sheriff excused himself and came back into the house. "What the devil is a manufacturer's agent?" he whispered.

"It's a fancy name for a salesman," Grandfather said.

"Sounds fishy to me. Everything about this fellow sounds fishy. I'll give you odds he's wanted somewhere."

"He's not wanted here," Grandfather said, "but as long as it's only for a week, I'm not saying anything."

"I'll keep an eye on him," the sheriff said. He went out the back way, but when he got around to the street I saw him stop and take a good, long look at Mr. Allen.

Mr. Allen certainly wasn't any trouble. When I got up the next morning, he'd already been over to Main Street for his breakfast. He was sitting on the porch, smoking his pipe. He hadn't even complained to Mom about Grandfather's snoring which meant that he either was a sound sleeper or awfully polite.

I sat down and talked with him for awhile, and I liked him right away. He had a soft voice and a kind of shy smile that made his whole face light up. He really was good looking, and he'd done a lot of traveling to foreign countries, and he sure was interesting to talk to.

After while he got up and took a look at the sky, which was clouded over, and said, "It's cooler than it was yesterday. How about a game of tennis?"

I stared at him. "Tennis?"

"I don't cover much ground these days," he said, "but I like to bat a ball around. How about it?"

"Borgville's got no tennis court," I said. "There was some talk, once, about building one at the high school, but nothing came of it."

"No tennis court?" he said. He looked at me the same way a traveling man did, once, when I told him Borgville had no liquor store. "You should have a tennis court."

"Yes, sir," I said. "We also should have a bowling alley, and a moving picture theatre, and a skating rink, but we haven't."

He thought about that a while, then he said, "What do you kids do to pass the time?"

"We go fishing," I said. "And we play baseball, and do some swimming."

"Where do you swim?" he asked.

I told him there were some good places close to town, like the swimming hole on Borgville Creek, and Mr. Grant's quarry.

"Borgville," Mr. Allen said, "should have a swimming pool."

I didn't have anything to say.

"I think I'll take a walk," Mr. Allen said.

I didn't see him again until after lunch, when I went over to Main Street with Grandfather. Grandfather borrowed the morning paper from Mr. Snubbs, who runs the Snubbs Hardware store, and since it was a nice day he went over to the bench in front of Jake Palmer's barber shop to read it. We met Mr. Allen coming out of the barber shop, and the three of us sat down on the bench together.

Since word had got around that Mr. Allen was a confidence man, all the men who passed slowed down to have a good look at him, but that was nothing compared with what the women did. First came Margaret Snubbs, who is Mr. Snubbs's sister. She has got up close to forty without being married, partly because she thinks she is too cultured for the men around Borgville, but mostly because the men agree with her. I'll swear she was about to drop her handkerchief right at Mr. Allen's feet, but then she happened to look at Grandfather, and she changed her mind.

Then came Mrs. Beyers, who is past sixty, and she was so intent on Mr. Allen as she walked by that she didn't even notice Grandfather and me. Miss Phillips, who runs the Town Shop and who is close to forty like Margaret Snubbs, only in the other direction, actually had the nerve to stop and ask me to introduce her. Mr. Allen stood up very politely and told her, yes, he liked Borgville, and no, he was afraid he wouldn't be able to stay long.

It went on like that afternoon. It seemed half the women in Borgville heard Mr. Allen was sitting there in front of the barber shop and had to hurry down to see him. For the farmers' wives who happened to be in town, it was a sort of a bonus. They all slowed down when they passed us, even Mrs. Wallingford, who is a war bride from Vietnam. Mrs. Wallingford probably had not looked at any man but her husband since she got to Michigan, and maybe not even at him, because he treats her like dirt and works her like a hired man, but she looked so long at Mr. Allen that her husband got ahead of her and she had to run to catch up. If he'd caught her at it he probably would have beat her when they got home.

Finally Mr. Allen got tired being stared at. He nudged me and said, "Johnny, let's take a walk."

We walked out to the edge of town, which took awhile because of the funny limp Mr. Allen had. We turned off to inspect the Borgville Park, which was a little patch of weeds beside the Borgville Creek, and Mr. Allen marched straight across it to the barbed wire on the other side.

"That tennis court and swimming pool we were talking about," he said. "Right over there would be a good place for it."

"That's Old Man Edward's pasture," I said. "If you start building a tennis court in there, he'll run you out with a shotgun."

"Edwards?" Mr. Allen said. "I'll have to have a talk with him." We walked back up town. I left Mr. Allen at Arnell's law office and went over to the barber shop where Grandfather was still reading the paper.

"Mr. Allen is going to build a tennis court and a swimming pool in Edwards' pasture," I told him.

"That," Grandfather said, "is something I would like to live long enough to see."

That evening Mr. Allen invited Old Man Edwards to have dinner with him at the Star Restaurant, and afterward both of them went over to see Lawyer Arnell. The next morning Mr. Allen and Lawyer Arnell went to talk with Mr. Hanson, who is village president as well as president of the bank, and the whole town was wondering what they were up to.

By afternoon Mr. Hanson had notices up in the bank window and the post office and most of the stores, announcing a public meeting at the high school auditorium, and from the way people turned out you'd thought everyone in Borgville was interested in civic improvements. A lot of farmers came, too, though they had to hurry their chores to get there on time, and Sheriff Pilkins, when he heard Mr. Allen had something to do with it, came and brought four deputies. Grandfather and I went early and got seats right down in front.

Mr. Hanson started out by introducing Mr. Allen, and Mr. Allen said a lot of nice things about Borgville and how he liked it and wanted to do something for it, and then he said, "I have an option on fifteen acres of the Edwards pasture adjoining the Borgville Park. I intend to purchase this land and deed it to Borgville, on the condition that Borgville agrees to build a tennis court and a swimming pool and a baseball field and maintain the whole as a park."

He sat down, and Mr. Hanson let the audience chew that one over among themselves. People around me seemed confused. In Borg County, folks usually don't give things with conditions attached, and from the remarks I heard not many people had much of an itch for playing tennis or swimming in a pool.

Mr. Hanson thanked Mr. Allen for his generous offer and said that he was sure interested citizens would donate the necessary labor, but the treasury had no money for the materials, so the project would have to be financed by donations or there wouldn't be any project.

Doc Beyers made a little speech, then, saying that outdoor recreation and exercise were good for everyone, and Mr. Grove, who is a farmer from out west of town, got up and said if his boys wanted outdoor recreation and exercise he could give them plenty of it, right on his farm. Jake Palmer got up and said he'd always got all the swimming he wanted, when he was a boy, without any swimming pool, and if the kids were given tennis courts and swimming pools the next things they'd want would be golf courses and TV stations and automobile race tracks. Quite a few chimed in along the same line, and it looked as though Mr. Allen was about to be told what he could do with his fifteen acres and his conditions.

Then the women took over.

Miss Phillips got up. "I think it's a marvelous idea," she said. "It's about time Borgville had a few improvements. I'll donate one hundred dollars."

I heard Jake Palmer say afterward that she only did it because she stood to sell a lot of swimming suits in her Town Shop if a pool got built, because until then swimming suits were something we boys mostly got along without. But at the time I don't think Miss Phillips had swimming suits on her mind unless she was thinking about how Mr. Allen would look in one. Anyway, she sure started something.

Margaret Snubbs was on her feet before Miss Phillips sat down to give away a hundred dollars of her brother's money. Then Doc Beyers tossed in another hundred, though I personally saw Mrs. Beyers kick him first. Mrs. Ferguson, whose husband owns the Borgville Pharmacy, gave two hundred, and Mr. Hanson interrupted to say he'd donate two hundred, and after that donations came so fast that Mrs. Hanson, who was taking notes, had a hard time getting them all written down.

Every woman there seemed to think she had to give something, even Mrs. Wallingford, who was wearing the same old dress she'd worn ever since she came to Borgville and who looked as if she'd just come from pitching hay in the barn, which may have been true. She stood up to say something, but her husband hauled her back down before she could open her mouth. He didn't actually slap her face, but he threatened to.

But things kept humming until there was over three thousand dollars in pledges, and a Borgville Improvement Committee had been formed, and a lot of committees had been set up to think up ways to raise more money. Mr. Allen was offered a job on the committee, but he turned it down. Mr. Hanson was elected president.

On our way out, Sheriff Pilkins stopped Grandfather in the hallway. "Want to talk to you," he said. "Principal's office."

I tagged along and got to stay, maybe because the sheriff was too excited to notice me. He had Mr. Hanson there, and a few of the other men, and he said, "Allen has the women in this town hoodwinked, but at least we know what he's up to. Three thousand already, and more to come. And when he thinks the pot is big enough, he scoops it up and runs."

"How?" Mr. Hanson wanted to know. "The money will be in the bank. No one is going to hand it over to him."

"And just who is the treasurer of this here committee?" the sheriff asked.

"Miss Phillips," Mr. Hanson said.

"Ha! She's daft about the guy. So is Margaret Snubbs, and she's second vice president. So are all the women. Even that poor Mrs. Wallingford went off her nut, and I wouldn't be surprised if there's a homicide on the Wallingford farm before morning. Those women would clean out the treasury for Allen any time he asked them."

"No check can be drawn without my signature," Mr. Hanson said. "I'm not daft about him."

"He'll figure a way to beat that," the sheriff said. "These pros know all the angles. He's probably traveling about the country picking one town clean after another. It'll take some doing to catch him, and I'll need all of you to help me."

Grandfather asked, "Hanson, did he actually buy that fifteen acres?"

"Why, no," Mr. Hanson said. "He told us he'd work out the details with Arnell so the property would be available when we were ready for it."

The sheriff let out a snort. "What'd you expect? This guy is not in the giving-away business. He's in the taking-away business. We'll have to keep our eyes open, or Borgville will be took for plenty."

When I got up the next morning, one of Sheriff Pilkins's deputies was sitting across the street on the Smith's front porch keeping his eyes open. He sat there all day, except when Mr. Allen went up town to eat or went for a walk, and then he followed right along.

Outside of that, nothing much happened that day. The people who'd pledged money at the meeting were wondering how they were going to pay it, and the town was unusually quiet until Miss Phillips started a scandal along about supper time. She met Mr. Allen up town and invited him to eat with her at her apartment. Somebody heard her, and when it turned out that she hadn't invited anyone else, people drew their own conclusions, though Miss Phillips claimed she was going to invite a lot of people if Mr. Allen accepted. Anyway, he turned her down.

The next day was Saturday, and when Mom and I got home from shopping, Sheriff Pilkins was there talking with Grandfather. "I'm telling you," Grandfather was saying, "I don't know anything about it."

"I'm going to can Steve Carling," the sheriff said. "He left his car parked way up the street, and when Allen came sneaking out and drove away, Steve lost him."

"What happened?" I asked.

"Allen went somewhere last night," Grandfather said. "Pilkins wants to know where. I don't know why he thinks *I'd* know. Allen doesn't ask my permission when he wants to go for a ride, and I was sound asleep at the time."

"I know," the sheriff said. "Steve said he could hear you snoring clear across the street."

"That's a lie" Grandfather shouted.

"I thought maybe Allen was calling on one of those dames that's so daft about him, so I had Steve get both of them out of bed. But they hadn't seen him, or at least they said they hadn't. You've got no idea where he went?"

Grandfather shook his head.

"Then tell me this. Who does Allen know well enough in this town to be telephoning all the time?"

"It isn't me," Grandfather said.

"He's been making a lot of calls from the booth in the drugstore. I thought maybe it was one of those women, but they say no, and each thinks it must be the other, so they're probably telling the truth. I'd be a step closer to figuring out how he's going to grab the money if I knew who he was calling."

"Local calls?" Grandfather asked.

"Long distance I could check. Drat those new-fangled dials! Hanson says people are starting to pay off, and he's got over a thousand in the committee account. This darned thing has got me worried."

"Allen says he's leaving tomorrow," Grandfather said.

"Before the whole three thousand is collected? Maybe he will. A thousand wouldn't be bad for a week's work. And if I just knew how he was going to get his hands on it – well, he won't take any more night rides unescorted. I'll have twenty deputies planted around this town tonight."

I don't know what happened that afternoon, because I had a chance to go swimming over at Mud Lake, and I jumped at it. I got home late, and Grandfather already had eaten supper and gone away somewhere with Mr. Naylor, who lives next door. Sheriff Pilkins came by later, wanting Grandfather to help him keep track of Mr. Allen.

"Why don't you take me?" I asked. "I know Mr. Allen as well as anybody. I'd be more help than Grandfather would."

"You probably would," the sheriff said. "All right, if your Ma says it's okay."

She didn't, but I talked her into it. I waited in the house until Mr. Allen went up to his room to go to bed, and then I walked down to the end of the block where the sheriff had his car parked. It was pretty dark, by then, and our one street light didn't help much.

"He's just gone to bed," I said. "Do you really think he's a crook?"

"Naw," the sheriff said. "I'm just keeping twenty men up all night for kicks."

The sheriff did some checking on his radio, to make sure all his men were where he wanted them. And we waited. And waited. By the time the light went out in Mr. Allen's room, I was getting pretty tired of the whole business.

"Has your Grandfather figured out how Allen is going to get the money?" the sheriff asked.

"If he has, he hasn't told me," I said.

"You know what I think? I think he's figured it out, and he aims to nab Allen himself and give him to the State Police and make me look silly. He's been acting sly all day, and now he's run off without telling anyone where he was going. He's up to something."

We waited a while longer, and then the sheriff started his motor. Mr. Allen had come down off our porch. You couldn't miss that funny limp of his. He hurried out to his car and drove off, and the sheriff pulled out and followed him.

If Mr. Allen knew he was being tailed, he certainly didn't care. He drove a steady forty-five out Borgville Road, turned south on Hennings Road still going forty-five, and finally turned in at the Abe Meadows farm. As the sheriff drove slowly past, we saw Mr. Allen get out and go up to the house.

The sheriff parked down the road. He shifted some of his men around by radio, and then he said, "Johnny, run up to the house and see if you can look in. Find out what they're doing and come right back."

All the shades were up, so there was no problem finding out what they were doing. Mr. Meadows, and his married son Roger, and Mr. Allen were sitting around the kitchen table, talking and drinking beer. I went back and told the sheriff.

He scratched his head and asked, "What does Meadows have to do with it? He isn't even on the committee."

We waited for nearly an hour, parked down the road. Then the yard light came on, and Mr. Allen limped out to his car and drove off. He drove directly back to Borgville, never doing better than forty-five, and parked in front of our house.

But instead of going in the house, he walked off toward Main Street.

"Sheriff?" I said.

"Lemme think, dammit!" he said.

"He's not limping," I said. "He don't walk like Mr. Allen."

We would have got there quicker with the car, but neither of us thought of that. The sheriff jumped out and ran, and I was right behind him. We caught up with the fellow under the street light, and it was Roger Meadows.

"What the devil are you doing here?" the sheriff yelled.

"Why shouldn't I be here?" Roger asked.

The sheriff didn't wait for the explanation, if Roger had one. He tore back to his car and almost drove off without me, and I never heard a man swear so. He was doing seventy before he hit the edge of town, yelling into his radio as he drove.

When he finally quieted down, I said, "Out there at the farm, he walked with a limp."

The sheriff started swearing again.

"He's about the same build as Mr. Allen," I said. "The light wasn't too good, and from where we were he sure looked like him."

"Shut up!" the sheriff yelled.

What with the swearing and the sheriff keeping the accelerator flat on the floor, that was the wildest ride I ever had. We went screaming into the yard at the Meadows place, and the sheriff nearly kicked in the door before Mrs. Meadows opened it.

"Where's Allen?" the sheriff yelled.

"He and Abe went over to see Pete Farrell," Mrs. Meadows said.

She closed the door without waiting to be thanked, which is just as well, because the sheriff wasn't about to waste time being polite. It's all of ten miles from there to the Farrell place, and we made it in ten minutes, over one of the worst roads in the county. Mrs. Farrell came to the door in her nightgown, and she said yes, Mr. Allen and Mr. Meadows had been there, and her husband had gone with them. She didn't know where, but there'd been some talk about a poker game Bill Cummings was putting on.

The sheriff went back to his car and used the radio to send four deputies to the Cummings place. They called him back just as we were getting to the edge of Borgville. They said Mr. Cummings was playing poker for ten cent stakes with Grandfather and Mr. Wallingford and Mr. Naylor, and should they pick them up for gambling?

"By God, I'm tempted!" the sheriff said. But he told them to forget it and be on the lookout for Mr. Allen.

We tore down Main Street again, and as we passed our street I looked up toward our house and said, "Sheriff?"

"Shut up!" he said. "I'm thinking."

"I think Mr. Allen's car is gone."

He slammed on the brakes. We drove back to our house and got Mom out of bed. She said she hadn't heard a thing, but Mr. Allen's suitcase and all of his clothes were gone.

"That's strange," Mom said. "He told me he'd be leaving tomorrow."

The sheriff went to check with the deputies he'd left watching the Snubbs house and Miss Phillips apartment, and then he had to go over and get Mr. Hanson out of bed to make sure Mr. Allen hadn't got away with the Improvement Committee's money. Mr. Hanson said, "Nonsense!" and slammed the door in the sheriff's face.

The sheriff drove back to our house, and we waited in his car until Grandfather came home about two o'clock, listening to reports from the sheriff's deputies, who were tearing all over the county looking for Mr. Allen's car. Grandfather said he'd won two dollars and forty cents and was too tired to talk.

"I know Wallingford and Cummings are poker nuts," the sheriff said, "but what were you doing there? You gave up poker twenty years ago."

"That's all you know about it," Grandfather said.

Grandfather hauled me off to bed, then, so I don't know what the sheriff did after that, but when we saw him after church the next morning he certainly looked as though he'd been up all night.

He was waiting for us on the front porch, and he said, "I want to talk to you, Rastin."

"No," Grandfather said, "I want to talk to you."

"Talk, then," the sheriff said.

They sat down in the parlor, and Grandfather began, "Back in the spring of '68 –"

"Let's talk about Allen," the sheriff said.

"I am. Back in the spring of '68 there was a young fellow in the army in Vietnam, and he met a pretty girl there, and they fell in love." The sheriff grunted.

"They wanted to get married," Grandfather went on, "but before they'd even made a start at untangling the red tape, the boy was shot up pretty bad. He lost a leg and almost lost his life. His friends thought he was dead, and that's what they told the girl. He was in a hospital for a couple of years, healing up and then learning to walk with an artificial leg. As soon as he could he wrote letters to the girl, but he never got an answer. When he got out of the hospital he went back to Vietnam to look for the girl. The town she'd lived in had been smashed and no one knew what had happened to her. But he kept looking, and finally he found out that she'd married some GI and gone to America.

"Eventually he traced her to Borgville, Michigan, so he came here. He didn't intend to see her, or anything like that. He just wanted to make sure she was happy. But you know what he found?"

"Wallingford called in this morning," the sheriff said. "Said his wife had run out on him."

"Allen didn't like what he heard about Wallingford," Grandfather went on, "but he didn't want to cause talk and maybe make trouble for Mrs. Wallingford until he found out how she felt about it. He kept telephoning the Wallingford farm, and if Wallingford answered he'd hang up. The few times he caught her in the house alone, they had to be careful what they said on a party line. He tried to get her to meet him somewhere so they could talk, but she was too scared of her husband to do it.

"Meanwhile, Allen was afraid people would be suspicious and connect him with Mrs. Wallingford, so he decided to give Borgville a park. Turned out not to be a good idea. Attracted attention to him and put your deputies on him. At that point I had a talk with him and found out what was going on. All he wanted was a chance to talk with the girl. So I had Bill Cummings arrange that poker game. You know how crazy Wallingford is about poker. That got him out of the house, and some other people helped out to get your wolves off Allen's heels, and he saw the girl, and she packed the few belongings she had, and Meadows drove them out to Highway 27 where his son was waiting with Allen's car, and they took off. They're at least four states away, by now, so you can turn your wolves out to pasture."

"Allen?" the sheriff said. He didn't sound as though he'd believed a word of it. "Allen – and Mrs. Wallingford?"

"Well, she was a real pretty girl when she first came here. If she gets shut of that pig of a husband she has, maybe she'll be pretty again."

The sheriff banged on the table. "Look here. Allen stole another man's wife. That's worse than stealing money. And you helped him, which makes you an accessory."

"Horsefeathers!" Grandfather said. "Allen didn't *steal* her. He gave her a chance to get away, and when she found out she could do it without getting her neck broken, she jumped at it. The cows on Wallingford's farm got better treatment than his wife, and you know it. Allen has money, and he says he'll help her get a divorce if she wants it, and she's old enough to decide that for herself. It's none of the law's business."

The sheriff sat there for a moment, maybe thinking about the night's sleep he'd lost, and then he got up and started for the door. He snarled over his shoulder, "Stealing another man's wife! I should have locked him up."

Last week we had a nice letter from Mr. Allen, and he sent us a picture of Mrs. Wallingford and him, only now she's Mrs. Allen. She was dressed nice, and she'd gained weight and looked real pretty again. Mr. Allen had his arm around her, and they both seemed happy.

Mr. Allen said he was sorry about the fuss he'd stirred up in Borgville, and he'd written to Lawyer Arnell, telling him to go ahead and get those fifteen acres from Old Man Edwards and deed them to Borgville. And he wanted to help out with the park. There was a check with the letter, for five thousand dollars, made out to the Borgville Improvement Committee.

Sheriff Pilkins came over to see the letter. He read it through, and looked at the picture for a long time, and then he said, "I still think the fellow is a swindler."

Grandfather took the picture from him. "Could be." He grinned at the sheriff. "Could be. But if he is, this is the best swindle Borgville ever had."

THE GREAT HORSESHOE MYSTERY

The old order changeth, yielding place to new; And God fulfils himself in many ways, Lest one good custom should corrupt the world.

You can read that in Lord Tennyson's Idylls of the King. *Every kid attending Borgville High School does, and he graduates thinking it represents the pinnacle of human wisdom. (That's the way it has to be described in Miss Sussman's final exam for eleventh grade English. Question: "What sort of human wisdom is represented by the lines, "The old order changeth, yielding place to new; etc." Answer: "The pinnacle of human wisdom.")*

Grandfather Rastin says that's nonsense. A good custom never corrupted anything, and even if one accidentally did, that leaves a whole lot of completely innocent good customs that Lord Tennyson has yielding place to new just on general suspicion. Grandfather thinks we should preserve and cherish and learn to reject the bad before it has time to do any corrupting.

The problem is to agree on what should be preserved and cherished. Some of Grandfather's choices can be highly disconcerting. ...

Borgville's new park was dedicated on the Fourth of July, with an all-day community picnic. Everyone in Borgville attended, and there were farmers and their families from miles around, and businessmen from neighboring towns, and I guess all the politicians from four counties. The Park Committee tried to get the Governor of Michigan to give the dedication speech, but he'd already signed up to talk somewhere else. So they finally settled for Mr. Dombrowski, who is our County Drain Commissioner.

It was an important day for Borgville, and my family did all right, too. I won a white ribbon in the hundred yard dash for boys 15–18, and Mom took the red ribbon in the rolling pin throwing contest – Mrs. Pobloch beat her by ten feet – and even Grandfather Rastin got a ribbon. Mr. Hanson awarded it to him before the field events started.

He said there weren't any events for men over eighty, but if there were he was sure Grandfather would win all of them, so the committee had voted to award him the first blue ribbon. Grandfather said afterward that the real reason was to get him to stay on the sidelines and give the younger men a chance.

It was a busy day for me, and I didn't see much of Grandfather until late in the afternoon, when he came over to watch me being eliminated in the tennis tournament.

"Tennis," he said afterward, "isn't much of a game."

I'd had my tennis racket for just three weeks, and I thought tennis was a fine game.

"I like games of skill," Grandfather said. "There isn't much skill called for in hitting a ball with a bat that big."

I tried to explain that it was where the ball went that counted, but Grandfather wouldn't have any of that. "How can you miss," he asked, "when you use a bat the size of a wash tub?"

"What'd you play when you were young?" I asked him.

"Horseshoes," Grandfather said. "That's a real game of skill."

"Especially for horses," I said.

Grandfather grabbed my arm and glared at me. "What's wrong with horseshoes?"

It took me a moment to realize that he wasn't joking. "You mean there really is a game?" I asked.

He hauled me off through the crowd. We upset three picnic baskets and one thermos jug, tipped over a charcoal burner, and trampled several small children, but Grandfather didn't stop until he got me over to where the Park Committee was awarding ribbons. He elbowed everyone out of the way and stood me up in front of Mr. Hanson.

"Hanson," he said, "what this park needs is a horseshoes court."

Mr. Hanson stared at us. It took him a little time to get the idea in focus, and then he grinned. "Who'd use it?" he asked.

"Lots of people would Grandfather told him. "Finest game in the world. Just what these kids need. Imagine – Johnny didn't even know there was such a game!"

The members of the Park Committee were indulging in same head scratching. Probably they'd thought of a lot of bright remarks, but they were keeping them in until they figured out whether Grandfather was serious or pulling their legs.

"We have plenty of room for a court," Mr. Hanson said, "but there wouldn't be any sense in spending money an it if it wouldn't be used. You find a dozen people who want to pitch horseshoes, and *then* we'll consider it."

"Easy," Grandfather said.

He got a piece of paper from Margaret Snubbs, who was keeping records of who won the ribbons, and he signed his name at the top. Then he went looking for horseshoe pitchers. When I saw him again, a couple of hours later, he was so mad he'd stopped wearing his blue ribbon. He had just two names on his paper – his and Nat Barlow's – and I knew that Nat didn't want to pitch horseshoes. He's a frail old man in his seventies, and he doesn't look as if he could even lift a horseshoe. He just signed because Grandfather asked him to.

I offered to sign the paper myself, so there'd be three names, but Grandfather wouldn't let me. He was so disgusted that he went home before the fireworks started, and he spent all of the next day up in his bedroom, rocking in his rocking chair and snarling when anyone tried to talk to him.

I'd begun to feel curious about this wonderful game of horseshoes. I looked it up in the dictionary and in my encyclopedia, but the authors didn't seem to know that horseshoes were anything but footwear for horses. That would have been the end of it if I hadn't chanced to be looking through a mail-order catalog a week later, and darned if it didn't have a game of horseshoes listed. I drew eight dollars out of my savings account and sent off the order. I figured on giving it to Grandfather for his birthday in September, but when it came I couldn't wait. I wrapped it up in some paper left over from Christmas and put it at Grandfather's place at the breakfast table.

"It's a late Christmas present," I said, "or an early birthday present. Take your pick."

Grandfather made a face at me. He's always tickled pink to get presents, but he doesn't like to show it. It took him about ten minutes to get all of the paper off and folded up for next Christmas, and all the time he was fidgeting with curiosity because the package was so heavy. Finally he got the box open, and there they were: two red horseshoes and two blue horseshoes and two stakes.

"Well!" Grandfather said. I'd never seen him look so pleased.

Mom threw up her hands. "Keep those things out of my garden," she said.

"We'll set it up out by the alley," Grandfather said. "Right after breakfast. It's a fine game for character-building."

Mom winked at me. "Isn't it a little late for you to start building your character?"

"I was referring to Johnny," Grandfather snapped, "and you know it."

So we drove in the stakes out by the alley, where the grass is pretty thin anyway, and I had my first lesson in pitching horseshoes.

In case you've never played the game, I'll tell you a little about it. The idea is to stand at one stake, which is located at what looks to be a country mile from the other, and throw a horseshoe so it comes down around the other stake. This is called a ringer. A horseshoe is something smaller than a hoola hoop, and more than a mite heavier, and after a morning of throwing horseshoes back and forth there were blisters on two of my fingers, and muscles I never knew I had were sending up surrender signals.

"I've had enough," I said, when the biggest blister broke.

"Bah!" Grandfather said. He cut loose with another horseshoe, and it floated through the air like a feather, flat and turning slowly, and came down with a *clump* right around the stake. "Bah! You kids are all ice cream and soda pop."

"We sure are," I said, rubbing my arm.

I went in to get my blisters patched up, but Grandfather stayed out there until lunch time, throwing horseshoes back and forth. After lunch, he asked, "Ready to try again?" I held up my bandaged fingers, and he let out a snort and walked off toward Main Street.

Most afternoons when the weather is nice, Grandfather borrows the morning paper from Mr. Snubbs, who runs the Snubbs Hardware Store, and sits on the bench in front of Jake Palmer's barber shop to read it. That afternoon he didn't bother with the paper. He was back twenty minutes later, bringing Nat Barlow with him. The two of them went out to the alley, and I hurried after them, mainly because the spectacle of Nat Barlow throwing a horseshoe, or anything else, was one I didn't want to miss.

"You first," Grandfather said.

Nat picked up a red horseshoe, closed his eyes, and let fly. The horseshoe landed in the middle of the alley, roiled in a big circle all the way to the stake, and plopped down there as pretty as anything you could imagine.

Nat jumped up and down and clapped his hands. "Ringer!" he yelled.

Grandfather squinted at the far stake. "No, it isn't," he said. "Not quite."

"It is too," Nat said.

The three of us walked down to the other stake. Grandfather proceeded to demonstrate scientifically that the horseshoe wasn't quite far enough around the stake to be a ringer. Nat waved his arms and shouted that Grandfather was trying to cheat him. Grandfather explained again, being very patient with Nat, but there is something about Grandfather being patient that would make an angel swear.

Nat stomped his foot a couple of times and threw away his other red horseshoe, making a much better toss than he had with the first one. It sailed clear across the alley and through the door of Merton's barn.

Nat went back up town by way of the alley, and Grandfather returned to the house, muttering to himself. I went over to the barn to retrieve Nat's red horseshoe.

Merton's barn is really a big old stable that the Mertons built to keep their horses in back about 1920, when Mr. Merton's old man thought the future of the automobile didn't look very bright. The stalls were knocked out long ago, to convert it to a double garage, but it still has the loft where hay and feed and stuff were kept. For years the Mertons used the space for storage, until the loft got so overloaded with junk that Mrs. Merton was afraid to go in there after her car. Just a week before Grandfather's horseshoes arrived, Mr. Merton had the barn cleaned out and everything carted away. Now the place is so empty that the Mertons' two little foreign cars look like beans in a bushel basket. Fortunately neither of the cars were there when Nat threw the horseshoe.

I collected all four horseshoes and made myself four ringers while standing two and a half feet from the stake, and then I went in to see what Grandfather was doing.

"Imagine that!" he said to me. "A grown man behaving like a spoiled child!"

"It was pretty close to a ringer," I said. "Why didn't you let him have it?"

"What's the point in a game's having rules if you don't use them?" Grandfather asked.

I didn't have any answer to that, so I said, "Now you've got no one to play with."

"How's the hand?"

"Not so good," I said.

"Soda pop," Grandfather said. "And ice cream." He went up to his room, and I heard his rocking chair start up.

A couple of hours later Mr. Snubbs came by with the morning paper. "Thought maybe your Grandfather was sick and couldn't come after it," he said.

"He's not exactly sick," I said. "He's just mad."

"It amounts to the same thing," Mr. Snubbs said.

Grandfather called down from the head of the stairs. "That you, Snubbs? How about a game of horseshoes?"

Mr. Snubbs started to back away. "That's all right for a youngster like you; but me – I'm too old for such carrying on. Why, I haven't pitched horseshoes since –"

He never got to finish. Grandfather was down the stairs and had him by the arm, marching him through the house and out of the back door. I was curious to know if Mr. Snubbs could do as well with his eyes closed as Nat Barlow had, but I never got to find out. When we got to the alley, there weren't any horseshoes.

"What'd you do with them, Johnny?" Grandfather asked.

"I left them right there on that stake," I said.

"They didn't walk away by themselves," Grandfather said.

Mr. Snubbs giggled. "Maybe some horse came along and liked them."

"Grandfather didn't answer that. He stood there for all of a minute, thinking, and then he headed for the house at a full gallop.

Mr. Snubbs winked at me. "I think I'll go back to the store. Let me know if he finds them, so I can keep away from here."

When I got to the house, Grandfather was shouting at the telephone, "I want to see Sheriff Pilkins. Right away!"

The sheriff wasn't in. Grandfather told the deputy just what he thought of a sheriff that wasn't around when he was needed. He hung up grumbling, and before he got one good grumble rounded off the sheriff came walking up the front steps.

Grandfather and Sheriff Pilkins are not what one would call close friends, and this is only partly because Sheriff Pilkins is a Republican, and Grandfather would be Borgville's Democratic Chairman if there were enough Democrats in Borgville to need a chairman. I guess the main reason is that they just don't like each other. But Grandfather has helped the sheriff out quite a few times, and made a monkey out of him more than once, and the sheriff thought Grandfather wouldn't be telephoning him if it wasn't something important. He was all excited and out-of-breath. "What have you got?" he asked.

"It's what I haven't got," Grandfather said. "Someone just stole my horseshoes."

Sheriff Pilkins collapsed onto the sofa. "Would you mind saying that again?"

"You hard of hearing, or something? Someone just stole my horseshoes."

The sheriff buried his face in his hands. "All right," he said, talking through his fingers. "Someone stole your horseshoes. Any suspects?"

"No," Grandfather said. "I know derned well it was Nat Barlow."

"I doubt it," the sheriff said. "I saw Nat just now. He's over on Main Street sitting in front of the barber shop, and if he has any horseshoes in his pockets they don't show. Who else?"

"Nat stole them and hid them somewhere, just to be spiteful," Grandfather said.

"I doubt it, but I'll have a look. Where were they?"

We went out to the alley, and I showed the sheriff where I'd left the horseshoes.

"They shouldn't be hard to trace," the sheriff said. "They're the only playing horseshoes around here. All we have to do is wait until we see someone pitching horseshoes, and ask where he got them."

"There won't be anyone pitching horseshoes," Grandfather said. "Nat's hid them somewhere."

The sheriff looked the scene of the crime over very thoroughly. Suddenly he grinned. "Say – you don't suppose a horse came down the alley –"

"Shut up!" Grandfather shouted.

"Just a moment," the sheriff said. He walked all the way to the end of the alley, where it meets the alley that runs behind the stores on Main Street. When he came back he looked excited.

"There was a theft up town this afternoon," he said. "Jim Higgins was making up the Variety Store's bank deposit, and he was called to the telephone, and while he was talking someone sneaked in the back door and stole his moneybag. That's where I was when they told me you'd called. I thought maybe you had a line on who took it, so I came right over."

"Don't know a thing about it," Grandfather said.

"But look – this alley connects with the alley that runs behind the Variety Store. I was thinking that the thief could easily have come up this way after he took the money, and he stole your horseshoes, too. It sometimes happens that when someone steals something and wants to hide it he'll grab anything he can lay his hands on that's heavy."

Grandfather turned and stared at the sheriff. "Why?"

"To make it sink. Then he can toss the loot in the water, somewhere, and fish it out when the heat's off."

"Is that a fact?"

"Sure. I've read about it lots of times."

"How much money was in the bag?" Grandfather asked.

"Quite a lot. Nearly a hundred dollars worth of change. Higgins hadn't got around to his paper money, which is a lucky thing for him."

"You don't say," Grandfather said.

I knew what was coming. That is, I knew *something* was coming. It always does when Grandfather sounds so meek and innocent-like.

He went on, "Then maybe you wouldn't mind explaining why the thief needed my four horseshoes *to sink a bag full of metal money*."

The sheriff's face started getting red. Grandfather kept glaring at him until he looked the other way and got out a handkerchief to mop his face.

"No wonder crime runs rampant in this county," Grandfather said and walked away.

We met the sheriff up town that evening, when I was taking Grandfather's evening walk with him. "I talked with Nat," Sheriff Pilkins said. "He claims he doesn't know anything about your horseshoes."

"If he says he doesn't, then he doesn't," Grandfather said. "I've never known Nat to tell a lie."

"Probably some kids ran off with them," the sheriff said.

"They knew they'd be perfectly safe," Grandfather said, "considering who's sheriff."

Sheriff Pilkins started to sputter, and Grandfather walked away so fast I had to run to keep up with him. "If I thought it would do any good," Grandfather said, "I'd threaten not to vote for him. But he knows I've never voted for him yet, and I wouldn't vote for him even if he found the horseshoes. He knows that, too."

"So what are you going to do?" I asked.

"I guess I'll have to find them myself."

He went home and rocked on it. He was rocking when I went to sleep, and he was rocking when I woke up. He was mad enough to rock all night on it, and maybe he did, but as far as his horseshoes were concerned it was wasted mileage.

"Did you think of anything?" I asked him at the breakfast table.

"No," he said, and right after breakfast he went back up to his rocking chair.

I started for the park to see if I could find someone to play tennis with, and as I turned into the alley there on the first stake were four horseshoes – two red and two blue. I turned and ran back to the house.

"You can stop rocking," I told Grandfather. "Whoever took your horseshoes brought them back."

He didn't say anything until he'd worked up a little more speed. Then he asked, "Are you joking?"

"Nope," I said. "They're right there on the stake where I left them."

Grandfather rocked a little faster. "This is ridiculous. Bringing them back makes even less sense than taking them."

"The sheriff stirred up a lot of dust," I said. "Maybe the thief got scared."

"Pilkins wouldn't scare a thief, but he might make him laugh himself to death. How's the hand?"

"Some better," I said.

So we spent the morning pitching horseshoes.

Sheriff Pilkins stopped by at ten o'clock – to report progress, I suppose – and when he saw us playing with the horseshoes he stood there watching for a long time while his face took on some colors that made me wonder if his blood circulation had a safety valve.

"So your horseshoes were stolen," he said finally.

Grandfather took aim and let fly with another ringer. "Fortunately," he said, "we didn't have to depend on you to get them back."

"Who had them?"

"Don't know," Grandfather said.

"Then – how'd you get them back?"

"Whoever took them brought them back."

"Did you get a look at him?"

Grandfather shook his head.

"If you hadn't been in such an all-fired rush to start using them, we could have checked for fingerprints."

"That so?" Grandfather said. "What would you charge him with if you caught him? Borrowing my horseshoes overnight?"

Sheriff Pilkins considered this. "It wouldn't make much of a case," he agreed. "But you might have thought about that before you kicked up so much fuss."

"I wasn't after blood," Grandfather said. "All I wanted was my horseshoes back."

"So you got them back. And the next time you have a dastardly crime to report, don't."

The sheriff left, and Grandfather went over and sat down on a cement block that Merton had saved out of the junk that was in his barn. "Johnny," he said, "there's something mighty queer about this."

"I can't see that there's anything to worry about," I said. "We have the horseshoes back, and I won't make the mistake of leaving them out here again."

Grandfather didn't say anything.

"Too bad you didn't like tennis," I said. "If I'd got you a tennis racket we wouldn't have had all this trouble."

"If you'd eat more potatoes and less ice cream," Grandfather said, "you'd be able to pitch a shoe within ten feet of the stake."

He got up and walked down the alley, looking around carefully. Then he came back and stood in the doorway of Merton's barn, looking the place over carefully. "It was Jerry Stark, wasn't it, that Merton had cleaning this place out?"

"Sure," I said. "He worked on it two days."

"Jerry still living over at the old Hurth place?"

"If Old Man Hurth hasn't thrown him out, he is."

"Tonight," Grandfather said, "I'll have a job for you."

He went back to the house. I followed him, and this time I brought the horseshoes along and left them on the back porch.

It was almost midnight when I got out to the Hurth place. It's an old wreck of a house that stands a couple of miles north of town. It'd been boarded up for several years when Jerry Stark rented it. Grandfather said it wasn't fit for human habitation, but I guess Jerry wasn't in any position to be particular.

Jerry had a pretty good job in a factory in Wiston; and then the factory moved to Tennessee or Arkansas or somewhere and left Jerry with a wife and three small kids and no job. He worked at what he could find, which wasn't much, and when the mortgage was foreclosed on the house he was buying in Wiston, he rented the Hurth place because it came cheap. Only the word I got was that he wasn't even able to pay that rent, and Old Man Hurth was talking about throwing him out.

I left my jalopy parked down the road and tiptoed through a couple of acres of weeds to get to the front door. There was a light in one of the rooms, though not much of a light. Old Man Hurth never put electricity into that house, so it had to be a candle or a kerosene lamp. There was a baby crying, and as I stood by the porch listening, one of the older kids chimed in.

I felt sorry for Jerry. It would have made sense to me if Grandfather had suggested that he was the Variety Store thief. Not that he'd ever done anything dishonest, but he sure needed the money. What I couldn't understand was where the horseshoes came into it.

But they were Grandfather's horseshoes, and all I could do was hope he knew what he was about. I had them wrapped in a burlap bag, so they wouldn't make any noise, and I took them out one at a time and laid them in a row at the edge of the sagging old porch. Then I went home.

Grandfather was waiting up for me, and I told him the mission was accomplished.

He grunted. "Anyone see you?"

"I don't think so."

"All right. Go to bed."

"I'd still like to know why you're giving your horseshoes away," I said. "Even if Jerry isn't working, he probably doesn't have time to waste pitching horseshoes. And if he has, he'll need the stakes to go with them."

Grandfather grinned at me. "Go to bed," he said. So I went to bed.

I slept in the next morning, and Mom finally woke me up at nine thirty and wanted to know what Grandfather and I had been up to the night before.

"Did you ask him?" I asked her.

"Yes. He said I'd have to ask you."

"He told me not to tell anyone," I said. We laughed. "What's he doing this morning?" I asked.

"He's out pitching horseshoes."

"*What?*"

"I said he's out –"

I tore downstairs, barefoot and in my pajamas, and ran out to the back yard. Sure enough, Grandfather was out there pitching with all four horseshoes.

"Where'd you get them?" I called.

"Someone left them on the stake," Grandfather said. "Just like he did yesterday."

"Then it must have been Jerry that took them."

Grandfather missed a ringer by a hair and muttered something to himself. "Do you think so?" he asked me.

"What are you going to do? Tell the sheriff?"

Grandfather shook his head. "Tonight," he said, "I'll have a job for you."

It was the same job. I took the four horseshoes back to the Hurth place and left them in a row on the front porch. Grandfather didn't bother waiting up for me that second night, and I didn't bother to wait for him the next morning. I was the first one out of bed, and I pulled my clothes on and ran down to look for horseshoes. There weren't any.

Grandfather was just getting up when I got back upstairs. "If you're planning on playing horseshoes this morning," I said, "don't. He's convinced that you want him to keep them."

"Good," Grandfather said, and he went down to breakfast whistling.

I'd had enough horseshoe mystery, so right after breakfast I went over to the park to play tennis. I came home at eleven-thirty, dead tired, and found Grandfather out by the alley pitching horseshoes with Jerry Stark.

"We're waiting for you, Johnny," Grandfather said. "Take your car and help Jerry move."

"Move where?" I asked.

"To the Ashley farm," Grandfather said. "Jerry's going to work for Ashley."

"Not right away, he isn't," I said. "I'm hungry."

"After lunch, then."

Mom fixed an early lunch for the three of us, and then I drove Jerry back to the Hurth place. He didn't have much to say along the way, except that he thought Grandfather was a great guy.

"He certainly is," I said, "but don't ever make the mistake of trying to figure him out."

"I asked Ashley for that job at least a dozen times," Jerry said. "He wouldn't even talk to me about it. Your Grandfather makes one telephone call, and the job's mine."

"I didn't know you knew anything about farming," I said.

"I don't," Jerry said. "That's why Ashley wouldn't hire me."

Jerry's wife fell all over him when he told her the news. We loaded her and the kids into my jalopy, and tossed as much stuff as we could carry in on top of them, and drove over to the Ashley farm. Ashley has a little cottage he once built for one of his sons, and Mrs. Stark took charge of it. It wasn't much of a house, but compared with the place they'd been living in it probably seemed like a palace.

Jerry borrowed Ashley's pickup truck, and the two of us got the rest of his stuff moved in a hurry. There wasn't much to move. Then Old Man Ashley started giving Jerry a lesson in driving a tractor, and I headed back to town.

Grandfather was sitting on the bench in front of Jake Palmer's Barber Shop, reading Mr. Snubbs's morning paper and keeping one ear on the conversation of the men standing around, just in case they needed straightening out about anything. It wasn't the proper time to be asking questions about reappearing horseshoes, so I went on home. Grandfather had left the horseshoes on one of the stakes when he finished using them, and I put them on the back porch. I wasn't going to have *that* business starting up again.

Grandfather wasn't much interested in talking about horseshoes when he came home. He had another job to be done that night, and he wouldn't talk about that, either. He did it himself, walking off toward town just after dark, and coming back an hour later looking as smug as a dog that's just had puppies.

He wouldn't tell me anything about it. I went and checked the horseshoes, just in case, but all four of them were on the back porch where I'd left them.

Grandfather and I were pitching horseshoes when Sheriff Pilkins came by the next morning. "I want to talk to you," he said to Grandfather.

Grandfather waited with a horseshoe poised to throw, and said, "Talk."

"I've just seen Higgins," the sheriff said. "He says the stolen money was returned to him during the night. Someone dropped it in through the mail slot."

"Nice of you to let me know," Grandfather said. "Though I imagine I would have heard about it sooner or later. Or did you think maybe I could tell you who returned it?"

"I don't know what to think," the sheriff said. "Your horseshoes are stolen, and apparently they walk back by themselves. Higgins's money is stolen, and it comes back anonymously. Without a penny missing. It doesn't make sense."

"It makes two crimes you don't have to solve," Grandfather said.

"Look here. Just because the stolen goods were returned doesn't mean there wasn't a crime committed. The whole setup looks screwy, and I wouldn't be surprised if you and Higgins cooked it up just to pull my leg."

Grandfather took the time to pitch a horseshoe. He missed. "What's screwy about a crook's conscience bothering him?" he asked.

"It takes more than a conscience to stuff a bag of coins through a mail slot. I suppose the thief did it a penny at a time."

"Maybe he did," Grandfather said. "What did Higgins say about that?"

"He didn't say anything. He just grinned at me."

"That surprises me."

"It does?"

"It sure does," Grandfather said. "I'm surprised he didn't laugh himself silly."

Grandfather turned around and pitched the other horseshoe. A ringer. We walked down to the other stake, and when we turned around Sheriff Pilkins was gone. Grandfather stooped down to pick up his horseshoes.

"Just a moment," I said. "It's time you let me know what's going on, I've got part of it figured out. I know Jerry Stark took the money and you talked him into returning it and got him a job. Right?"

"Right," Grandfather said. "Only I didn't have to talk him into returning the money. He was glad to return it. He'd spent ten dollars for groceries, and I loaned him that so he could return all of it. It's a sad thing when a man has to steal to feed his family. But he'll be all right, now. He'll work his head off for Ashley."

"That settles everything except what the horseshoes had to do with it."

"Come here," Grandfather said. We walked over to the door of Merton's barn. He pointed. "See that?"

It was dark in the back part of the barn, but finally I made out what he was pointing at. It was a rope, dangling down from the opening to the loft.

"Sure," I said. "There's a pulley up at the roof, and Jerry was using that last week to lower stuff down from the loft."

"Still need an explanation?"

"Just one. What did the horseshoes have to do with it?"

"Look," Grandfather said. "Jerry was making his rounds asking people for work. He walked through the back door of the Variety Store. Higgins wasn't in the back room, and there was the bag of money. Jerry hadn't earned a penny that day, and his family didn't have a thing in the house to eat. He took the money and beat it down the alley."

"But it was broad daylight, and a hundred dollars in change won't fit into a watch pocket. Jerry had to get rid of the bag right away, and he figured he was as good as caught if anyone saw him with his pockets bulging. He turned up this way, and here was Merton's barn. He knew all about it, from cleaning it out.

There wasn't a soul around. He tied the money bag to one end of the rope and hoisted it up to the roof, where it was just about invisible. But he had a problem keeping it there because there wasn't anything to tie the rope to. He looked across the alley, and there was just what he needed – four horseshoes.

He looped the rope around them, piled the loose ends on top so the horseshoes wouldn't be seen, and got out of there. He couldn't have found a safer hiding place, and it was the easiest thing in the world for him to come back after dark, lower the money, and return the horseshoes.

"He thought he'd got away with it until the horseshoes turned up on his porch. Then he didn't know what to think. I suppose it was mean of me to scare him that way, but I figured it'd be best if he came to me for help, rather than – what's the matter?"

"But that's just what the sheriff said!" I exclaimed.

"What did the sheriff say?"

"He said the thief came down this way, and stole your horseshoes, and –"

Grandfather sighed. "That's the trouble with Pilkins. Even when he does get a good idea he gives it such an idiotic twist that the Almighty Himself couldn't see any merit in it. Horseshoes to sink a bag of coins – phooey. Took me until the next day to remember that weights hold things *up*, as well as *down*. Now let's pitch horseshoes."

THE PAIR OF KNAVES

A visitor once asked Grandfather Rastin what Borg County's leading tourist attraction was, and he answered that it doesn't need a tourist attraction because it doesn't get any tourists. Unfortunately, that's the story of Borg County's life. Its one large lake is called Mud Lake, for obvious reasons. People passing through aren't asked to stop for a scenic view, because Borg County doesn't have scenic views, and if it had one there wouldn't be any place to see it from. The highest point in Borg County has such gradual slopes in all directions that you can walk right over it without noticing it.

This doesn't mean that there are no spectacles in Borg County. One or two of our annual events are even spectacular enough to attract a fair crowd of visitors from outside the county. As Grandfather says, that's why they're spectacles. …

That Labor Day spectacular was one I'd just as soon forget. I should have hung a black flag over our front door and nailed a quarantine sign under it. My Grandfather Rastin has the most *contagious* dumps you ever saw, not to mention the fact that he was mad enough to bite somebody.

For weeks we'd been looking forward to the annual water carnival on Mud Lake. Grandfather had four invitations, including one to sit in the judges' stand, but that morning at breakfast he announced that he wasn't going. When I told him he was being a poor loser he hit me in the face with a piece of toast, which fortunately he never butters.

We talked him into coming along, and then we spent the whole afternoon wishing we hadn't. His grumbling all but drowned out the motorboats, and nothing, not even the chance that he might see Sheriff Pilkins blow himself up, would make him stay for the fireworks. So we went home and went to bed, and that should have been the end of it.

A little after eleven the telephone rang. I answered it, and a voice whispered, "This is Mrs. Hanson. Tell your Grandfather to come out here right away. He's needed."

And hung up.

"Maybe she really wants a doctor," I told Grandfather. "It sounded like laryngitis."

"She whispered so her husband wouldn't know she was calling me. Let's go."

We got dressed in nothing flat, and went.

The trouble started, believe it or not, back in 1936. That was the year that Hiram Mills, who had charge of Borgville's Fourth of July fireworks display, was suddenly taken sick. My Grandfather Rastin stepped in without hardly any practice, and did so well that the 1936 display is still remembered as the only one in Borgville's history where nobody got burned and nothing got set on fire.

Hiram handled the display the next few years, and then his son took over, and not even Grandfather's best friends realized that this one experience had given him an insatiable appetite for setting off fireworks. I doubt that he realized it himself until last winter, when word got around that the promoters of the Mud Lake Water Carnival had decided to add a fireworks display.

Grandfather didn't waste any time in making it known that his services were available. He cornered Mr. Hanson, who is president of the Borgville Bank and a member of the Carnival Committee, and reminded him about 1936, and Mr. Hanson practically promised Grandfather the job. Grandfather filled his room with books and magazines and catalogs and started planning the best fireworks display in the history of Borg County.

Then it occurred to Sheriff Pilkins that a lot of voters would turn out to watch the fireworks. The sheriff pulled a few political strings and offered to finance the display, and before Grandfather knew what was going on, the sheriff had the appointment. Grandfather said publicly that as long as the sheriff's salary wasn't buying us any police work we might as well have the fireworks, but I could see that he was awfully disappointed.

Before he got over being disappointed he started to get mad, and from there all roads ran in one direction – down. By the time Mrs. Hanson telephoned, he had hit absolute bottom. If he'd known what she wanted he would have gone back to bed, but the only thing on his mind that night was fireworks. He was certain that Sheriff Pilkins had goofed up the Mud Lake fireworks, and to his ears Mrs. Hanson's whisper was a clarion call for assistance. Neither snow nor rain nor heat nor the gloom of night could have stayed him from the swift accomplishment of his appointed route to the Hanson cottage. It was the first time since I learned to drive that he bawled me out for not going fast enough.

I did everything but massage my jalopy's radiator cap, but it still took us half an hour to get out to Mud Lake, and another fifteen minutes to find the Hanson place in the dark. The driveway already had four cars in it, so I parked out by the road and was a very bad second to Grandfather in getting up to the door.

Mr. Hanson came to the door, and the look on his face made it obvious that we weren't expected. He was less shocked than he would have been to find the President of the United States or the Prime Minister of Afghanistan knocking on the door of his lake cottage at that time of night, but not by much.

"What's wrong with the fireworks?" Grandfather demanded.

"Why – nothing is wrong with the fireworks," Mr. Hanson said. "They all were shot off hours ago."

"Horsefeathers!" Grandfather roared. He doesn't often use a stronger swear word than that, but the way he says it never leaves much doubt about what he means.

Mrs. Hanson's voice came from somewhere inside the house. "Is that Mr. Rastin? I asked him to come."

"Oh," Mr. Hanson said. "Well, come on in. We have a kind of missing person problem, and we didn't know whether to call you or the sheriff. I decided on the sheriff, because if there's anything to it we'd end up calling him anyway, but evidently Mae –"

"Who's missing?" Grandfather asked, making it sound as if he couldn't have cared less.

"That's part of the problem. We don't know."

Labor Day house parties are a Mud Lake tradition, and the Hansons had a housefull of guests from Detroit. The men were in one room and the women in another, and I was at least an hour getting the husbands matched up with their wives. When I finally managed it, it came out like this:

Mr. and Mrs. Nolte. They made a fine Mutt and Jeff team. Mrs. Nolte was the tall, skinny one.

Mr. and Mrs. Keefer. This was another pair of opposites, but in a different way. Mrs. Keefer was young and nice-looking, and maybe even pretty enough to be on television, and she was already wearing the makeup for it. Her husband wasn't young, and he could have posed as the *before* picture in almost any *before-and-after* advertisement you could name.

Mr. and Mrs. Urschel. They looked like everybody's favorite grandparents.

Mr. Baldridge. He acted like a college boy, and he would have looked it if it hadn't been for the gray in his hair. He's the reason I had so much trouble getting the couples matched up, because there wasn't any Mrs. Baldridge.

Mr. and Mrs. Hanson, the hosts. They looked too young to be grandparents, and their seven grandchildren prove how misleading looks can be.

Sheriff Pilkins arrived before Mr. Hanson finished all the introductions. I expected the sheriff to shoot off a few more fireworks when he saw Grandfather, but the most scintillating thing on *his* mind was getting back home to bed. We didn't find out about it until later, but he'd had a hard night.

The fireworks, which he shot off from a raft in the middle of the lake, went over pretty well; but at one point in the proceedings he absent-mindedly put a piece of lighted punk in his pocket, and when his pants started to smoke, one of his deputies got excited and pushed him into the lake to put out the fire. I was sorry Grandfather wasn't there to see it, though I doubt that it would have made him feel better. It would have taken a major conflagration to cheer him up.

Mr. Hanson ran through the introductions again, and the sheriff said, "Yeah, I already know Rastin. What's the trouble?"

"It's the funniest thing I've ever had happen to me," Mr. Hanson said. "This man walked in here this morning and introduced himself. Said his name was Dick Scott. Everyone was arriving about that time, and I just naturally thought someone brought him."

"And we thought he was Mr. Hanson's guest," Mr. Urschel said. "Then tonight during the fireworks he vanished."

"Did you check to see if he got lost in the woods or fell off the dock?" the sheriff asked.

"The only 'woods' is that little grove of trees," Mr. Hanson said. "He would have heard us calling him. And there isn't two feet of water around the dock. It wasn't until after the fellow disappeared that we got to comparing notes and found that none of us had met him before today."

Grandfather looked around for a rocking chair and finally had to settle for one of those modern things that look like a lunatic's idea of a better mousetrap. He sat down and started whispering with Mrs. Hanson.

The sheriff scowled. "He could be one of your neighbors' guests."

"Then why did he spend the whole day here with us? Anyway, we've checked with everyone on this side of the lake."

The sheriff thought for a moment, scratching at his bald spot. I haven't a doubt in the world that if Grandfather hadn't been there he would have promised to look into it the next day and gone home. He actually got as far as saying, "Well, in the morning –"

Then he saw Grandfather grinning at him.

He backed into the nearest empty chair and said grimly, "Tell me everything that's happened. Right from the beginning."

The beginning was when the missing man walked around the corner of the house and said, "Hi. I'm Dick Scott." Mr. Hanson shook hands with him and told him to make himself at home, which he did so thoroughly that a little later he was telling the invited guests to make themselves at home. "He was a friendly bloke," Mr. Hanson said. "Life of the party and that sort of thing. A good talker. I rather liked him."

Heads nodded.

"He complimented me on my dress," Mrs. Nolte said. "It's been years since a man did that. Why, my husband –"

Someone shushed her.

"What'd he look like?" the sheriff said.

"Heavy-set fellow," Mr. Hanson said. "Curly hair, good looking. In his forties, I'd say. Dressed expensively. I've seen neckties like his marked twenty bucks, and his jacket –"

"All right. So he walked in and made himself at home. What have you been doing all day? Sitting around and talking?"

"Mostly. We watched the water skiing and the stunts. We had some motorboat rides and some of us went down to the other end of the lake to watch the boat races. Keefer and Baldridge went fishing."

"Without catching anything," Mr. Keefer grumbled. He really was a funny-looking little fellow, with bushy gray hair, and he kept arching what would have been his eyebrows if he'd had any. "Mud Lake is the name for it. There's nothing out there but mud."

"I told you the boats would spoil the fishing," Mr. Hanson said. He went on, "We had a chicken barbecue this evening, and then the ladies talked and we played poker until the fireworks started. That's all."

The Sheriff stiffened like a bird dog catching a scent. "*Poker!* How much did he win?"

"He didn't win anything. He was the worst poker player I ever saw."

"How much did he lose, then."

"I haven't any idea, but it must have been plenty. He said he'd never played before, and I believe it. Once he called on a pair of tens, when he knew it took jacks or better to open. He couldn't get it through his head that three of a kind beat two pair. I've never seen such a lousy poker player, but he was darned good company. Enjoyed himself all the time. Seemed to have more fun losing than most men would winning."

"Sure. How much did he lose?"

"Well, let's see –"

"I'd make it at least three bucks," Mr. Urschel said.

The sheriff snorted. "What stakes were you playing for?"

"Nickel limit. And he didn't win a pot."

The sheriff snorted again. "Even so, I doubt that he ran out on his poker losses. What happened next?"

"We went outside to watch the fireworks," Mr. Hanson said. "He kept wanting to start another game. We told him to keep his shirt on until the fireworks were over, and the next thing we knew he was gone."

"He was a poker nut," Mr. Nolte said. "One of these guys that can't stop. A compulsive gambler, maybe – he never won, but he wanted to raise the limit to a dime. I think he wandered off looking for another game."

"Let's go outside," the sheriff said.

Mud Lake is really is a nice-looking lake. It's another of those cases where a rose by any other name would smell as sweet, except I have to admit that sometimes Mud Lake does smell a little odd. The mud is mostly on the bottom and doesn't interfere with the fishing and boating, but the lake will never take any prizes as a place to wade. There are lots of expensive cottages around it, because it's the only real lake Borg County has.

There wasn't much to see at that time of right. Mr. Hanson put on a couple of yard lights, and then the sheriff made him turn them off because he wanted things exactly the way they were when this Mr. Scott disappeared.

We felt our way down to the lake shore, which was about a hundred feet from the cottage, and in that hundred feet I fell over eight lilac bushes and seventeen pieces of lawn furniture. Finally the sheriff had to have the lights turned on again so the Hansons and their guests could find the chairs they were using during the fireworks.

Mr. Scott had been sitting off to one side, near the trees. The only persons close to him were Mr. Baldridge, on his left, and Mrs. Urschel, in front of him, and they were too far away for polite conversation. The Noltes had been sitting in a row of chairs down by the water, with Mr. Keefer and Mrs. Hanson. Mr. Hanson and Mr. Urschel had been sitting nearby, with Mrs. Keefer in a glider way off on the other side.

"Are you sure Scott came out here?" the sheriff asked. "What with the dark, and everyone looking up at the fireworks, you wouldn't have missed him."

"We all came together," Mr. Hanson insisted. "And I told you – he kept wanting to play poker."

"All right. What happened next?"

"Later someone said Scott had gone back to the porch and had the hands all dealt for another game."

"That was me," Mr. Baldridge said. "He practically dragged me back there and said, 'Let's play,' and started to deal. I told him two-handed poker was a bore, so he dealt six hands and I came back to tell the others. No one wanted to play, so I stayed down here. Then Scott yelled, 'Let's play poker!' and someone called to him –"

"I did," Mr. Keefer said. "I told him to come back and watch the fireworks."

"Did he come?"

"I don't know."

"I'd better have a look at the porch," the sheriff said. He galloped back to the cottage, with the rest of us stringing after him. There was a long screened porch with a door at one end and a cement patio outside the door. At the far end was a round table with six chairs. At each place was a hand of poker, untouched.

"Is that the way you left it?" the sheriff asked.

"It's the way *he* left it," Mr. Hanson said. "We started looking for him and just never paid any attention to it."

"Where was he sitting?"

"There in the corner," Mr. Hanson said, pointing.

"*Don't touch the cards!* Was it his deal when you stopped playing?" They had to think about that. "It was mine," Mr. Nolte said finally.

The sheriff circled the table and very carefully peaked at each of the poker hands. "Only one hand has anything," he announced finally. "His own. He dealt himself a full house. Sixes and jacks."

When the men finally digested that, it broke them up. Mr. Urschel laughed until he had to take off his glasses and wipe his eyes. Mr. Nolte flopped onto a sofa and buried his face in his hands. Mr. Hanson bent over and clutched at his middle. He doesn't have much stomach, but what was there he grabbed. Mr. Baldridge was late getting back and didn't hear the joke, but when they told him he laughed louder than anyone else.

"Lost all evening," Mr. Hanson gasped. "Didn't win a single pot. Couldn't take it any longer so he came back here and slipped himself a full house. Then he got ashamed and beat it. If we'd thought to look at the cards, I wouldn't have bothered to call you."

"Then I'm glad you didn't look," the sheriff said. He hadn't cracked a smile all the time they were laughing. He moved over to a glider and started to swing, and the longer he swung the grimmer he looked.

"We'd better find this guy before we go any further," he said finally. "I'll send for some help. See how many flashlights you can find."

"If you say so," Mr. Hanson said. "The way I see it, it's a waste of time. He's an hour and a half further away than he was the last time we looked."

"You were looking for a guy who'd maybe wandered off and got lost. This time – well, my hunch is that he's an hour and a half deader than he was when you looked before."

The sheriff sent for four deputies, and Mr. Hanson rounded up an armful of flashlights and a few neighbors to help out, and when everything was ready we started off. Mr. Hanson found the body himself, just inside the little grove of trees that stood between his cottage and the one on the west.

Scott had been stabbed in the back with an ice pick, which turned out to be one that had been in Mrs. Hanson's kitchen drawer since before the cottage had electricity.

The sheriff had the men tiptoe up one at a time for a look – Mr. Hanson's guests to identify the body, and the neighbors to find out if they'd ever seen the man. None of them had.

Then Steve Carling, one of the deputies, herded us back to the cottage, and we settled down for a long wait.

"If I'd known what I was getting you into, I wouldn't have called," Mrs. Hanson told Grandfather.

"Then I'm glad you didn't know," Grandfather said with a smile. "It's worth losing a little sleep to see Pilkins trying to play detective."

"That was a pretty shrewd piece of detection," Mr. Hanson said.

Grandfather nodded. "That's what worries me. If a man's just naturally wrongheaded, a right guess is the worst thing that can happen to him."

"He seems like the most competent sheriff I've ever seen," Mr. Baldridge said.

"You'll know him better before morning," Grandfather said dryly.

By that time we were all pretty much on edge. Mrs. Keefer got into an argument with her husband about which of them had wanted to come to Mud Lake in the first place, and she slapped him. The Noltes didn't seem to be speaking to each other, and the Urschels didn't seem to be speaking to Mr. and Mrs. Hanson.

Grandfather moved around trying to get everyone quieted down, and Mrs. Hanson, who is one of those people who think the right thing to do in any crisis is eat, hurried to make sandwiches. Grandfather passed out the sandwiches and coffee, and put me to cleaning up the mess when Mrs. Keefer spilled hers, and found matches to keep Mr. Urschel's pipe lit, and a spare carton of cigarettes for Mr. Nolte, who was chain-smoking like he was trying to set a record, and generally got things under control.

He also got in a few licks of detective work, like making Mrs. Hanson show him where the ice pick had been buried under a pile of junk in the back of the knife drawer, and getting one of the neighbors to fill him in on the current Mud Lake gossip.

Finally Sheriff Pilkins came back. "Sorry to keep you folks waiting," he said. "I only want one of you, but I thought I might as well get statements from the rest while you're all together.

Just then Mrs. Keefer spilled her coffee again, getting some of it on Mrs. Nolte. Mrs. Nolte dropped her lighted cigarette onto the carpet, and Mr. Urschel tripped over Mr. Baldridge trying to get to it and spilled another cup of coffee. All of that made quite a diversion, and it was some minutes before the sheriff's remarks got through to everyone.

"Just what do you mean – you only want *one* of us?" Mr. Hanson demanded.

"What I said. Sorry, Hanson. One of your guests is a liar and a murderer."

"The ice pick," Mr. Hanson muttered. "But I've known all of these people for years –"

"And you didn't know one of them was a knave. That's usually the case." Mrs. Nolte suddenly wanted to go home, and Mrs. Urschel seconded the motion. "The party's ruined anyway," she said.

"Some party," Mrs. Keefer said, glaring at her husband.

The sheriff ignored them. "Dick Scott was a knave, too. Just like that poker hand, you've had two knaves in a full house. Your guest isn't a thief, though – if that's any consolation. He left more than five hundred dollars in Dick Scott's wallet."

"Who are you calling a knave?" Mr. Urschel demanded.

"I'll ask the questions," the sheriff said. The room got deadly quiet. "Dick Scott didn't accidently wander in here on foot with five hundred dollars in his pocket looking for a place to play nickel poker. One of you brought him, and he came here for just one purpose. He was a cardsharp, out to make a killing on a small-town banker and his hick friends."

"Now wait a minute!" Mr. Hanson sputtered. "One of my guests brought –"

"A cardsharp. A professional gambler, crooked variety. Couldn't you guess it just by looking at him? Expensive clothes, everybody's pal, and let's raise the limit. The person who brought him here is the person who murdered him, and chances are it wouldn't take the Detroit police long to find out which of you knew him. It also would embarrass and inconvenience the rest of you, so I'm glad I don't have to ask them. I suspected foul play as soon as I saw that poker hand, and I knew who did it. All I want from you now is some careful thinking, to see if you remember anything I can use for evidence. Mr. Urschel, is one of those cars in the driveway yours?"

Mr. Urschel nodded.

"You drove out here this morning?"

Mr. Urschel nodded again. "It was supposed to be a week-end party, but the Hansons had a death in the family last week and had to be out of the state. So we just came today, for the carnival and fireworks, and we were all going home tomorrow morning."

"What time did you arrive this morning?"

"A little before ten. Maybe five of."

"Did you have any passengers?"

"My wife, of course. And Mr. and Mrs. Keefer."

"Who was here when you arrived?"

"Just the Hansons."

"Not Dick Scott?"

Mr. Urschel hesitated. "I couldn't say. I don't remember seeing him until later."

"Was he a passenger in your car?"

"Certainly not."

"Mrs. Urschel, was Dick Scott a passenger ... Mr. Keefer? ... Mrs. Keefer? I take that as established. I doubt that all four of you would lie, and anyway, I know who the murderer is. Obviously none of you saw the other cars arrive, or there wouldn't have been any mystery about Dick Scott. You'd have seen who brought him. Mr. Baldridge, is one of those cars yours?"

Mr. Baldridge nodded.

"What time did you arrive?"

"Ten, fifteen minutes after ten."

"Did you have any passengers?"

"I did not."

"Mr. Nolte?"

"About ten-thirty, and the only passenger was Mrs. Nolte."

"Then you got here last. My crucial question is for you: *was Dick Scott here when you arrived?*"

Nolte frowned. "I really couldn't say. I stopped by the side of the house to talk with Baldridge, and it was some time before I got around to the patio. By then –"

"But he was!" Mrs. Nolte exclaimed. "He was the first person I saw. He introduced himself, and that was when he complimented me on my dress."

"Thank you," Sheriff Pilkins said. He turned back to Baldridge. "Well, sir, I do believe that you are elected. Would you like to tell us about it?"

Mr. Baldridge was either the guiltiest person west of Detroit or the most astonished person north of New Orleans. His jaw worked, but no words came out.

"See that he stays put," the sheriff said to Steve Carling. "No, no—the hammer lock shouldn't be necessary. Just keep an eye on him. How much money had Scott won from you, Baldridge? More than you could pay, obviously. He wanted his money or a satisfactory equivalent, and of course there was a threat of some kind. You're a stock broker, aren't you? Did he threaten to take your IOU's to your employer?"

Mr. Baldridge still wasn't able to talk.

"The satisfactory equivalent was an introduction to some rich suckers. So you brought Scott here, and he maneuvered your friends into a poker game. I'm sorry I wasn't here to see it. Scott was expecting to win big from these innocents, and they held the limit at a nickel to keep him from losing so much and finally called the game off to watch fireworks. It's a wonder he didn't make you eat all those nickels, Baldridge. While the others were getting settled down there by the lake, he invited you for a little walk. Knowing what was coming, you had the foresight to take the ice pick along. What sort of an ultimatum did he give you?"

Baldridge spoke for the first time. "You're absolutely insane!"

"Are you tired, Baldridge? You've had a busy night. You didn't dare show a light in the woods, so I suppose you brought Scott's wallet back here to look for your IOU's. Did you remember to wipe off your fingerprints when you returned the wallet? We'll soon know.

"Then came the play-acting. You dealt those hands yourself, and went down to the lake to tell the others Scott was dealing and wanted to play, sneaked back here and shouted in a voice something like Scott's, and hurried back to the lake. And the others, sitting there in the dark and watching and listening to fireworks, and maybe doing some *ooing* and *ahing*, never realized that Scott's voice was really yours, or that you were covering a lot of ground behind their backs."

"You're absolutely insane," Baldridge said again.

"Save that one for yourself. Your lawyer may want to plead insanity, and I hope it's true. I hope you weren't in your right mind when you brought that crook out here to fleece your friends."

"I never saw him before," Mr. Baldridge protested. He turned to Grandfather. "Now I see what you mean. Wrongheaded? This guy's plain nuts!"

The sheriff glared. "You had one stroke of luck. Scott made his living being friendly with strangers, and he didn't wait for you to introduce him. It must have been a real pleasant surprise when you found out the others didn't know he came with you, but your mistake with the cards more than cancelled that out."

"What about the cards?" Mr. Hanson asked.

The sheriff smiled. "I'm sure Mr. Rastin saw it as soon as I did."

Grandfather, who was whispering with Mrs. Hanson again, looked up in surprise. "The cards? No, I can't say that I did. I can't even say that I do yet."

The sheriff's smile broadened. "Shame on you, Rastin. Scott let these suckers win every hand. When they got greedy enough, and the stakes got high enough, he would have cleaned up – and made it look like he was a stupid poker player having a run of luck. When they started playing again he wasn't about to discourage them by winning the first hand himself, and he certainly wouldn't have risked making them suspicious by dealing out of turn and giving himself a full house when no one else was at the table.

"As soon as I looked at that hand I knew Scott didn't deal it. Since Baldridge said he *saw* Scott dealing, then Baldridge was lying. A man doesn't lie for no purpose. I didn't have to shake those facts many times before the pieces started falling into place."

"I'll be doggoned!" Mr. Hanson exclaimed. "But now that you mention it –"

"Double doggoned!" Mr. Nolte said. "But – Baldridge? Ted, did you –"

"Take him away," the sheriff said. Steve Carling got up and applied his hammer lock.

Then Grandfather spoke. "*Horsefeathers!*"

Grandfather got up slowly and faced the sheriff. "I have a question or two."

"Make it snappy," Sheriff Pilkins growled.

"I will," Grandfather promised. "Hanson, your guests are staying overnight. Where's Scott's luggage?"

That got him a room full of blank looks. "He didn't have any luggage," Mr. Hanson said.

"Isn't that peculiar," Grandfather drawled. "He came to an overnight party without pajamas, or razor, or even a toothbrush."

"Nuts," Sheriff Pilkins said. "He left his luggage in Baldridge's car, and Baldridge has had plenty of time to dispose of it."

Grandfather smiled. "Don't waste your time looking for it. When you want to know where it is, I'll tell you. About this poker hand. Baldridge, when Scott was dealing that last hand, where was he sitting?"

"In the platform rocker," Mr. Baldridge said.

Grandfather nodded. "The hand with the full house is on the other side of the table, where Scott was sitting before the fireworks."

Baldridge stared at him. "It is? But the sheriff said –"

"That was a typical Pilkins investigation," Grandfather said. "Maybe Scott hoped to change his luck, or maybe he was tired of that hard folding chair and wanted something more comfortable like the rocker. So when he returned to the porch, he changed chairs, and you were the only one who knew that, though the sheriff might have guessed it if he'd taken a careful look at the table."

Sheriff Pilkins wasn't giving an inch. "Nonsense," he growled. "Now that Baldridge knows how he goofed, he'll naturally say Scott was sitting somewhere else."

"Think so? I'd enjoy watching you explain to a jury why Baldridge went to all that trouble to create the impression that Scott dealt those hands – *and then left the deck of cards on the opposite side of the table.* Wait – you can look at it later. I have one more question. Mrs. Keefer, why did you kill him?"

I think everyone held his breath. I know I did. Then Mrs. Keefer's face puckered up, and she bawled as if her heart was broken, which it may have been. She was trying hard to say something, and it was a long time before anyone could understand her.

Then she had to say it twice before Steve Carling would let go of Mr. Baldridge. "I didn't mean to," she sobbed. Over and over.

At first I thought the sheriff was going to arrest Mr. Baldridge anyway, but finally he had to admit that in most courts a confession would take precedence over his detective work. He took Mrs. Keefer away, and Mr. Keefer, after he called his lawyer in Detroit, insisted on going along even though there wasn't anything he could do until morning. Mr. Urschel went with him to lend moral support.

By then it was nearly four o'clock. Mr. Hanson offered beds to Grandfather and me, but Grandfather said he wasn't in the mood for housepartying.

"We aren't, either," Mr. Hanson said with a sigh. "But I guess we're stuck with it. Just tell us how you knew."

"A lot of little things," Grandfather said. "It wasn't a rational crime. If the murderer had thought about it at all, he – she – would have waited until Scott got back to Detroit, where there's an unlimited number of suspects. Baldridge impressed me as being a rational person."

Mr. Baldridge grinned and thanked him.

"Pilkins thought Scott looked like a cardsharp," Grandfather went on. "Could be, but he also looked like one of those rich playboy lady chasers. All of you ladies are charming to me, but a youngster like Scott is likely to have a narrower outlook. To put it frankly, Mrs. Keefer was the only lady present he was likely to chase, and yet Mrs. Hanson tells me he spent the day paying compliments to all of the ladies *except* Mrs. Keefer. That seemed so fishy that I got to wondering if it maybe wasn't an act so you wouldn't suspect that Scott and Mrs. Keefer knew each other.

"Then there was the question of where Scott came from. Your neighbor tells me the third cottage on the west is empty this week. He understood it'd been rented and was surprised nobody moved in. There's a car there now, but he hasn't seen anyone around. Of course it was Scott that rented it, and that's where his luggage is. He came over here as soon as he arrived. And he really hadn't played poker before. I doubt that a cardsharp would pretend to be *that* stupid about the game, or sit calmly watching water skiing and boat racing all day without trying to get a game started, or play all evening without suggesting a hand or two for really big money."

"He suggested raising the limit to a dime," Mr. Hanson said.

"That was only because he'd used up all his nickels and got tired asking for change," Mr. Nolte said.

"I guess it was, at that. What else?"

"If a man had wanted a weapon in a hurry, he'd have taken one of the knives. He wouldn't pull the drawer all the way out and paw through that junk at the back hoping to find something better. The knives were right in front. A woman could have seen the ice pick when she was working in the kitchen. During the fireworks Mrs. Keefer was sitting off by herself in that glider, as if maybe she expected someone to join her or wanted to be where she could slip away without anyone noticing. Just little things, but they all added up. Also, I've been watching you folks for hours. I'm surprised she didn't break down sooner. Didn't you notice how the cup shook when she tried to drink coffee. If she wasn't guilty, I was willing to eat Pilkins's poker hand."

"She's always had a terrible temper," Mrs. Urschel said softly. "And there *have* been rumors – no name mentioned, but rumors. I hoped they weren't true. Mr. Keefer is such a nice old thing, such a dear, but with a young and pretty wife, well –"

"Even so, I don't understand why she killed him," Mrs. Hanson said.

"Hell hath no fury," Grandfather murmured. "You introduced Scott to a game he'd never played before, and it fascinated him. Maybe they hadn't been able to see each other lately, so they went to considerable trouble planning things so he would be at this party and they could sneak in a rendezvous or two, and then when the opportunity came, Scott was saying, 'Let's play poker!' I don't condone what she did, but I can't say that I blame her. If he was tired of her he should have picked a more diplomatic way of letting her know, and he shouldn't have gone for a walk in the woods with her immediately afterward, There aren't many women who wouldn't feel outraged if they found themselves playing second fiddle, to a nickel poker game."

"Poor Keefer," Mr. Hanson said. Then he laughed. "Poor Pilkins."

"Oh, Pilkins," Grandfather said disgustedly. "He's pretty good at shooting off fireworks, but he's always pairing up the wrong knaves. Let's go home, Johnny."

THE AUTOMATION MYSTERY

In Borgville, Michigan, a nice day in March usually doesn't last a day. That one held on for most of the afternoon, and when I came home from school my Grandfather Rastin had his rocking chair out on the porch enjoying the sunshine. I sat down to give him the latest scandal from Borgville High School, about how one of the white mice in the science lab had a mixed brown and white litter, and Mr. Harwick was giving Jerry Ardnow an "F" for not conducting a properly controlled experiment. While we were talking, one of those funny little foreign cars came snuffing up the street and stopped in front of our house.

Except for the fact that he was bald-headed, the man that got out had a build just about right for the car, but his face was a couple of sizes too small for his glasses. He stood there for a moment, counting the houses from the corner to make certain he had the right one, and then he strutted up our walk and took the six front steps in three jumps.

He squinted at the two of us while fishing a piece of paper from his pocket. "You're –" He moved the paper to arm's length and focused the squint on it. "You're William Rastin?" He had a large voice that tapered away to a squeak at the end of a sentence.

"That's my name," Grandfather said.

"You're the one that's behind this idea about running a slate of college professors for county offices?"

"I believe I was the one who first suggested it," Grandfather said. "I stand for intelligence in government."

"And just what will that accomplish?"

"Hard to say. It's never been tried before."

The stranger snorted. "Run anyone you please for office. That's not why I'm here. I've tried to get statements from the present office holders, and they won't talk. The professors referred me to you. What do you have to say about this?"

He passed a newspaper clipping to Grandfather, who glanced at it and handed it back. "Who are you?" he asked.

"Jim Davey. Organizer for the International Brotherhood of Sand and Gravel Workers. This is an outrage, and no one in Borg County seems to care. I want a statement from you in behalf of these eggheads you're running for political office."

"I see. Well. A statement? You may say that my slate of candidates stands firmly for the right of every man to have a job who wants one, and it also stands for the right of any businessman to invest his capital according to his own best judgment."

"You can't have it both ways."

"Why not?"

"Because," Davey boomed, pointing a trembling finger, "automation is the curse of the working man, and the working man is going to do something about it. It's time the politicians woke up to the fact that working men vote and machines don't. Ten jobs eliminated, just like that!" He snapped his fingers. "Those ten men vote, and all of them have relatives who vote, and the relatives have relatives, and by the time I've finished every working man in this county is going to understand that he may be next. I'm telling you, Election Day in Borg County is going to be a day of judgment!"

"Did you ask Elmer Vaughan about this?"

"He laughed at me. Typical businessman attitude. He fires ten workers and replaces them with a machine, and he thinks it's funny."

"You're after the wrong politicians. What could the County Drain Commissioner do about a thing like this even if he wanted to?"

"Ha! If local politicians have guts and put the heat on, they can accomplish plenty. Want to change that statement?"

Grandfather shook his head.

"You won't elect any of your professors. Not one. I'll see to that." He stomped down the steps, hitting each of them with a thump, and drove away.

"What was that about?" I asked.

"I don't rightly know."

"What was in the clipping?"

"Says the oldest continuously operated gravel pit in the State of Michigan has succumbed to automation. Its owner, Elmer Vaughan, has acquired a new loader that will do the work of ten men. Borgville date line. Strange."

"It's a lot better than that," I said. "It's hilarious. This labor guy will have a great time tracking down the ten men the new loader's doing the work of. I never heard of Elmer hiring even one man. Did you?"

"Not in the last thirty years. The strange thing is that Elmer could buy a new machine without it being talked about. Wish I'd thought to ask this fellow what newspaper that clipping is from. Things like that usually are picked up from local papers, but there hasn't been a whisper in the *Gazette*. Find out what Maggie knows about this."

Maggie Cross writes up the Borgville news for the *Borg County Gazette* and also for the *Wiston Journal* when the *Journal* wants any Borgville news, which isn't often. She's an invalid and has to do all her reporting from her bedroom, but no one would say she doesn't do a thorough job. On account of that, and also because she is Elmer Vaughan's niece, she should have known about this new loader if anyone did. She hadn't heard a thing and couldn't imagine where an out-of-town paper got the story. She started asking questions, as though she meant to write one herself, and I told her she'd better get her information from a more authoritative source.

"She doesn't know anything about it," I told Grandfather. "A machine like that would be expensive. Where would old Elmer get the money?"

"He took out a second mortgage a short time back. He'd maybe have enough for a down payment." Grandfather stepped his rocking up a notch. "But it doesn't make sense that it would get into an out-of-town paper when no one around here knows about it."

"Maybe the manufacturer told the paper."

"Maybe," Grandfather said, rocking faster. "The Borgville Service Station couldn't acquire a new tire gauge without me knowing about it. Why hasn't someone mentioned this machine of Elmer's?"

I didn't answer.

"Johnny. Go over to Wiston and look through the *Wiston Journal*. The public library should have it."

"*Now?*"

He nodded. "Check back at least four weeks. While you're at it you might as well stop at Elmer's and have a look at that new loader."

I raised my nose and sniffed deeply. Mom was frying chicken for supper. "Now?" I asked again.

"Now."

I got my jalopy and went.

The Vaughan farm has a big old stone house and a much bigger stone barn. Elmer Vaughan hadn't farmed for years, but Joe Wills, his neighbor, rented the barn along with the best farm land. The house, where Elmer had lived alone since his wife died four years ago, was a mess. No one came to the door and Elmer's car was gone, so I drove down the road to the entrance to the gravel pit.

The gate was locked and there was a big NO TRESPASSING sign nailed to it. The lane didn't look as if much traffic had passed that way, but that wasn't surprising in March. It was a long way to the pit, which was out of sight behind a hill, and Elmer had been known to blaze away with a shotgun at trespassers, no questions asked.

I thought I knew a way to see the loader without walking all that distance to the pit and maybe getting shot, so I drove as far as the first cross road, turned, and came to a very sudden stop. Parked by the road a short distance from the corner was that funny little foreign car of the labor organizer, Jim Davey.

Joe Wills was working there by the road, fixing fence, so I walked over to him. He grinned and pointed at the car. "Think maybe somebody's dog dragged that out here?"

With Mom's chicken waiting for me, I wasn't about to waste time laughing at corny jokes. "Have you heard anything about this new loader of Elmer's?" I asked.

Joe shook his head. "I'm not old enough to remember when Elmer had anything new." He pointed at the car again. "Any idea who owns that thing?"

"A labor organizer," I said.

"That so? What's a labor organizer doing out here?"

As if to answer his question, from the direction of Elmer's gravel pit came a big *B-O-O-M!* I turned in time to see a conglomeration of wheels and rods and assorted unidentified parts fly into the air and go soaring off in all directions. Before either of us could say a word, Jim Davey came scooting along the road, jumped into his car, and drove away.

"Well, now you know what he was doing," I said. "And you saw what was left of Elmer's new loader."

"I'm going to call the sheriff," Joe said. He started for his house at a run. I drove over to Highway 29, stopped at the first filling station, and telephoned Grandfather. "I got there too late to see the loader," I said. "That labor organizer just blew it up."

"Horsefeathers!"

"I saw it with my own eyes."

"I don't believe it. Go on to Wiston and see if your eyes work any better on newspapers."

I went to Wiston and looked through six weeks of the Wiston Journal, which is a shattering experience on an empty stomach. Wiston is the closest thing to a big city that Borg County has, and the Borgville housewives wouldn't wrap garbage in some of the things that get into the *Journal*. I wasn't about to have Grandfather making further remarks about my eyesight, so I looked carefully at every column of every page. Elmer's loader wasn't mentioned. For that matter, neither was Borgville. The people in Wiston like to pretend that Borgville doesn't exist.

By the time I got home, Grandfather had taken his rocking chair back upstairs to his bedroom. He was rocking at full speed with his door closed. I opened it long enough to tell him the *Journal* hadn't mentioned Elmer's loader, and all he did was grunt. Mom warmed up some chicken for me.

Fred Devers, who runs the Borgville Motel over on Highway 29, telephoned while I was eating. Grandfather had called him earlier to ask if Jim Davey was staying there, so he thought Grandfather would like to know that Davey came back and checked out without even using his room, and just as he was about to drive away, one of Sheriff Pilkins's deputies drove up and arrested him.

Tuesday it rained. Grandfather was waiting for me on the porch when I got home from school. He stomped down the steps, bundled up in his raincoat and rain hat and galoshes and carrying an umbrella, and climbed into my jalopy. "Wiston," he growled, and glowered all the way there, with me wondering whether he was mad at the weather or Sheriff Pilkins.

Finally I asked him, and he said, "I can't make head nor tail of this. For one thing, this labor organizer doesn't impress me as the type who blows things up. For another, even if he was he wouldn't go around announcing his presence and purpose ahead of time. Than there's that newspaper story, which doesn't make any sense at all. I've got to talk with Davey."

"If you're going to tell the sheriff Davey isn't the type who blows things up, you'd better trade that rain hat for a crash helmet," I said.

I expected an explosion when we walked in, but the sheriff shook hands with both of us, invited us into his private office, offered a cigar to Grandfather, who doesn't smoke, and asked, "Do you have any idea how I can get that labor punk out of my hair?"

I looked at his hair. It's thinner than it was a few years ago, and the bald spot on top is getting bigger. Incidents like this make me wonder if growing up is all that it's cracked up to be. The older a man gets, the less hair he has and the more things keep getting into it.

"Davey giving you trouble?" Grandfather asked.

"Before he was in this place three minutes he'd started organizing a prisoners' union. He's already got a hunger strike going to protest the food, and this afternoon he hit me with two pages of supplementary demands. Among other things, he wants a TV set in every call."

The sheriff blew a blast into his handkerchief. "As if that weren't enough, now he's trying to organize my deputies." The sheriff sounded as if he couldn't quite believe it.

"TV in every patrol car?" Grandfather asked.

"Johnny," the sheriff said, "did you see this fellow on Elmer Vaughan's property?"

I shook my head, suddenly understanding why he was being so polite to us. I was about to be a witness, and he was sounding me out to see whose side I was on.

"Or climbing the fence?"

I shook my head again. "There's a hill there, and I didn't see him at all until he came over the top on his way back to his car."

"But he was running?"

"Like a scared rabbit."

"That's what Joe said. Davey hasn't acted very scared since then. He's making noises about suing me for false arrest, and I'd feel better with a better case."

"Do you have a case?" Grandfather asked politely.

"I think so. Davey went around trying to get someone to do something about that machine of Elmer's and threatening dire consequences, and then two witnesses saw him running from the direction of the gravel pit just after the explosion took place. It's a case, but I'd be happier about it if someone'd seen him on Elmer's property."

"Is the machine repairable?" Grandfather asked.

"All I saw of it was small pieces scattered over about ten acres. I'd say no, but I'll get an expert opinion as soon as Elmer recovers enough to answer questions."

"Where'd Davey get the dynamite?"

"I figure it was Elmer's. He usually kept some in his work shack, which wasn't locked."

"Doesn't Elmer know if there was dynamite in the shack?"

"Elmer's a mess. All he does is blubber that he's ruined and nobody cares. According to what little sense I can make of what he says, he doesn't know anything about anything, except that he heard the boom and nearly got clobbered by pieces of his beautiful machine."

"It's a queer case," Grandfather said.

"It sure is. Imagine – that labor organizer blowing up a machine to save ten men's jobs when Elmer hasn't had even one employee since about 1935."

"That's a lucky thing for you."

"Why?"

"Because that's why Davey won't sue you for false arrest. I'd like to talk with him."

"You're welcome to try. I'll tell you now that anyone who talks with him mostly ends up listening."

To stop all of that organizing activity, the sheriff had moved Davey to the most remote cell in the jail, but we could hear his big, booming voice and squeak punctuations as soon as we stepped into the place.

"That's right," he was saying. "Television cameras. They spot them along the corridor, maybe even put one in every cell. One man can run a jail ten times this size. He can watch the whole place, and if anything happens he takes care of it by pushing buttons. When they install that kind of setup here, you'll be out of a job. You guys better organize right now."

He was talking with Steve Carling, one of Sheriff Pilkin's deputies "Steve!" the sheriff bellowed.

Steve tiptoed away quietly. The sheriff said, "Ring the bell when you've finished," and followed him.

"Oh, it's you," Davey said. His clothes were wrinkled, his bow tie was crooked, and he needed a shave, but he acted just as cocky as he had on our front porch.

"I hear you've been giving the sheriff a lively time," Grandfather said.

Davey grinned. "Do you know how many people are in prison or jail in the United States? More than two hundred thousand. I got one of the deputies to call the library and ask. This could be the largest completely unorganized group in our population. It's time someone did something about that. Two hundred thousand!"

"I doubt that very many of them spend much time worrying about the threat of automation," Grandfather said.

"Automation is the curse of twentieth century civilization," Davey snapped. "Directly or indirectly, it affects everyone."

"It affects most people for the better," Grandfather said. "Even if it didn't, blowing up machines wouldn't be the way to solve the problem."

"Bah. I never went near the old man's precious machine. The only time I ever set foot on his property was yesterday morning when I called at that pig pen he calls a house, and he laughed me off the place."

"Then why did you run?"

"I figured it might be a trap, and I figured right. Business interests will go to any length to give the labor movement a black eye."

"You weren't on Elmer's property when it happened?"

"Nope. Parked my car and walked along the road trying to find a place where I could see that dratted machine. I didn't, and I was walking back to my car when the thing blew."

"Where'd you get that newspaper clipping?"

"One of our members spotted it and sent it to us."

"What paper did it come from?"

Davey scratched his head. "I don't know. Does it matter?"

"It matters."

"As soon as I get back to headquarters I'll try and find out for you.

"Thanks," Grandfather said.

We walked to the other end of the corridor and rang the bell. Sheriff Pilkins was still bellowing at Steve Carling in his private office, and another deputy let us out.

We stepped out into the rain. Grandfather opened his umbrella and said disgustedly, "We should have stopped at Elmer's on the way here. By the time we get back there it'll be dark."

"I have a flashlight in the glove compartment," I said.

"What good is a flashlight on a night like this?"

We splashed across the parking lot, and Grandfather slammed my jalopy's door so hard I was tempted to get out and put splints on it.

"All right," he said, a moment later. "I'll use your flashlight if I have to. But first, let's stop at Elmer's house."

The wind came up and it started to rain harder, and by the time we got there it was so dark I had trouble finding Elmer's drive. There was a feeble crack of light showing at one of the windows, but Grandfather banged on the door three times without getting any response. He opened it.

Jim Davey had been wrong. No pig with a smidgen of character would have stayed in that house for an instant. There was junk everywhere, dirty dishes, old worn-out furniture, dust, dirt, garbage, and in the middle of it all old Elmer sat at a table by a kerosene lamp with his face in his hands.

Grandfather said, "Elmer!"

Elmer jumped up, grabbing a shot gun, and there was nothing junky about that. It looked shiny and ready for action.

Grandfather said sternly, "Don't point that gun at me!" Elmer lowered the gun.

"That's better. Now tell me about your loading machine."

Elmer sat down again. He buried his face in his hands and started to sob, and between sobs he sputtered, "Get out. Get out. Get out."

Grandfather tried twice more, but all Elmer would do was sob and sputter, so we got out.

We drove down the road to the gravel pit entrance. Grandfather took my flashlight, and we climbed over the gate, using Elmer's NO TRESPASSING sign for a foothold. Grandfather led the way up the lane and along the sloppy ruts that pointed down into the pit, and I kept looking over my shoulder expecting Elmer to come charging out of the night with his shotgun.

"I hope the sheriff looked the place over good," I said. "If there were any clues, they've washed away."

"What would Pilkins do with a clue even if he found it?" Grandfather asked.

Eventually Grandfather located the place where the explosion took place, and we circled out from there, trying to spot pieces of the loading machine. When the sheriff said it was spread over ten acres he wasn't exaggerating. All the flashlight picked out was a gear wheel, a few hunks of metal, and a couple of gadgets I didn't recognize.

"Humpty Dumpty sat on a wall," I said.

Grandfather grunted.

"Humpty Dumpty had a great fall. All the sheriff's horses and all the sheriff's unorganized deputies –"

"We might as well go home," Grandfather said.

"Not enough light? I could go get another flashlight. Or borrow Elmer's lamp."

"No. Let's go home. I can't do anything more tonight."

As I drove up Main Street on my way home from school the next day, I saw Jim Davey's car parked at the curb in front of Jake Palmer's barber shop. I swung in beside it and got out. Grandfather and Davey were sitting there on the bench. Davey's clothes and whiskers needed attention worse than they had the night before, but Davey looked cocky as ever.

"I'll send you some literature," he was saying. "I'd like to straighten you out on this thing."

Grandfather chuckled. "You're welcome to send it, but you'd be wasting both the literature and the postage. I'm to old to be doing any automating, but I'm perfectly willing to accept the benefits from those who do."

"Benefits!" Davey shouted. "Try talking benefits to the guys that get fired!"

Grandfather handed some coins to me and jerked his thumb at the barber shop door. Jake Palmer has put in one of those machines that sells pop in cans, and I went in and bought us a round of drinks.

"Here's a perfect example," Grandfather said, as I passed out the cans. "An automatic vending machine. It increases the sales of pop by making the product instantly available, anywhere, any time. That means more jobs. It helps small merchants by giving them a new source of income that they wouldn't have time for if they had to handle the sales themselves. It creates a whole new industry in the manufacture, sale, servicing and operating of vending machines. Progress always has made more jobs and income then it destroys, and it always will."

Davey snorted. Then he looked at the can of pop I'd handed to him and let out a screech that would have curdled it if it'd been milk instead of root beer.

"Look at that!" he yelled, pointing a trembling finger. "A zip-top can! Self opening cans, self opening bottles – and you say progress means more jobs! What about the poor guys that were making can openers and bottle openers? What are they doing now?"

Grandfather pulled the tab on his own can, inspected his fingers for wounds, tilted the can to take a couple of swallows of ginger ale, inspected his fingers again. "They're manufacturing band-aids," he said, "for the people who open the zip-top bottles and cans."

When Davey stopped laughing he drank his pop, shook hands with Grandfather, promised again to send him that literature, and drove away. "What's he doing here?" I asked.

"I told Pilkins if he'd bring him to Borgville and turn him loose here, I'd convince him that he should forget that false arrest suit."

"Did you?"

"Easily. If word got around that Davey had come all the way to Borgville to organize ten non-existent workers, he'd be a laughing stock."

"What about Elmer's loader?"

"The case is closed."

"You mean – Sheriff Pilkins caught the dynamiter?"

"Not really. He agreed to close the case when I told him who it was. The dynamite part was simple. It was the newspaper clipping that was complicated. It took me almost two days to track that down."

"So where did it come from?"

"It's like this," Grandfather said. "Elmer's lost most of his gravel business. This year, after maybe twenty-five years, he's going to lose the county road business. Trucks waste too much time waiting to be loaded, and the drivers have to pitch in and help. The business doesn't amount to much, but it was all Elmer had. He mortgaged half of his farm land to pay his wife's medical bills, and he's had to mortgage the rest, piece by piece, to meet his mortgage payments."

"Maggie Cross heard about him losing the county business, and she tried to help her uncle out by making up a story about him getting an automatic loader. She sent it to the *Wiston Journal*, hoping that the County Road Commission would see it and maybe reconsider."

"The *Journal* people spotted the oddity about an old gravel pit going automated, so they put it out on the wire service and a few papers around the country picked it up; but because it was from Borgville, the *Journal* didn't use it. Maggie's lie didn't help a bit, which is usually the case with lies, and she didn't want to admit what she'd done because she was afraid she'd be getting into trouble over nothing."

"You mean – there wasn't any loader?" I exclaimed.

Grandfather shook his head.

"But I saw it – saw the pieces!"

"You'd been told Elmer had a new loader, so you saw a loader."

"Look," I said. "*Somebody* blew up *something*. I saw that."

"Well, all that fuss about a loading machine he didn't have put Elmer off his noggin a little. He was ruined, and he thought people were making fun of him. When he saw the union man snooping around a second time, he put all the dynamite he had under his bunk pile and blew it up. Wanted to scare the guy away, he said, and he certainly did that. He was pretty badly worked up about it, but he'll be all right now.

His sons didn't know he was having such a tough time. They'll help him out."

"Junk pile?" I said.

"Right. You see, Elmer new threw anything away, and –"

"Of course," I said disgustedly. "Anyone whose seen the junk in his living room should know he'd have a mountainous pile of junk at his gravel pit. But look here. Elmer probably had enough parts there to *build* a loading machine if he'd known how. The sheriff looked the place over in broad daylight, and he thought it was a loading machine. You made one swing around there in the dark, in a driving rain, with only my little flashlight –"

"Oh, that," Grandfather said, looking modest. "The junk pile was spread awfully thin by the time the sheriff got there, and like you, he'd heard there was a loader. So he found pieces of a loader. I was just trying to find out what had been blown up. And I don't need much light to recognize parts of Elmer's old Model T Ford."

A CASE OF HEREDITY

I was walking home along Borgville Road, having tried all the fishing holes in three miles of the Borgville Creek without catching anything. These strangers had stopped their car along the highway where there's a picnic table under a shade tree. They were standing by the fence looking out across Old Man Wallace's corn field as if ten acres of stunted corn was something worth seeing.

The girl smiled at me when I came up to them. "Hi, sonny," she said.

I am past the age where I enjoy being called sonny, especially by strangers, but when the girl smiled at me I didn't mind. She was very pretty, with dimples in both cheeks and dark hair that was cut short-like around the back. None of the Borgville girls wear their hair that way. She had on a pretty flowered dress and one of those big real-leather pocket books with a strap that goes around the shoulder. She looked like some of the girls that pose for pictures in Mom's mail order catalogs.

"Is the next town Borgville?" she asked.

I told her it was.

"I suppose there are Borgs all over the place," she said.

I told her there used to be a lot of them, but now there were only a couple of families left. The man said something, or maybe he just snorted. He kept his back to us and stood there looking out at the corn field.

"We need an umpire," the girl said. "How'd you like to settle an argument for us? Just because his father was in jail, once, he won't marry me. Don't you think that's silly?"

"He was in jail five times," the man said. "At least five times."

"Phoey," the girl said. "What does that have to do with you?"

The man turned around. He was grinning, but it wasn't a real happy grin. He was a fine-looking fellow, though. He had dark, curly hair, and he was tall and husky, like some of the State Police troopers that come through Borgville now and then.

"Ever hear of the Fisher family?" he asked.

I gulped. "Charlie Fisher?" The words slipped out before I thought what I was saying.

He turned to the girl. "You see? Dad died before he was born, but Borgville never forgets. Probably the mothers are still using Dad's name to make their kids be good." He pointed across the field, and then I saw what he'd been looking at, all that time. "What's that over there?" he asked.

"It burned down before my time," I told him. "I've heard that it's the old Fisher place."

"The ancestral home," he said. "Nothing there but a clutter of stones and a piece of chimney, but I'll bet the kids still think the place is haunted. Don't they?"

A lot of them did, but I didn't say anything.

"Who was Charlie Fisher?" the girl asked.

I was too embarrassed to answer, but the man snapped at me, "Say it!" So I said it. "He was a crook. Everybody knows that."

"There you have it. Like father, like son."

"Jeff!" she said. "That isn't so, and you know it." She turned to me. "Don't you think he ought to marry me?"

"I don't know, Ma'am," I said. "But my Grandfather might."

"Does he live in Borgville?"

"Yes, Ma'am."

"Don't call me Ma'am," she said. "It makes me feel old and decrepit. Let's talk to the boy's grandfather, Jeff. You might as well hear about your father first-hand."

They put me and my fish pole in the back seat of their brand new convertible – I looked, and it only had 172 miles on it – and they drove me to town. It was a hot afternoon, and I was glad to get out of walking that mile and a half, but that wasn't the real reason I suggested that they see my Grandfather Rastin. I thought maybe I could work it into a joke on him.

This always is a dangerous thing to try, but at that particular moment Grandfather had it coming. He'd got onto a *faces* kick – looking at faces on television, and in pictures in newspapers or magazines or wherever he could find them. He'd even had a crack at all the neighbors' family albums. Though he's past eighty, he has wonderful eyesight, and he keeps saying he never forgets a face.

As near as I could figure it out, he was studying all those faces, and classifying them, because he had some kind of notion about reading character from a person's face. Everyone I asked about it said the idea was a hundred years out of date. I'd got tired hearing Grandfather talk about faces, and I thought maybe handing him these strangers, with the problem of whether the girl should marry the son of a crook, might shut him up for awhile.

Grandfather was in his usual place on the bench in front of Jake Palmer's Barber Shop, and Nat Barlow was sitting there with him. We parked right in front of them, and I led the two strangers over to Grandfather and said, "These people want to know if they should get married."

Grandfather looked the girl over first, studying her face until she blushed a little. Then he turned to the man.

"It isn't quite as simple as it sounds," the man said. "You see, my name is Fisher."

Grandfather kept looking at him and studying *his* face. "There's no law that I know of against Fishers getting married," he said.

"I was one of the Borgville Fishers," the man said. "They were all crooks, you know. I've been checking up on them."

Grandfather remarked that he'd heard of people looking up their ancestors and bragging about how they landed on Plymouth Rock, or fought at Vicksburg, but he'd never heard of anyone trying to shake down the crooks from his family tree. Nat Barlow had been looking the fellow over, too, and suddenly he cut loose with a whoop and yelled, "You're Charlie Fisher's boy!"

"That's right," the man admitted. "Jeff Fisher is the name."

"I'll be derned!" Nat said.

Jake Palmer stuck his head out the door of his barber shop and looked around. "Did I hear you say that rat Charlie Fisher's come back?"

"Naw," Nat said. "This here's his boy. Jeff Fisher."

"Oh," Jake said sourly. "You're gonna give him a parade, I suppose. I say if there's a Fisher anywhere in the county, call the sheriff." He ducked out of sight and banged the door.

Jeff Fisher looked at the girl. "You see how it is," he said.

"Jake's still sore about the five hundred your old man did him out of," Nat said.

"It doesn't make any difference," the girl said to Grandfather. "Tell him it doesn't make any difference. I wouldn't be marrying his family. Besides, they're all dead, now."

The girl sat down on one end of the bench, and Jeff Fisher sat down on the other end, and they told us all about it. Fisher was an orphan, he said, and he never knew who his parents were. He never cared much, either, until he met this girl and decided to get married, and then he thought he should be fair to her and check up, to make certain there wasn't any insanity, or leakage of the heart, or such things, in his family. He went back to the orphanage and found out that his dad was Charlie Fisher, formerly of Borgville and lastly of the state prison, where he died when Jeff Fisher was a kid.

He had some people investigate, and he found out a few other things, too. Such as how Charlie Fisher's dad, Joe Fisher, was not exactly an upstanding citizen, even though he was once elected township supervisor in what later turned out to be a vote fraud. And he found out that Charlie's granddad was a convicted horse thief.

All of this had him worried. After all, if his great-granddad, and his granddad, and his dad were all crooks, he wondered if being a crook might run in the family, and sooner or later something would bust loose in him and he'd end up behind bars himself. If that was going to happen, he certainly didn't want to marry the girl.

We had quite a crowd around us by this time. Mrs. Pobloch stopped on her way back from shopping, and old Mr. Gregory had happened by, and Bill Wallace, who runs the Borgville Service Station, and Doc Beyers's wife, and Mr. Hanson, the bank president, and some others I don't remember.

Grandfather said, "Seems to me I've heard of a lot of fellows turning out decent in spite of what their dads or granddads might have done."

Jeff Fisher shook his head. "I've put myself through college, and I know a little about psychology. No one is a crook by heredity, but certain tendencies can be inherited, and if there are three generations of crooks in my family, those tendencies must be pretty strong. I have a good job, with the Harling Machine Tool Company, in Detroit. I keep their books for them, and look after their money, and how do I know when I'll get the urge to walk off with some of it?"

"If you've been all right up to now," Grandfather said, "I don't think you've got much to worry about." He turned to the girl. "If I was you, I'd marry him."

"I'm convinced," she said. "He's the one that needs selling."

"Aw, marry the girl," Mrs. Pobloch said. "She'll make you a fine wife."

The crowd was getting bigger, and it wouldn't have taken one of those public opinion experts to see that it was pretty much in favor of instant wedding bells.

"You ought to get married right here in Borgville," Mrs. Beyers said. "It would kind of be like wiping the slate clean. We'll give you a nice wedding and a good sendoff."

Mr. Hanson was all for calling in Reverend Adams and getting things moving. There was some talk about the license and what could be done about the waiting period, and I was so interested in what was going on that I didn't notice when Grandfather slipped away. Suddenly I saw Mr. Gregory, who runs the Star Restaurant, sitting in Grandfather's place, and I looked across the street and saw Grandfather coming out of Snubbs's Hardware Store.

He walked off down the street, and I ran and caught up with him. He went up to Doc Beyers's office and borrowed the doctor's Detroit telephone book, and then he walked on down to the Borgville Service Station and got a map of Michigan. The discussion had built into quite an argument by the time we got back, with the girl and everyone else pushing the idea of getting on with the honeymoon plans, and this Jeff Fisher just scowling and shaking his head.

Grandfather elbowed his way through the crowd, and Mr. Gregory saw him coming and got up and let him have his seat back. Grandfather sat down with the telephone book and the map of Michigan on his lap and asked, "How do you know that this crook Charlie Fisher is the Charlie Fisher that's your dad?"

Jeff Fisher stared at him without noticing that his mouth was wide open. "You mean there's more than one Charlie Fisher from Borgville?"

"Three, that I know of," Grandfather told him. "Fisher isn't an uncommon name, you know. Look here."

Together they went through the Detroit telephone book counting Charles Fishers and Charles Fischers, and there was a pile of them.

"There," Grandfather said. "How do you know you aren't related to one of these?"

"They told me at the orphanage it was Charles Fisher from Borgville," Jeff Fisher said.

"There are lots of towns in Michigan with a 'ville' in them," Grandfather said. "Look here."

He unfolded his map, and nothing would do but they had to go through the whole list of towns in Michigan, and all those with a 'ville' they had to compare with Borgville to see if Jeff Fisher had misunderstood, or if maybe the people at the orphanage had been mixed up. It took some time, and when they'd finished, Grandfather folded up the map and asked, "How do you know they didn't get it wrong?"

Jeff Fisher didn't know, and I could see that Grandfather had made his point.

"And even if it is Borgville," Grandfather said, "it might not be that Charlie Fisher. It's a common name around here, and as I said, I can remember three. This Charlie Fisher – the crook, I mean – wasn't a bad boy.

He went off to the city and got to be pretty successful. He was selling stocks, and pretty soon people around here were after him every time he came visiting to tell them where to invest their money. He finally gave in and sold them some gold mine stock. Turned out there wasn't any gold mine, so he went to jail. I can't see what his granddad or his dad could have had to do with that, but I can tell you one thing for sure. You don't look a bit like that Charlie Fisher. There was another Charlie Fisher worked on a farm north of town. I believe you do favor him a little."

The girl clapped her hands, and Jeff Fisher was looking a lot less like the son of a crook and a little more like a possible bridegroom. He asked, "Can you tell me anything about him?"

"Not a thing," Grandfather said. "Don't know where he came from, or where he went."

"Maybe I was making a fuss about nothing," Jeff Fisher said, grinning for the first time. "One crook wouldn't have bothered me, but when I found three – and Lord knows how many there might have been before that – I began to get worried. Val's folks are pretty particular, too. They'd raise the devil if they thought she was going to marry a convict's son. And I wouldn't want to make her unhappy."

"I wouldn't give it another thought," Grandfather said. "That crook Charlie Fisher had hair that was as straight as a string. He wouldn't have had a curly-haired kid like you. Go ahead and marry the girl. It's the right thing to do."

"Thanks," Jeff Fisher said. "You know, I think I'll do that. If she's still willing, that is."

The girl let out a real gooey, "Oh, Jeff!" and he kissed her right there on Main Street with half the town standing around and applauding. There was another motion to send for Reverend Adams, but Jeff Fisher said there wasn't that much rush about it. The important thing was that they'd made up their minds about it – what he really meant was that he'd made up his mind – thanks to the kind people of Borgville, and he'd be grateful all his life. But he was sure Val's folks would want her to have a real dressed-up wedding in her church at home. Mrs. Beyers said of course, that was the only way to get married, and everyone lined up to shake hands with Jeff Fisher and the girl, and then the two of them walked on down the street hand in hand to have a look at Borgville.

"Aren't they a handsome couple!" Mrs. Pobloch exclaimed.

I happened to look at Nat Barlow, and he seemed to disagree. He was glaring at Grandfather, his face was red, and he was breathing in little short gasps and seemed about to explode.

"Bill Rastin," he said, "you're a dirty liar!"

Grandfather, who had his eyes on Jeff Fisher and the girl, said quietly, "A liar, but I'm as clean as you are."

"There never was but one Fisher family around here," Nat said. "And I never knew anyone to be sorry about that. And as for Charlie Fisher having straight hair –"

"I know," Grandfather said. "Charlie was short and fat, and he always looked like a born crook to me. You can be sure he didn't get any of my money. It was different with Charlie's dad, Joe Fisher. Joe was really a good-looking man. And –" He shrugged his shoulders. "This young fellow is a dead-ringer for his granddad."

"You oughtta be ashamed of yourself," Nat said. "Telling that girl to marry him, and then going through all that monkey business to talk him into marrying her."

Mrs. Beyers leaned over and patted Grandfather on the shoulder. "It was a fine, noble thing to do. And they certainly make a good-looking couple. I'm so happy for them."

Grandfather didn't say anything. Jeff Fisher and the girl had stopped to look at something in the window of the Town Shop. Grandfather jumped up and waved in their direction as Sheriff Pilkins zoomed past with a load of his deputies. The deputies were out of the car before the sheriff got it stopped, and by the time Jeff Fisher saw what was happening, there wasn't anything he could do but turn around with his hands up.

The sheriff searched Fisher and went through the girl's pocket book, and then he packed the two of them off to the county jail with the deputies. He walked back up the sidewalk toward us and no one said a word to him. Everyone was too stunned to ask what was going on.

He shook Grandfather's hand. "Nice going, Bill. I'll let you know about the reward."

"Hang the reward," Grandfather said.

Mrs. Pobloch had backed herself up against the barber shop window, and she started to mop her face with her handkerchief. Mrs. Beyers had turned an unhealthy-looking white. She said, "Ed Pilkins, would you mind telling me why you arrested that fine young man and his girl?"

"Quite a few reasons," Sheriff Pilkins said. "They both have records that would fill a book. Here's a pretty good reason right here. Twenty-five pay roll checks of the Harling Machine Tool Company, all made out to Jeffrey C. Fisher, all of them for $127.83."

"Why, that's the place he works," Mrs. Beyers said. "What's wrong with him having those checks?"

"Worked," Sheriff Pilkins said. "Worked, not works. And he wasn't exactly a long-standing employee. Matter of fact, he only worked there one night, night before last, and he worked just long enough to steal a bunch of checks and a check-writing machine. He and the girl are a couple of real professionals. That was a darned clever thing to do – come back here where his family lived and put on that act of theirs. He'd of cashed one of these checks at every business place in town, no questions asked, and been gone before Borgville knew what hit it."

"Then he was a crook!" Mrs. Beyers exclaimed. She turned on Grandfather. "You told the girl to marry him. And you convinced him he should marry her. You ought to be ashamed of yourself!"

"They've been traveling all over the country together," Grandfather said. "I figured it would be best if he married her – even if he is a crook."

"They're both crooks," Sheriff Pilkins said. "And if it'll make you feel any better, they've been married seven, eight years, though they get married again whenever it helps whatever line they happen to be passing out."

He shook Grandfather's hand again and walked away. Mrs. Beyers and Mrs. Pobloch disappeared in a hurry, and all up and down Main Street I could see people getting together to talk about what had happened to the last of the Fisher family.

Grandfather and Nat Barlow sat there on the bench for a long time without saying anything. Finally Nat nudged Grandfather. "You called the sheriff?"

Grandfather nodded. "I used Snubbs's phone. Pilkins told me to keep them occupied until he could get here, so I got the phone book and the map and gave them a spiel."

"You wouldn't dare call the sheriff just because of that heredity business," Nat said. "How'd you know they was crooks?"

"It's a new art he's discovered," I explained to Nat. "He reads a person's character by studying his face. I'd have to admit that this was quite a demonstration."

"Demonstration, nothing," Grandfather said. "A year ago they stole some money orders from a little post office in Wisconsin. Their pictures have been up in the Borgville post office for the last six months. If you two looked at the post office bulletin board regular each week, like I do, you'd know what's going on in the world."

THE UNMURDERED PROFESSOR

When Mr. Obermeyer, who is principal of Borgville High School, yanked me out of my history class to talk on the telephone with Sheriff Pilkins, I knew right away it had something to do with the way I drive my jalopy. I thought about it all the way to the office, but as near as I could remember I hadn't run a stop sign for at least three weeks, and reckless driving and speeding were out of the question. There are one or two laws that my jalopy might be seduced into violating, but the worst intentions in the world wouldn't make a speeder out of it. As for reckless driving, my Grandfather Rastin has said more than once that merely backing that car out of the garage constitutes reckless driving, but I don't think he meant it the way the law does.

Mrs. Fletcher, who is Mr. Obermeyer's secretary, was standing by the counter holding the telephone. She handed it to me, and she and Mr. Obermeyer cocked their ears and waited.

"Where's your Grandfather?" Sheriff Pilkins shouted.

I relaxed. "Oh," I said. "Is that all?"

"Isn't that enough?" the sheriff asked.

"He's at Professor Alford's house, in Wiston," I said.

"That's what you think. Where was he going from there?"

"He wasn't going anywhere from there. I took him there this morning, before school, and I'm supposed to pick him up right after school."

"Ha!" the sheriff said. And hung up.

I held onto the telephone for a few seconds, making up my mind, and then I hung up. "Emergency," I said to Mr. Obermeyer and got out of there before he could start asking questions. I looked back as I went down the walk to the parking lot and saw him watching me out of the window. Probably he was trying to make up his mind whether my action constituted what he liked to call A SERIOUS BREACH OF DISCIPLINE, or whether it was just bad manners. The next day I found out what he decided, but that's another story.

I drove directly to Professor Alford's house, which is a big old place near the Wiston College campus. Mrs. Alford was talking on the telephone, but she didn't have any trouble handling a conversation with me at the same time. She told me she'd just got home, but she thought Professor Alford had taken Grandfather over to the college.

"Everything is in a turmoil around here," she said. "Professor Pritchard was murdered this morning."

"Gosh!" I said. "That's probably why Sheriff Pilkins –"

"He's in a coma, and I don't think he's expected to live."

"*Sheriff Pilkins*? But I just talked with him –"

"Professor Pritchard. He has a fractured skull."

I thanked her over my shoulder as I was going out the door, which probably was another serious breach of discipline. But I just don't know how to go about making conversation with a woman who says someone's been murdered and isn't expected to live.

I found Grandfather standing on the steps of the Wiston College Science Building. Under his arm he had a shiny leather briefcase that I knew wasn't his, and he was holding it as though it were something he'd shoplifted and would like to return.

"What are you doing here?" he demanded.

"Sheriff Pilkins called me at school," I said. "He wanted to know where you were. I think he's going to arrest you."

"Horsefeathers! Pilkins is an idiot."

"Sure. I thought I'd better tip you off and find out whether you'll need a lawyer."

Grandfather told me one or two things I hadn't heard before about what he thought of Sheriff Pilkins, but he was interrupted by a student who galloped up and handed him a stack of papers. Grandfather stuffed the papers into his briefcase. The student dashed up the steps to the science building, and Grandfather followed him. Another student was standing nearby, taking it all in, and I asked him what was going on.

"Beats me," he said. "They're making some kind of survey."

"What are they surveying?"

He laughed and said a couple of thousand people were trying to figure that one out. He hurried off after a coed who didn't seem to know him nearly as well as he knew her, and I went into the Science Building.

Grandfather was waiting by the open door of a classroom. The teacher was studying a piece of paper with a puzzled look on his face, and the student who'd handed Grandfather the stack of papers was standing by looking as if he'd just presented a summons. Finally the teacher laughed and said to the class, "Ladies and gentlemen, President Channing insists that I administer a Loyalty Test. Take paper, please. Write your name and residence, this class – which in case you've forgotten is Physics 103 – and my name, which has been Mr. Stevenson all semester. Below that you will write the words of the Wiston College Alma Mater. All three verses."

Someone in the back of the room started to sing the Alma Mater, and the whole class took it up. Mr. Stevenson rapped for order. "No talking," he said. "The instructions say I am to administer this test as severely as I would a final examination. I would very much regret having to flunk one of you for cheating on the words of Alma Mater."

"We took this loyalty test last hour," a girl said.

"Then you will take it again this hour," Mr. Stevenson said. "The instructions say everyone, including the instructor." He sat down and started to write.

Grandfather moved on, and I followed him. "If it's the words to the Alma Mater you want, you didn't need to bother all these people," I told him. "I've sung or heard them myself at least a thousand times, and I think I could even give them to you backward, if that'll help any."

Grandfather stopped and looked at me. "That's an idea," he said. He fished a blank piece of paper from the briefcase. "Here – put your name at the top and write down the words. All three verses."

"Backward?" I asked.

He walked away without saying anything, and I put the paper up against the wall and wrote, but not backward:

Hail to Wiston College! Hail!
Alma Mater fair and strong,
Old in wisdom, young in courage,
You we praise in deed and song.
Watch! As down your hallowed pathways,
'Neath the unfurled banners bright,
Wiston's valiant sons come marching,
Soon to put their foes to flight.
Hail to Wiston College! Hail!
Honored may you live, and long.
Old in wisdom, young in courage,
You we praise in deed and song.

The bell rang as I was finishing. Students came charging out of the classrooms and nearly knocked me off my feet. I fought my way upstream and finally got clear to chase after Grandfather. He'd met Professor Alford, the head of Wiston College's Psychology Department, in front of the building. Students were coming from all directions to hand papers to Grandfather, and he was stuffing them into his briefcase.

"Have we got everyone?" he asked.

"No," Professor Alford said, giving his goatee a couple of tugs. "But we got everyone who's had a class during the last three hours, and just about all the specials. We'll do a repeat tomorrow morning, and that should get almost everyone."

"Tomorrow will be too late," Grandfather said. A janitor was moving slowly along the walk, carrying a ladder. Grandfather pointed. "What about him?"

Professor Alford nodded at one of the students. "Custodians," he said. The student went loping off.

"And what about him?" I asked, pointing to another man who was hurrying toward us. It was Sheriff Pilkins.

The sheriff made a tactical error that was unusual even for him. He started bellowing at Grandfather when he was too far away for us to make out what he was saying. And then when he came within range he was too winded to do anything but pant loudly.

Finally he managed a question. "Where is it?"

Grandfather nodded at Professor Alford, and Professor Alford took a folded slip of paper from his inside pocket and handed it to the sheriff.

The sheriff glanced at it, glanced a second time, looked at Professor Alford, turned to look at Grandfather. "Is this all?"

"What'd you expect?" Grandfather demanded. "A signed confession?"

The sheriff didn't say anything.

"Don't you recognize it?" Grandfather asked.

"Can't say that I do."

"This is no place to talk," Professor Alford said. "Let's go over to my office."

We headed for the psychology department, with Sheriff Pilkins trailing along with more determination than enthusiasm, and when we got there Professor Alford turned Grandfather's briefcase over to some students and took Grandfather and the sheriff and me into his office. He found chairs for all of us, and then he sat down at his desk and tilted back with a big grin on his face.

"One of the neighbor women found that paper behind a chair cushion after they took Pritchard away," he said. "She was cleaning the place up, and there was plenty of cleaning to do. He bled quite a lot, as you may have noticed. Anyway, my wife was there helping out, and she sent it over to me to find out whether it had anything to do with the assault on Pritchard."

"I don't suppose it occurred to her that I might be interested," the sheriff grumbled. "I didn't even hear about it until this afternoon, which is a good four hours wasted."

"She knew you'd be interested," Professor Alford said, still grinning, "but she wasn't sure you'd know what to do with it."

"Thanks!"

"What *would* you have done with it? Or, now that you have it, what are you going to do with it?"

The sheriff took out the paper and unfolded it. "Well, there's the handwriting –"

"Obviously disguised."

"And then, there's fingerprints –"

"A couple of dozen people, have handled it, including you."

The sheriff gave it the hot potato treatment and then picked it up again, carefully, by one corner. He scratched his head while giving the paper a long, careful look. That time I managed a look for myself. Someone who was obviously was in a hurry and couldn't write very well had scribbled, *Dishonored will you die and fast.*

"You still don't recognize it?" Professor Alford asked.

Sheriff Pilkins shook his head.

"Do you know the Wiston College Alma Mater?"

The sheriff snorted. "Who doesn't?"

"Exactly. Who doesn't? I didn't see the connection myself, but Rastin did. Third stanza, second line. 'Honored may you live, and long.' It poses a couple of intriguing questions."

"What sort of questions?" the sheriff asked, scratching his head again.

"For one thing, Pritchard wrote the Alma Mater. Did his attacker know that, or was he just making a play on words?"

"I thought that fellow Mueller wrote the Alma Mater."

"Professor Mueller wrote the music. Pritchard wrote the words. And then – the change from *long* to *fast* is understandable, and of course *honored* to *dishonored* and *live* to *die*, but we were intrigued by the change from *may* to *will*."

"Seems to me he was saying just what he meant," the sheriff said.

"Perhaps. But it wasn't a *necessary* change, and since there obviously is an intention to paraphrase that line of the Alma Mater it does seem strange. Rastin thought there was a possibility that the person who wrote this wasn't overly familiar with the Alma Mater – hadn't learned it correctly – or he would have written, 'Dishonored *may* you die and fast.' So we've spent the afternoon following up that idea."

"Following it up how?" the sheriff asked.

"We've been trying to find out how many people around Wiston and environs don't know the Alma Mater."

"There isn't anyone," the sheriff said. "No one in this part of the state could help learning that thing. Do you have any idea how many times a year –"

Professor Alford was still grinning. "A fairly good idea. Every athletic event, every college program, every ceremony has the Alma Mater sung once and sometimes twice. Every radio station in these parts plays it several hundred times a year. Every frat house and sorority house has a recording, and so do half the students who aren't frat or sorority members. Not only that, but it's a catchy tune and a wonderful barbershop quartet number. I've heard the thing as many as a dozen times in one evening over at *The Broken Pretzel*. The students like to sing it, and so do the town people. There shouldn't be anyone in these parts who doesn't know the words perfectly, but the fact remains that *someone* wrote *will you* instead of *may you*. As I said, it's intriguing. We aren't claiming any more than that for it."

"I see," the sheriff said, looking at the piece of paper again. "If you find someone who thinks the words are *will you* instead of *may you*, then that might be the person I'm looking for."

"It might. We really don't expect anything that dramatic, though. At least, I don't. Rastin never says much about what he expects, but then – you know Rastin."

"You're darned right I know him," Sheriff Pilkins said. "Well – thanks for the help. I wouldn't have thought of it myself. You'll let me know right away if you come up with anything?"

"Right away," Professor Alford promised.

The sheriff shook hands with him, scowled at Grandfather, and left. Grandfather didn't even bother to scowl back at him, and you may have noticed that during the entire conversation he hadn't said a word. To me this was a lot more intriguing than all that *may you – will you* business.

Professor Alford got his pipe lit, and tilted his chair again, and aimed a cloud of smoke at the ceiling. "Poor Pritchard. He's an opinionated crank, but basically harmless. Who could have done such a vicious thing to him?"

"You're the psychologist," Grandfather said.

"Find me the person who did it, and I'll analyze his psychology for you."

"Incidentally, Pilkins might come storming back here to call you a liar. Are you a liar?"

Professor Alford's feet came down with a bang. "I don't recall any recent indulgence in mendacity. Why?"

"Then you didn't know that *Mrs.* Pritchard wrote the words to the Alma Mater?"

Professor Alford dropped his pipe. It spilled hot ashes all over his dust blotter, and he didn't even notice. "*Madge* Pritchard wrote those words? Where'd you get an idea like that?"

"Professor Mueller told me. Mrs. Pritchard wrote the poem, and he set it to music, and the copyist wrote down only the last names of the composer and poet. When the thing got to be a hit, everyone assumed that Pritchard was the author, him being a professor of English and all. He's been taking bows for it ever since."

The blotter started to smoke in a dozen places, and Professor Alford noticed the ashes. He mashed them out and then leaned back trying to puff on an empty pipe. "As the philosopher said, learn one new thing each day and you'll stay young. I haven't felt so youthful in years. I do recall hearing something about Madge Pritchard dabbling in poetry. Not that it really matters – or does it?"

"Pilkins would think it does. By his idiotic reasoning, it provides a motive."

"Madge meditated on the injustice for twenty years and then she used a poker on her husband? Not even Pilkins would swallow that!"

"Look at the note," Grandfather said. " 'Dishonored will you die.' Pritchard would be dishonored if the truth got around, wouldn't he?"

"He certainly would," Professor Alford admitted. "At least, he'd *feel* dishonored, which amounts to the same thing."

"So the note is maybe a significant clue. Given a clue, and a strong motive that fits it, all Pilkins has to prove is opportunity. Who had the best opportunity?"

"I suppose Madge did," Professor Alford said, still puffing on the empty pipe.

"Right. Pritchard was working in his study. Mrs. Pritchard was in the garden digging up her glad bulbs. She claims she had her back to the house, but I had a look at the place where she was digging. Either she was facing the house, or she was reaching around a rosebush, which is not only inconvenient, but hazardous. The attacker was interrupted when your wife rang the doorbell. He forced open a French window that hadn't been used for years and jumped out not forty feet from where Mrs. Pritchard was digging up bulbs, and she didn't see or hear anything – she says. I'm wondering how long it will take Pilkins to decide that she dug up a few bulbs to give herself an alibi, went into the house to whack her husband, was interrupted by the doorbell, and left through the French window herself."

"I can't believe it."

"Why was your wife calling on the Pritchards this morning?"

"Madge invited her over."

"Pilkins will make it fit," Grandfather said. "He'll say Mrs. Pritchard set the stage very nicely. Your wife would ring the bell, walk in anyway when no one answered, and find the body. Only the timing was messed up, and your wife got there before Pritchard was entirely dead. It's as good a case as Pilkins has ever had."

"Nuts to Pilkins. Do *you* think Madge Pritchard would try to kill her husband because twenty years ago he took the credit for a poem she wrote?" Grandfather snorted. "How long have they been married?"

"Thirty years, at least."

"In thirty years any husband gives his wife at least a thousand reasons for murdering him, if she wants to take them that way. Let's go have another look at the place."

My jalopy was in the general parking lot on the other side of the campus, and I didn't catch up with Grandfather and Professor Alford until they were almost at the Pritchard house. Then when I saw the traffic jam in front of the house I was afraid I might have to go back to the campus to find a parking place. Professor Alford drove right into the driveway, so I followed him, and sat in the car for a moment to see if anyone would object.

From the front, the house looked like something swiped from a southern plantation, and from the side and back it looked as if the guy that stole the front should have gone back for the rest of it. We cut across the lawn and pushed through a crowd of people on the big front porch. The only men there were a deputy sheriff and a slick little fellow with a mustache.

Professor Alford nudged me when he saw him. "That's Professor Labey," he whispered. "If Pritchard dies, he'll be head of the English Department."

"Does that make him a suspect?" I whispered back.

Professor Alford laughed. "You and your Grandfather!"

Mrs. Alford met us at the front door. Her face was white, but she hadn't been frightened by anything. She was just doggone mad.

"The sheriff wants to arrest Madge!" she said.

"It must be that new deputy – the college fellow," Grandfather said. "Pilkins couldn't possibly be this efficient on his own hook."

"What are we going to do?" Mrs. Alford asked. "Madge was just getting over the shock of what happened this morning, and now she's broken down completely."

"Have her doctor tell Pilkins to go soak his head," Grandfather said.

"I already did, but the sheriff has one of his deputies sitting on a chair right outside her door. He wanted him in the room – said she might try to commit suicide. The idea!"

"Is there any word about Pritchard?" Grandfather asked.

"Just that he's still unconscious."

"Where's Pilkins now?"

"I don't know, but I'll tell you one thing. He's keeping out of *my* way."

We went into the living room, where Professor Pritchard's niece, Marcia, a Wiston College student, was glumly sitting on the sofa with her fiancé. Mrs. Alford introduced us, and the two of them nodded and went right on looking glum. Professor Alford was called to the telephone, and he came back talking to himself, which was not unusual for him.

"They've finished checking over the whole batch," he said.

"The whole batch of what?" Grandfather asked.

"That test you and I spent the entire afternoon running. They didn't find a single mistake in the crucial line – which is all they were looking at."

"Oh. I'd forgotten all about it."

"So had I, after your very convincing analysis. Would you mind telling me why we went to all that trouble, when you already had this thing figured out?"

"I don't know," Grandfather said. "I guess my mind can be perverse in several directions at the same time."

"It certainly can."

"Say, you two," Grandfather said, speaking to Marcia Pritchard and her fiancé. "Do you know the words to the Wiston College Alma Mater?"

They stared at Grandfather. John Wikel was a moderately homely young man, but I should add that Marcia Pritchard was not about to win any beauty contests, though she seemed like a nice girl. They turned to look at each other, and then they laughed and started to sing.

"All right," Grandfather said. "Skip it."

"Are you asking a *music major* at Wiston if he knows the Alma Mater?" John Wikel asked. "Do you have any idea how often –"

"I'm getting a better idea all the time. I saidskip it."

"You aren't being consistent," Professor Alford said. "There's no reason why they shouldn't take the test."

"Then you give it to them," Grandfather said. "I'm going to look around."

I followed him out of the front door, and we circled the house, walking slowly. "If Professor Pritchard regains consciousness, maybe he'll be able to tell who it was," I said.

"Maybe," Grandfather said, "but they're not counting on it. They think he was clobbered from behind."

"Is Mrs. Pritchard strong enough to beat a man up that way?"

"I'd say she is. Mrs. Alford keeps referring to her as 'little,' and she isn't very tall, but she's well-developed in other directions."

We walked over to look at the rosebush, and I saw right away what Grandfather meant. It was a small bush, but if Mrs. Pritchard had her back to the house she was either reaching around it or sitting on it. I tried it both ways, at Grandfather's request, and I can offer testimony to the effect that a young rosebush can be just as prickly as an old one.

Mrs. Alford saw us and came out to investigate. "Is it possible that Madge did it?" she asked.

"Of course it's possible," Grandfather said, "but that isn't saying she did it. Whatever happened, she certainly didn't use her head. All she had to do was tell Pilkins she saw a stranger disappearing around the corner of the house, and Pilkins would have run in circles for a month trying to catch him."

"What's this about giving Marcia and John a test?"

"To find out if they know the words to the Wiston College Alma Mater."

"Of course they know the words! They're Wiston students, aren't they? John is a brilliant music student. He plays first trumpet in the band and orchestra, and the orchestra is going to play a composition of his on its Christmas concert."

They went on talking, but I lost interest because just at that moment I saw Sheriff Pilkins playing Indian. There were several big lilac bushes scattered about, and separating the Pritchard yard from the next one was a thick hedge. Sheriff Pilkins went sneaking from lilac bush to lilac bush, and when he got close to the hedge he pounced.

"Got you!" he shouted.

"What in the world!" Mrs. Alford exclaimed. "Why, that's Professor Klotz!"

"Right," Sheriff Pilkins said. "We've been looking for him all day. He's the third corner in as neat a triangle as you've ever seen. His wife died a couple of years ago, and his living next door to the Pritchards gave him plenty of opportunity to get mighty friendly with Mrs. Pritchard. Right, Klotz?"

This Professor Klotz looked more like an automobile mechanic than a professor, and if Sheriff Pilkins had some idea of frightening him into a confession, he'd picked the wrong man. Professor Klotz shook off the sheriff's hand, brushed his sleeve a couple of times, and faced the sheriff squarely. "Dummkopf!" he said. He sounded more like a judge handing down a verdict than a criminal calling the arresting officer names.

"Either Mrs. Pritchard did it herself, or she's covering up for someone," the sheriff said. "Neighbor on the other side of Klotz saw him coming through the hedge this morning, just about the time that Mrs. Alford was ringing the Pritchards' doorbell." He turned to Klotz. "Well?"

Klotz folded his arms and regarded him haughtily. Having already rendered his verdict, he had nothing further to say.

"Do you know the words to the Wiston College Alma Mater?" Grandfather asked him.

"Of course," he said. "Who doesn't?"

"You might test him on it," Grandfather told the sheriff.

"I will," Sheriff Pilkins promised. "On that and a lot of other things."

The sheriff marched him away, and Mrs. Alford said, "Now if that isn't the most ridiculous thing – both of them over fifty, and he thinks he's found a triangle!"

"People never get too old to make fools of themselves," Grandfather said.

We went back to the house. Grandfather stayed in the kitchen to talk with Mrs. Alford, and I went to the living room to see how Professor Alford was making out with his tests. He handed the papers to me.

"Flying colors," he said.

Both of them had written, "Honored may you live," but if they were pleased at having passed the test they didn't show it. They were holding hands and looking as glum as they had before.

I took the papers to Grandfather and told him they tested loyal. He nodded and stuffed them into a pocket without looking at them. I went back down the hall to investigate the scene of the crime, which was Professor Pritchard's study.

The Professor's desk placed him with his back to the door, and the rack by the fireplace was real handy in place a potential poker murderer forgot to bring his own weapon. The poker was missing, but there were a couple of other gadgets that would have served the purpose just as well. The French window looked out into the back yard, and from the study door I could see the rosebush.

I turned away just in time to see Mrs. Pritchard coming down the stairs. The deputy was right on her heels, but she wasn't paying any attention to him. She was wearing a wrinkled housecoat, and her hair was a mess, and she didn't look like the kind of person who'd be holding down one end of a triangle. She looked like a stout little old woman with problems.

At the bottom of the stairs she looked toward the living room, and then toward the kitchen, and then she said to me, "Where are they taking Howard?"

"Howard?" I said.

"Professor Klotz."

"Sheriff Pilkins just arrested him."

"The fools! All of them are fools! Roger is a fool, too."

She went into the living room and sat down and buried her face in her hands.

I went back to the kitchen. "Who is Roger?" I asked.

"That's Professor Pritchard," Mrs. Alford said. "Why?"

"Mrs. Pritchard just said he's a fool."

"Did she? Oh – the poor dear!" She hurried away.

Grandfather went outside again to commune with the rosebush. Mrs. Alford got Mrs. Pritchard back upstairs, and then she came down and gave me a glass of milk and two small cookies, and since it was getting close to supper time I sat around feeling hungry and wondering how long it would be before Grandfather decided to give up and go home.

Grandfather returned to the kitchen just as Sheriff Pilkins came prowling through the place, back from third degreeing Professor Klotz. The sheriff exchanged glares with Mrs. Alford and went out through the dining room door. "Pritchard's regained consciousness," he said, over his shoulder. "He has a nasty fracture of the skull, but he'll recover."

"Can he talk?" Grandfather asked.

"He will talk. They won't let anyone see him yet. I have a man waiting at the hospital."

"Did you ask Klotz about the Alma Mater?"

"He wrote it for me twice," the sheriff said disgustedly. "In English and in German. The English is all right, and I'm taking his word for the German. He says he makes all his students learn it in German. Fit *that* into your dratted theory!"

He banged the door after him, which wasn't absolutely necessary, and Grandfather took the two loyalty test papers from his pocket, glanced at them, and pocketed them again. I asked him if he still thought Mrs. Pritchard was the attacker.

"Seeing as how Pritchard is going to be all right," he said, "I'd like to forget the whole business. Arresting somebody for this just might create more problems than it solves."

"You won't have an easy time selling that idea to the sheriff," I said.

"No, but I might be able to sell it to Pritchard. Let's find Professor Alford."

He was on the front porch talking with Professor Labey. "Just for the record," he was saying, "where were you at eleven-fifteen this morning?"

"Walking home from class," Professor Labey said. "Why do you ask?"

"I'm collecting alibis."

"Is that so?" Professor Labey said, with a nasty grin. "And just where were you at eleven-fifteen?"

"Lecturing to about fifty students," Professor Alford said.

"At least *you're* safe. I hear Klotz bolted his ten o'clock German class this morning. Interesting, don't you think?"

"I heard he went home early with a headache."

"Did you?" Professor Labey said, still with the nasty grin. "I heard Pritchard had the headache."

Grandfather tugged at Professor Alford's arm. "Come on," he said. We walked down the steps and around to the drive. "Where are we going?" Professor Alford asked.

"To the Wiston Hospital. Know anyone there?"

"I know everyone there. Why?"

"I've got to talk with Pritchard before Pilkins gets to him."

"We can try, I suppose. Is it important?"

"I've never done anything more important," Grandfather said. "Let's go."

It wasn't easy. First there was a nurse with a long nose and thick glasses who thought she was playing *Horatius at the Bridge*. Then there was a doctor who argued the case for fifteen minutes before he let slip the fact that Professor Pritchard wasn't his patient.

While we waited for someone to smoke out the professor's doctor, Grandfather slipped off by himself. He came back to report that a deputy sheriff named Steve Carling was roosting on a chair outside the professor's room. "If you haven't got a good, solid 'in' with someone higher up," he told Professor Alford, "we might as well go home."

Eventually Professor Alford got ahold of the right doctor by telephone, and was referred to still another nurse. She went to have a peek at Professor Pritchard and came back to tell us nothing doing. The professor was asleep.

We sat down to wait. The hospital's kitchen was just up the corridor, and every cart of food they were sending to the patients rolled right past my nose on its way to the elevator. I spent the next hour trying to figure out a way to get myself admitted to the hospital in time to get some supper.

Professor Pritchard's doctor turned up about six-thirty. Grandfather left the argument to Professor Alford, interrupting only when the professor said five minutes with the patient would be enough.

"Two minutes," Grandfather said. "And all Pritchard will have to do is lie there and listen."

"It's against my better judgment," the doctor said. "Besides, I promised Sheriff Pilkins he'd be the first to talk with the patient."

"How can you tell which is your better judgment?" Professor Alford asked, making like a psychologist.

The doctor grinned. "I'll only let one of you in."

"As far as I know," Grandfather said, "there's only one of me."

That took care of everything except Deputy Steve Carling. When he found out that Grandfather was going to see Professor Pritchard, and he wasn't, he threw a noisy fit right there in the hospital corridor. I was surprised that the doctor didn't throw him out, because some of his remarks were not exactly sanitary.

Finally he ran out of threats and had to telephone Sheriff Pilkins for a new supply, and the doctor took Grandfather into Professor Pritchard's room. I timed him, and I think the doctor did, too, because they came out right on the two minute mark.

"All right," Grandfather said. "We can go home."

"What happened," Professor Alford asked the doctor. "I know *he* won't tell me."

The doctor shrugged. "I was just there to make certain he didn't excite the patient. Anyway, they whispered."

We took the elevator to the lobby, and we met Sheriff Pilkins at the front door. His face was as red as I've ever seen it, and he barged right past us without even favoring us with a glance. The elevator was waiting, but he didn't seem to notice it. He tore across the lobby and took the stairs, four of them at the first jump, and disappeared.

"The exercise will do him good," Grandfather said. "He's putting on weight, and not in his head, where he needs it. They'll have to let him see Pritchard, so let's wait for him."

We sat down in the lobby, and about five minutes later the sheriff was back again, still using the stairs. He stopped when he saw us and glared at Grandfather. "Bah!" he said. And left.

"Just what does that mean?" Professor Alford asked.

"It means," Grandfather said, "that the case is closed. Pritchard told him that he wouldn't sign a complaint, and if the sheriff arrests anyone, no matter who it is, he'll testify in court that it's the wrong person. Now let's *really* go home."

Late that night Professor Alford drove over to Borgville to see us. Grandfather had gone to bed, but he came down in his nightshirt, and told the professor to make himself at home, and brought him a bottle of cold beer.

"I know you don't usually make social calls after ten o'clock," he said, "What's on your mind?"

"I had a talk with Madge Pritchard," Professor Alford said. "She told me who did it. I thought you'd like to know."

"I already know."

Professor Alford sputtered all over the place and delayed the conversation while he dry-cleaned beer from his goatee. "Who do you think it was?" he asked finally.

"I *know* it was John Wikel."

The professor sputtered again, though he hadn't taken any more beer. "How the devil did you figure it out?"

"Easy," Grandfather said. "I used the Loyalty Test."

"But Wikel passed the test! He got every word right!"

"Naturally. He wasn't in school this afternoon, but word about what we were doing got around fast. He guessed he'd slipped up somewhere, and by the time you gave him the test he'd had a chance to get the words right."

Professor Alford held his glass under his nose for a good minute without taking a drink. "That may make sense to you," he said finally, "but it doesn't to me. Go on."

"Don't you know what Wikel is studying?"

"Certainly. He's a music student."

"Right. Kind of a star music student. Plays a horn in the college band and orchestra. Do you need any more explanation?"

"I certainly do!"

"Think about it. Whenever the Alma Mater is sung at a college function, what's Wikel doing?"

Professor Alford didn't say anything.

"He's blowing on his horn, that's what he's doing. He's *played* the Alma Mater hundreds of times, but he's probably never *sung* the Alma Mater in his life. No wonder he got the words screwed up!"

"You devil you!" Professor Alford took a fast gulp of beer, and then he had to dry clean his goatee again. "Pritchard disapproved of his niece's romance," he said. "He would. I doubt if he even understood young love when he was young. He was going to make her break her engagement, and he also was going to ship her off to a girl's college in the East. Wikel went to make a last appeal, and Pritchard ordered him out of the house. Young love being what it is, the poor kid lost his head. He really is a fine young man with a promising future, and he's feeling a lot worse about this than Pritchard does. Imprisoning him could easily ruin his life, and the niece's, too. Maybe even Pritchard's, because Madge would never forgive him. Just by a twist of luck the doorbell rang with Pritchard only half killed. What'd you say to him?"

"I asked him if he wanted his niece married to a jail-bird and his wife arrested for obstructing justice. He didn't. I told him he had a choice between ruining several people's lives, including his own, and doing something generous, for once in his life, and he agreed. Maybe the poker knocked some sense into him. Now if you don't mind, I'm going to bed. Let him finish his beer before you throw him out, Johnny."

Grandfather went back upstairs. Professor Alford tried to drink his beer, but he had to stop to chuckle between swallows, and then he got to laughing so hard he couldn't swallow.

"Your Grandfather," he said, "is a remarkable person."

"Sure," I said. "He usually doesn't strike people as being that funny, though."

"But he is. I never thought I'd live to see the day, but he is. John Wikel used the poker, *but he didn't write that note*. He wouldn't have had time to write it. Madge Pritchard wrote it. She was in the back yard, talking with Klotz, when Wikel left by the French window. They got to Pritchard before my wife walked in. They understood immediately what had happened, and they decided to salvage what they could from the situation.

Klotz hurried off to get ahold of John Wikel and tell him to calm down and act innocent and everything would be all right, and Madge tried to point the sheriff in the wrong direction, only she was so rattled she botched the job. Her writing those words, under those circumstances, would make a wonderful psychological study, though unfortunately it couldn't be published. Your Grandfather –"

He drained his glass. "Poor Madge. She was in a turmoil all day because she didn't know what Pritchard would tell the sheriff, and she was afraid if she insisted on seeing him first – alone – the sheriff would be suspicious. She's ready to hang a metal on your Grandfather, and I'm going to enjoy this as long as I live. The trouble is I'll never be able to share it with anyone. I'll give you five dollars, Johnny, if you'll promise not to tell him."

"You don't have to bribe me," I said. "I couldn't take your money."

"All right, Johnny. Word of honor, anyway. This is the best day I've had in years."

I showed him to the door, and then I tore up the stairs to see Grandfather. I hadn't promised the professor a thing, and I wasn't going to miss a chance to have a good laugh at Grandfather myself – only I wanted him to know about it.

I turned on the light, which made him bellow at me, and I said, "About those words John Wikel messed up –"

"I know," he said. "Madge Pritchard wrote them."

"You were listening!"

"Wasn't."

"Then how did you know?"

"I doubted that the assailant had time to be writing poetry. And then-Madge Pritchard was the only person of any consequence who didn't take the test. I wondered if maybe she'd got so sick of her poem she didn't remember the words. I called Professor Mueller. In her original version she wrote *will you*, and he thought it struck a false note. He changed it to *may you*. They had quite an argument about it at the time."

"Then why did you make up that fairy tale for Professor Alford?" I asked.

"I owed it to him," Grandfather said. "I wasted a whole afternoon for him and his students, and maybe made him look ridiculous to the college administration, and he's entitled to some compensation. Psychologists are always happiest when they catch someone being brilliant and absolutely wrong, so I gave him something to be happy about. Anything else?"

"You haven't explained anything," I said. "If you knew John Wikel didn't write those words, how did you figure out he was the one that bashed Professor Pritchard?"

"Professor Pritchard told me," he said. "Now turn off the light and go to bed."

THE LESSER THING

Mr. Obermeyer, who is principal of the Borgville High School, is a nut on quotations, and one day last winter he wrote on the board, "We find great things are made of little things, And little things go lessening till at last Comes God behind them."

I remember that one because I copied it down on the chance that I'd be able to figure it out later. I still don't understand it, but if I did I think it might explain the connection between an old almanac, and a bet on a horse, and Borgville's first murder in twenty years. Grandfather Rastin says there isn't any connection, and Sheriff Pilkins says there is, but there wouldn't be if Grandfather didn't talk so much.

The almanac belonged to Mr. Snubbs, who runs the Snubbs Hardware Store, and Mr. Snubbs was trying to throw it away when Grandfather got it. Every afternoon except Sunday Grandfather walks over to Main Street to see if Mr. Snubbs is finished with the morning paper, and Mr. Snubbs always is, or if he isn't he says he is. When Grandfather went after the paper one day last spring, Mr. Snubbs had a big pile of junk ready to be carted away, and a 1948 Almanac was on top, so Grandfather took it home to read.

I always thought an almanac was a place to look up something, like who won the 1929 World Series, or what time the sun is going to rise on Easter Sunday. I thought Grandfather knew that, too, or I'd have told him, but before I found out what was going on he'd read the thing through from front to back and was scaring us half to death with some of the statistics he quoted at the breakfast table.

I don't know anything about the bet on a horse except what I've hear but I've heard plenty. Back about 1915, Joe Hammer, who then was only a kid, challenged the owner of the first automobile in Borgville to a race, the automobile against Joe's horse. Nat Barlow, who was a neighbor of Joe's, bet fifty cents on the horse.

People tell a lot of queer stories about that race, and they only agree on one thing: the automobile won by a radiator cap. Joe Hammer always claimed he lost because the horse threw a shoe crossing the Borgville

Creek bridge. Nat Barlow's version was that the horse had more sense than the rider and threw Joe Hammer crossing the Borgville Creek bridge.

That's how Borgville's famous Nat Barlow – Joe Hammer feud got started. Nat is now a frail old man in his seventies, and so gentle he wouldn't swat if a horsefly bit him, and all down through the years he's never seen Joe Hammer once without bringing up that race and his fifty cents.

And Joe Hammer, who is almost as old as Nat, threatened so many times to break Nat Barlow's neck that finally even Nat decided he was bluffing. There always are a few people around who take that kind of thing seriously, but most folks agree with Grandfather. Ever since 1915 he's been saying that it's nobody's business but Nat's and Joe's, and if those two youngsters want to fight it out, why – let 'em fight.

That's how things stood in May. Grandfather had been reading and rereading that almanac for a couple of months, and Nat Barlow and Joe Hammer had been feuding over that fifty-cent bet for more than fifty years, and if anyone in or near Borgville had murder on his mind, he was keeping it to himself.

It was Saturday, and a warm, sunny day – just the kind of day Grandfather likes. He left the house early, and when I got up town about twelve thirty he was sitting on the bench in front of Jake Palmer's barbershop, along with Nat Barlow and a couple of other old timers. There was quite a crowd standing around – Walt Pobloch, who lives above the barber shop, and Jeff Morgan, who works at Dimmit's Grocery Store and was on his way to the bank with a deposit, and Steve Carling, who is a deputy sheriff, and Joe Hammer's hired man Ed Seagrave, who had come to town to get a new head gasket for Joe's tractor and didn't seem in any hurry to get back, and a few others.

Grandfather hadn't gone after Snubbs's paper yet – he thinks it isn't ethical to take a man's morning paper away from him before one o'clock – so he was sitting there listening to the others jabber. In the middle of some talk about the fishing on Mud Lake, Grandfather grunted a couple of times, cleared his throat, and announced in a loud, clear voice, "This is 1973, and Borgville is going to have a murder this year."

That stopped the conversation. Steve Carling opened and closed his mouth three times and finally managed to say, "What makes you think so?"

"Logic," Grandfather said. "In 1946, there were 109 persons

murdered in Detroit. Estimating Detroit's population at that time as one and three-quarter millions, that figures out to about one murder for every sixteen thousand people. There are about eight hundred people in Borgville, which gives us one murder every twenty years. And –" Grandfather pointed a finger. "do you know when the last murder happened here?"

None of them did. "1953," Grandfather said, and leaned back on the bench and crossed his legs.

"Nuts!" Steve Carling said. As a deputy sheriff he naturally considered himself an authority on murder, even if he'd never solved one. "Crime in a big city isn't the same thing as crime in a rural area. And what does 1946 have to do with it?"

I could have told Steve about the almanac and the fact that crime statistics in a 1948 almanac are only complete through 1946. I could have told him, but I didn't, and it was a cinch that Grandfather wasn't going to.

Grandfather pointed his finger again. "When," he demanded, "did the last Borgville murder take place before 1953?" Steve didn't know. "1933," Grandfather said. "Exactly twenty years. Mary Randall killed her husband with his shotgun. He came home drunk, and beat her and the kids, and she shot him. The jury acquitted her."

"Coincidence," Steve said. "Anyway, Borgville's population wasn't 800 back in 1933."

"Was," Grandfather said.

"Anyway, crime statistics change from year to year. There are a lot more murders than that in Detroit now, and you can't predict a Borgville murder this year because of what happened in Detroit in 1946."

"If there are more murders now," Grandfather said, "that only means that Borgville is overdue. This is Borgville's year. 1973." He nodded his head.

Even I could see that Grandfather's deduction would not take any prizes as an exercise in logic. The fact was that he'd got bored with the conversation and decided to pull the legs of those present, especially those of Steve Carling, and the dangerous thing about leg pulling is that sometimes it gets taken seriously. These remarks didn't get a laugh from anyone. Steve muttered something about Grandfather being afflicted with hardening of the cranium and walked away. Everyone else sat or stood quietly waiting for someone to think of a way to change the subject.

"Nice day," Nat Barlow said finally.

As a subject-changer that didn't seem worth much, but everyone jumped at it. The weather got thoroughly analyzed, After a few minutes of that, Grandfather snorted and craned his neck to see the clock in the window of the Borgville Pharmacy. "Johnny," he said, "go see if Snubbs is finished with his paper."

I went over to the hardware store and got the paper for Grandfather. The crowd had broken up by the time I got back, but if you think that ended the matter you don't know Grandfather. He commands a lot of respect, even if he is the only registered Democrat in Borgville, and people listen to what he says. They listen even when he's pulling legs.

Less than an hour later I was over at the Borgville Pharmacy trying to talk Mollie Adams into putting an extra scoop of ice cream into my chocolate malted, and I heard Doc Beyers say to Mr. Ferguson, "Who do you think it will be?"

"That's easy," Mr. Ferguson said. "Nat Barlow. Who else?"

They were talking about who was going to be murdered.

Borgville had only one feud going, and just about everyone had heard Joe Hammer threaten Nat Barlow with everything from neck-wringing to head-bashing. Those who didn't take it seriously were willing to go along with a gag, and for a week or so the standing joke around Borgville was to ask if Nat was still with us. Nat didn't like it, and it made Joe Hammer so mad that a couple of times it looked as if he might pass up Nat and murder someone else. But nothing happened, and Grandfather's prediction might have been forgotten if some of the men hadn't enjoyed joshing him about it.

"When's the murder coming off?" they'd ask.

And Grandfather, who enjoys a laugh as much as anyone, would say, "Lots of time between now and December 31st." And then he'd tell them something about the number of murders in Baltimore and Fort Worth – in 1946, of course.

School let out the twelfth of June. I got a summer job in the Borgville Pharmacy and lost it five days later when I was horsing around with Mollie Adams after closing and tipped over a display and broke seventeen bottles of hair oil. Grandfather marched right over to Mr. Ferguson's house, when he heard about it, and told him he had no business making all that fuss over a few bottles of hair oil, and Mr. Ferguson told Grandfather that a bald-headed man had no right to any kind of opinion about hair oil.

I didn't get the job back, and the only result was that Mr. Ferguson ordered Grandfather out of his house, and Grandfather swore he'd never set foot in the Borgville Pharmacy again, and I guess we'll have to go all the way to Wiston the next time we need a prescription filled. None of that has anything to do with the murder except to explain how I happened to be loose up town the day it happened.

The afternoon was more than just sunny – it was hot. Grandfather was reading Snubbs's paper on the bench in front of the barber shop, and Nat Barlow was sitting there beside him, not saying anything because the quickest way to get Grandfather riled up is to try to talk to him when he's reading.

Steve Carling came coasting up in his car and angle-parked at the curb. He got out and stood there for a minute looking up and down Main Street, and then he walked over and said, "Afternoon, Nat."

"Afternoon," Nat said.

"Anything doing up town this morning?" Steve asked.

"Nothing much," Nat said.

"Was you here all morning?"

"Right here," Nat said, patting the bench.

"What time did you go home for lunch?"

"When I always go," Nat said. "Noon."

"Anybody see you sitting here after eleven o'clock?"

"Anybody that went by."

"Who went by?"

Nat shrugged. "Can't say. Wasn't paying much attention."

Grandfather lowered his paper. "What idiotic stunt are you trying to pull now?"

Steve said to Nat, "Where were you at twelve o'clock?"

"Here," Nat said. "And I started home right at twelve."

"All right. We'll check on it. Meantime, you're under arrest. Come along."

Nat didn't even protest. His face got all puckered up, and he was almost too shocked to breathe. Steve took his arm and steered him toward his car, but before they'd taken two steps Grandfather let out a bellow and got in their way. "What idiotic stunt –"

"Interfering with an officer of the law," Steve said, "calls for a jail sentence."

"Horsefeathers!" Grandfather roared. "You'll tell me what the devil you're up to, or I'll turn you over my knee and paddle you!"

Steve quieted down. Most people do, when Grandfather looks at them like that. "You ought to be happy," he said. "You got your murder. Joe

Hammer was stabbed in the back with a pitch fork. Nat did it. We got a witness."

"Horsefeathers!" Grandfather said.

But Steve got Nat into the front seat of his car and started around to the driver's side. Grandfather opened the back door and hopped in, and I hopped in right after him. Steve didn't make us welcome, but he got in without saying anything and drove off.

Joe Hammer's farm is on Hog Back Road, which intersects Borgville Road a couple of miles south of town. Hog Back Road is an insult to any respectable hog, it being all ups and downs and so crooked in places a car runs the risk of a head-on collision with itself. Steve took those curves at a good forty miles an hour, and Grandfather, who hates to ride in the back seat anyway, planted his feet wide apart and hung onto the door handle and the window crank and told Steve between curves just what he thought of his driving.

There already was a crowd of people at the Hammer place. Steve got Nat out of the car, and Sheriff Pilkins saw them and pointed to an empty corn crib. Steve nodded and led Nat away. Doc Beyers was talking to the sheriff, and a couple of deputies were making motions at keeping the crowd back. Grandfather barged past them and went storming up to Sheriff Pilkins.

"Your nose isn't needed!" the sheriff shouted. He called to one of the deputies, "Mort, get him out of here. Didn't I tell you –"

"I'm a deputy," Grandfather said. "I've got as much right here as you have."

Sheriff Pilkins and Grandfather never have been very friendly, but back in 1937, when the Borgville bank was robbed, the sheriff made Grandfather a deputy for a couple of days, and Grandfather still calls himself a deputy whenever it suits him or seems likely to irritate the sheriff. Sheriff Pilkins doesn't like that, but he learned long ago that arguing with Grandfather is a waste of time. So he told Mort to get back to the crowd, and he let Grandfather stay. I couldn't very well claim that I was a deputy, so I ducked behind a manure spreader where he couldn't see me.

Grandfather and the sheriff went over to the corn crib, and I went around to the side and looked through the slats. Ed Seagrave, the Hammers' hired man, was sitting on a milk can. Steve Carling was standing off to one side with Nat Barlow. The sheriff went in and stood looking down at Ed.

Ed isn't much more than twenty-five, a big, husky fellow and not bad looking. That day he looked older than Grandfather. His face was burned dark, from working in the fields, but there in the corn crib it had a sickly gray color. His hands were gripped together in his lap, and he didn't even look up at the sheriff.

"All right," Sheriff Pilkins said. "Talk."

"He was like a father to me," Ed said.

"Sure. You've worked here – how many years?"

"Five – six."

"Sure. Joe was like a father to you, but that won't catch me a murderer. Tell me what you know."

"I don't know nothing. I went in the barn, and there he was. The pitchfork was sticking straight up, like somebody'd stuck it in the ground, only it was –" He started to whimper.

Sheriff Pilkins reached out and slapped his face. "Snap out of it," he said. "I can't waste time on you."

"You've already wasted time," Grandfather said.

Sheriff Pilkins glared at him and turned back to Ed. "Give it to me. Everything that happened up to when you found Joe."

"I was cultivating corn," Ed said. "The south field. Joe came out about eleven to see how I was getting along. Wanted to know if I'd be through by noon, and I said I doubted it, but I might make it by twelve-thirty. So he said to go ahead and finish and we'd have a late lunch. So I did. I finished, and then I went back to the house. And Mrs. Hammer said Joe was in the barn, and would I call him to lunch, so I went out to the barn, and-and –"

"What time was that?"

"After twelve-thirty, but not much."

"Okay, Then you ran over to the Schmidts', and you found out they already knew about it and had called me, and you came back with them, right?

"I didn't know how to tell Mrs. Hammer, and I thought Mrs. Schmidt –"

"All right. I don't blame you. Why'd you run? It's all of half a mile. Why didn't you take the car?"

"I just didn't think."

"Anything else?"

Ed shook his head.

"Stick around," the sheriff said. "I might want you again."

Ed stumbled out the door and went over and sat down under a shade tree and buried his face in his hands. The sheriff turned to Steve Carling and told him to get Dave Schmidt in there.

Dave was about sixteen and a smart kid, but when Steve brought him in he did nothing but blubber for two minutes. I never saw anybody so scared. But the sheriff finally quieted him down and got his story. Seems that Dave admired the old sedan Joe had for a second car. He thought it would make a swell hot rod, but Joe wouldn't part with it. Then Mrs. Hammer had called him up about noon that day and told him Joe was griping about the cost of insuring two cars and if he came over right away Joe might be in a mood to let him have the sedan cheap. Dave got his dad's car and came right over. The barn door was open, and he looked in and saw Joe. That one look was enough. He jumped back in the car and took off for home. Only when he got there he was so excited and upset that it took his folks considerable time to get the story out of him. When they did, they called the sheriff, and then Ed Seagrave arrived and they all came back together.

"You didn't go in the barn at all?" the sheriff asked. Dave shook his head.

"Suppose he hadn't been dead?" the sheriff asked. "Suppose he was only hurt? Maybe you could have helped him."

"With *that* in his back?" Dave said indignantly.

The sheriff waved him away. As soon as Dave had gone, he turned to Nat Barlow. "Well, Nat. What about this little disagreement between you and Joe?"

Nat swallowed, making a regular production out of it. "It didn't amount to much."

"Ever since I was a kid I've been hearing about what Joe was going to do to you. You didn't maybe decide you'd do it to him first, did you?"

"No," Nat whispered.

"Maybe it was self-defense," the sheriff suggested. "He got you in the barn, and you knew what he was up to, so when you got a chance you used the pitchfork."

"No!"

The sheriff reared back and shouted, "Then what were you doing running away from the barn?"

"Wasn't," Nat said.

"Mrs. Hammer saw you."

"She didn't!" Nat squeaked. "I haven't been on this farm since 1915!"

Steve Carling spoke up. "He says he was sitting in front of the barber shop until twelve."

"All right. If he was there, somebody saw him. If he wasn't – take him in, and we'll start checking."

He turned, and there was Stella Hammer in the doorway. I'd always thought she was a nice-looking woman, though maybe a little on the skinny side, and her clothes always were classy, but that day she had on an old dress and her hair was a wild mess. She looked taller and skinner than I'd ever seen her. She kind of clawed at the air and made a gurgling noise. Then she screamed.

"He did it!" Her hands made clawing motions at Nat. "Stabbed Joe in the back and ran! I saw him running away!" She screamed again and pitched forward. Sheriff Pilkins caught her. By then the women that were supposed to be looking after her had missed her, and they came running and took charge of her.

Sheriff Pilkins got out a big red handkerchief and mopped his forehead. "Get Nat out of here," he said, and Steve took him away.

"Pilkins," Grandfather said, "you're an idiot."

The sheriff lit a cigarette and puffed it a couple of times, fast. "You and I don't admire each other much," he said, "but tell me this. Have you ever known me to be unfair to anybody?"

"Not intentionally," Grandfather growled.

"All right. Stella Hammer says it was Nat. No, strike that. *Now* she says it was Nat. At first she said she thought it looked like it might be Nat. She says she was looking out when Dave drove up. As he was getting out of the car she saw somebody run from the other side of the barn. She says he was wearing blue overalls and a straw hat, like Nat always wears; but it's a hell of a long way from the house to the barn, and it's only about twenty yards from the barn to the brush along the road, and he was running with his back toward her. Dave never saw him, because the barn was in the way, and he was hid by the time Dave drove off. Stella says maybe it was Nat, and there's been all this trouble between Nat and Joe, so I have to look into it. Of course I'll be looking into a lot of other angles, just in case. That's how matters stand right now, and you can't say I'm not being fair about it."

Grandfather grunted.

"As long as you're here," the sheriff went on, "you might as well make yourself useful. You know everything about everybody around here. Who's been having trouble with Joe lately?"

"Schmidt has," Grandfather said. "Something about a boundary line."

The sheriff got out his handkerchief again. "Now that's real interesting. We know it couldn't have been Dave Schmidt. Stella backs him up that he never went in the barn. She thought he asked Joe through the door about the car, and Joe said no, and he beat it. But the kid was powerfully upset. Do you suppose he did see someone running, and it was his old man?"

"I wouldn't know," Grandfather said.

"Anyone else?"

"Not worth mentioning."

"Any recent scandal about Joe and Stella?"

"It's a little late for scandal now," Grandfather said. "They just celebrated their twenty-fifth wedding anniversary last month. People talked when they got married, because Joe was past forty and she wasn't twenty yet, but I never heard but that they got along all right."

"What about Ed Seagrave?"

"He's not overly bright," Grandfather said, "as maybe you've noticed. Joe always said he's a darned good worker. Joe liked him, and I guess Ed liked Joe."

"Most everybody liked Joe," the sheriff said, "except Nat Barlow." He went over to the door. "Hey, Schmidt!" he yelled.

Mr. Schmidt came over. He was a big blond man, with a big face and a big smile, and he didn't look anything like Dave. He talks kind of funny. He said, "Ya?"

"Want to talk to you," the sheriff said.

Grandfather came out, looked around, and saw me. "Come on," he said.

As we walked away, the sheriff was saying to Schmidt, "I want to know everything you did today between eleven and twelve."

"Pilkins is an idiot," Grandfather said.

We bummed a ride back to town, and Grandfather went right up to his room and closed the door, and a moment later I heard him rocking. The madder he is about something, the faster he rocks, and this time it sounded like a freight train overhead.

The next morning Grandfather was up early, and after breakfast he walked over to Main Street. He was home before noon, looking as glum as I've ever seen him.

"They can't find any witnesses for Nat," he said. "With him sitting on a bench right there on Main Street, you'd think *someone* would have noticed him, but he's always sitting there, and people have stopped looking at him. They say, 'Sure, I saw him,' and then when they think about it they can't remember whether he was there or not. It's like asking about a lamp post. Everyone knows it's there, but no one remembers *seeing* it."

"That's too bad," I said.

"Everyone else has an alibi. Schmidt was with his wife, eating lunch. Harvey Lennox was working in the next field, and he says Ed was driving the tractor right up to half-past twelve. Even Stella Hammer has an alibi. From eleven o'clock on she spent most of her time on the telephone. Pilkins has checked, and he doesn't figure she could have got out to the barn and back between calls. Not that he was suspecting her – women don't usually do their murders with pitchforks. It doesn't look good for Nat."

It didn't look good for Grandfather, either. I'd never seen him looking so miserable. "I've got to get Nat out of this," he said.

"All we have to do is find one person that saw him sitting there," I said.

After lunch we combed Borgville from one end to the other. I took the north half of town, and Grandfather took the south half, and when we met in front of Jake Palmer's barber shop at three-thirty neither of us was very happy.

Borgville on a Monday morning is not exactly dead, but it isn't kicking very much, either. Practically nobody had been up town that morning. Mr. Snubbs had seen Nat at nine, when he went out to clean his front window. Chuck Foster, who delivers bread to Dimmit's Grocery Story, had seen him there when he went by at ten-thirty. Mr. Hanson, our bank president, went into the barber shop for a haircut just before noon, but he said he was in a hurry and he didn't notice whether Nat was there or not. He often doesn't notice things. Grandfather said the fact that Nat was the first person in line when the run on the Borgville Bank started, back in 1933, probably had something to do with Mr. Hanson not seeing him, but I don't think he was serious.

"Your mother's calling farmers to find out who was in town yesterday morning," Grandfather said. "Let's go home and see if she's found out anything."

We went home, and she hadn't, and Grandfather went up to his rocking chair.

Sheriff Pilkins dropped in at noon the next day. He knew Grandfather was working on an alibi for Nat, and he wanted to know if he'd found out anything. He took one look at Grandfather's face and didn't bother to ask.

"It looks like it was Nat," he said. "Taking a shortcut, he could have got to the Hammer place in thirty minutes, easy, just strolling along. I tried it myself this morning."

"Didn't anyone see him going home for lunch?" Grandfather asked.

"Nope. His daughter was over at Wiston, and when she's gone he fixes his own lunch. So it looks like it was Nat, but like I said, I aim to be fair about it. I'll keep checking."

"Come up to my room," Grandfather said. "I want to talk to you."

The sheriff grumbled, but he went, and when they came back downstairs ten minutes later he almost seemed grateful. "This idea isn't half bad," he said. "I'm glad you thought of it. It might help, or it might make things worse, but I'll give it a try."

"When?" Grandfather asked.

"Right after lunch. I suppose you want to be there."

"I intend to be."

"One-thirty," the sheriff said. "Stella's staying with the Schmidts. I'll stop there and get her."

We got to the Schmidts at five minutes and thirty-seven seconds after one, and we'd have made it half an hour earlier if Mom hadn't put her foot down and told Grandfather his digestion was his own business, but I was still a growing boy and shouldn't be rushing my lunch. It was one of the few times Grandfather ever complained about my not driving fast enough.

Schmidt saw us drive up, and he came trotting down from the barn to see what we wanted. Mrs. Schmidt and Mrs. Hammer were sitting on the Schmidt's big front porch, Mrs. Hammer sewing something, and Mrs. Schmidt resting a mite, she said, after the noon dishes. Grandfather grabbed a lawn chair and announced that he was waiting for the sheriff. Schmidt was too polite to ask questions, so he sat down to wait with him.

Mrs. Schmidt came out to talk with Grandfather. She said Mrs. Hammer was taking it real well and wanted to go home and make sure things were being looked after properly, but she was going to keep her there until after the funeral. Mrs. Hammer could have heard what they were saying without stretching her ears, but she didn't seem to be paying much attention. She'd prettied herself up some and looked nice, sitting there sewing.

Grandfather decided he wanted to know how much of the Hammer farm could be seen from Schmidt's place. He found a spot at the far end of the yard where we could see one end of the Hammer barn, and he said, "If you'd been standing here, you could have seen that murderer running from the barn."

Schmidt said, in that funny talk of his, that maybe he could have, but he hadn't been there. He'd been in the house eating lunch.

"Too bad," Grandfather said.

We went back to the house. Mrs. Hammer still didn't seem to pay any attention to us, and I got the idea she wished people would stop bothering her. For one thing, she acted nervous. I noticed that when she tried to thread her needle. She was so long at it that I felt like going up and steadying her hand for her. Finally Mrs. Schmidt saw she was having trouble, and she went over and threaded it for her.

The sheriff arrived a little after one-thirty and took Mrs. Hammer into the house for a talk. She seemed glad to see him, and if she was nervous when they came out she sure didn't show it. We loaded the Schmidts into my jalopy, and the sheriff took Mrs. Hammer, and we drove over to the Hammer farm.

There were six deputies waiting for us, along with Nat Barlow and quite a few other men. There also was a message from the county attorney, telling the sheriff he wanted to see what happened and not to start anything until he got there. Sheriff Pilkins paced up and down and used language not fit for women and children, but it was all right. Mrs. Hammer and Mrs. Schmidt had gone in the house, and I was the youngest one there, and he didn't use any words I hadn't heard before.

"I want to look around," Grandfather told the sheriff. "I'll be back."

"Don't exert yourself," the sheriff said. "Nobody'll cry if you don't make it."

We found Ed Seagraves behind the house, talking with Mrs. Hammer – except that Mrs. Hammer was doing all the talking. She was giving it to him but good, and by the time we got there Mrs. Schmidt was out trying to quiet her down.

"... shiftless, stupid bum," Mrs. Hammer was saying. "All these years, and he still doesn't know what needs to be done from one day to the next without someone telling him. I told you I was needed here."

Mrs. Schmidt coaxed Mrs. Hammer back to the house, and Grandfather grabbed Ed's arm and led him away in the other direction. Ed wasn't unhappy to leave. He mopped his face with a handkerchief, and allowed that he'd never had any trouble as long as Joe was running things, and if Mrs. Hammer was going to be that hard to get along with there were other jobs. Why, only yesterday Old Man Ashley had told him...

"Never mind," Grandfather said. "Where was it you were cultivating the day Joe was killed?"

Ed pointed. "There. Down toward the creek."

Ed led us down a lane and opened a gate, and we followed him across the cornfield, up a rise, and then down the long slope toward the creek.

"I was wondering if the murderer could have seen you out here," Grandfather said.

"Naw. When you're down here you can't even see the barn, and only the upper part of the house. He couldn't have seen me."

"He could hear the tractor, though," Grandfather said. "He'd know where you were, and he'd know that as long as he could hear the tractor you wouldn't be interrupting him."

"Yeah," Ed said. "I never thought of that."

We walked on down to the creek, and Grandfather looked around and scratched away at his bald head. "That's real interesting," he said. "You can see the top of Schmidt's house from here, though you can't see it from back there. Trees are in the way. And you can see the whole upper story of the Hammer house, but you can't see the barn at all. That's real interesting. Don't you think so, Johnny? Look."

I looked. The Hammer house, sticking up behind the hill, looked just like any house would look sticking up like that, and in the other direction all I could see was Schmidt's chimney and the peak of his roof.

"I'm going over to talk to Harvey Lennox," Grandfather said. "You wait at the house, Johnny, and come after me in a hurry if the county attorney shows up before I get back."

I went back to the house and waited around, trying to keep out of the way. More people kept arriving, and a bunch of kids showed up from town, riding bicycles. Dave Schmidt came over, looking for his parents, and then Grandfather came back bringing Mr. Lennox with him.

Grandfather took two of the kids aside – it was the Carson twins – and had a talk with them. I was getting pretty tired waiting, and so was everyone else, and the sheriff's face looked redder every time I saw him.

County Attorney Holder showed up about three-thirty and bobbed his white head around apologizing to everyone for being late. He even apologized to those who had no business there anyway, which seemed nice of him. The sheriff bustled around getting things organized, and finally it dawned on me what they were going to do.

Mrs. Hammer was in the house, standing at the kitchen window. Nat Barlow and the deputies and some other men were down in the barn, all dressed alike – blue overalls and straw hats. The idea was that they were going to run, one at a time, from the barn over to the bushes along the road, and Mrs. Hammer would tell the sheriff if she saw one that ran like the murderer ran.

Ed Seagrave was still hanging around, and he said to me, "Let's go down and watch."

I saw that Grandfather had picked himself a choice location, right under Mrs. Hammer's window, so I told Ed I'd rather hang around the house. Ed and the two Schmidts and a couple of others went down and sat on the rail fence by the barn. Then the sheriff decided everything was ready and waved his arm.

Nothing happened. I looked at the sheriff again, and as a result I almost missed the first runner. He was just vanishing into the bushes when I turned.

"No," Mrs. Hammer said.

The sheriff waved again, and we got Number Two.

To understand what was happening, you have to know that this was the house Joe Hammer built for his bride before they were married. She insisted on it. She was a town girl, and she was determined she wasn't going to have any barn smells in her house, and by gosh she didn't, even when the wind was right. Joe built the house that far from the barn.

So there we were, standing by the house and looking down the slope at the barn a good three hundred yards away. Those fellows didn't run very fast, but they all looked alike to me, and they were out of sight before I got more than a quick look at their backs. And every time one ran, Mrs. Hammer would sing out, "No!" and the sheriff would wave for the next runner.

We got as far as Number Seven before anything interesting happened. Then Mrs. Hammer wet out a squawk.

"That's him!" she yelled. "That's the one!"

"All right," the sheriff said, writing something in his notebook. He waved for the next runner. We got through Number Ten without anything else happening, and then the deputies herded all the runners back to the barn and started them over again. That round Mrs. Hammer squawked on Number Three, and the sheriff made a note of it and ran off the rest of them.

"Who were they?" the county attorney asked, after all ten had run a second time.

"Darned if I know," Sheriff Pilkins said. "Steve Carling is keeping a list. Here he comes."

Steve came trotting up waving a piece of paper, and the sheriff said, "Number Seven of the first bunch. Who was it?"

Steve looked at his list and blinked. "Nat Barlow," he said.

"Number Three of the second bunch."

"Nat Barlow."

"Well, now!" The county attorney's grin moved his ears back a couple of inches on both sides. "Well, now! That does wrap it up. That was a fine idea!" He pounded Grandfather on the back, and Grandfather looked in the mood to punch him right in the nose. "Thanks a lot, Bill," the county attorney said. "You've been a big help."

"I sure have," Grandfather said.

"You ready to admit it was Nat?" the sheriff asked.

"Nope," Grandfather said.

The sheriff glared at Grandfather. "You aren't?"

"Nope"

"Loyalty," the county attorney said, "is a fine quality, among friends. But when the duty of public office weighs heavily on a man's shoulders, his first loyalty belongs to all the people. To the principle of law and order. To justice. All men stand equal before the law, and even when the finger of guilt points to an old friend – and I want you to know that Nat Barlow is an old friend of mine, and a cherished friend at that –"

"Horsefeathers!" Grandfather roared.

"I fully understand your bitterness, but –"

"You're a tank-headed idiot," Grandfather told him. "You and Pilkins both. You're all set to convict an innocent man, and I'm almost tempted to let you do it and then show you up for the ignoramuses you are. But that time in jail, and a trial, would kill Nat, so I aim to straighten this mess out before I go home today. Let's go down to the barn."

They both started to argue, but Grandfather looked them right into the ground, and they quieted down and came along. All of us went except for Mrs. Hammer and Mrs. Schmidt, who stayed in the house. In the barn we met the crowd that had been doing the running, with a couple of deputies watching Nat Barlow as if he were some dangerous desperado. He looked pretty darned worried and unhappy, as if his last friend had just kicked him in the pants.

"Ed," Grandfather called, "come over here."

Ed Seagrave ambled over. Grandfather stood there for a minute, looking around as if he wanted to be sure he had everyone's attention, and he certainly had it. The sheriff and the county attorney weren't even breathing.

"Ed," Grandfather said, "we want to get a couple of things straight. You were out there driving the tractor until about twelve-thirty, and then you went up to the house. Mrs. Hammer told you Joe was in the barn, and you went down there and found him dead, and you ran over to tell the Schmidts. Is that right?"

"Right," Ed said.

"Now think. Beyond that, did you hear anything, or see anything – or anyone?"

"Nope," Ed said. "Couldn't hear anything above the tractor."

"Yeah. Harvey Lennox was working the next field, so we know you were running that tractor right through to twelve-thirty. All right. Now where are those kids?"

The Carson twins pushed through the crowd and stood there, looking plenty nervous.

"What were you doing Monday morning?" Grandfather asked.

Jerry spoke up. He always does the talking for the two of them. "We went swimming over at Old Man Ashley's swimming hole."

"That's the creek that cuts past this farm, isn't it?" Grandfather asked.

They both nodded.

"What'd you do when you got through swimming?"

"We waded up the creek a ways," Jerry said, and Harold nodded.

"What for?"

"Nothing much. We were catching frogs and stuff."

"See anything interesting?"

"When we got up this way we saw a tractor."

"What tractor?"

"Hammer's tractor," Jerry said. "It was sitting there in the field all by itself with the motor running."

"Is that all?"

"Well, then we saw Ed come tearing down the lane. He ran up and jumped on the tractor and started off."

"What time was that?" Grandfather asked.

"Don't know exactly. Along about noon, I guess."

"Where's Lennox?" Grandfather asked. "Harvey, could you see that tractor from where you were working?"

"Nope," Lennox said. "Just heard it, that's all. I was fixing fence over on the far side of the field. Couldn't see down into the draw from there. I heard the tractor all the time, but like I told you this afternoon, when I got to thinking about it, seems to me it was idling there for quite a spell, and then it started up again."

"How about it, Ed?" Grandfather asked.

Ed didn't say anything.

"You might as well tell us about it," Grandfather said. "Mrs. Hammer admits, now, that she saw you going down to the barn a little *before* Dave Schmidt got there. She says she doesn't know why you killed Joe, but once it was done it couldn't be undone, and she felt sorry for you."

If Mrs. Hammer had been present at that moment, there'd been another murder done. "That bitch!" Ed yelled. "The whole thing was *her* idea! She told me what to do!" It took the sheriff and three deputies to quiet him down.

"She pulled the shade down in an upstairs window to let you know Joe had gone out to the barn and everything was ready, didn't she?" Grandfather asked. "It's still down. Mrs. Schmidt carried her away afterward, and she forgot about it."

Ed talked, then, and spilled the works. How Mrs. Hammer had got real friendly with him, and how they took to carrying on when Joe wasn't around, and finally how Mrs. Hammer planned to get rid of Joe. She sent Ed out early Monday morning to knock down a stretch of Harvey Lennox's fence, and then about the middle of the morning she called Harvey to tell him it was down, knowing he'd have to fix it right away to keep his cows out of the corn. And then when Mrs. Hammer got Joe out to the barn, with Mr. Lennox working where he could hear the tractor and not see it, she gave Ed the signal with the window shade, and as soon as she saw him leave the barn she called Dave Schmidt with that lie about the sedan so Dave would discover the body before Ed came in from the field. Of course there wasn't any murderer running away. Mrs. Hammer made that up.

One of the sheriff's deputies got it all down, and when Ed was finished the two deputies turned Nat Barlow loose, and he came over and hugged Grandfather and cried on his shoulder. Just for a moment I thought Grandfather was going to cry, too. The way those two always jaw at each other, I never would have thought they felt that way.

"I really don't know what to say," the county attorney said.

"You usually don't," Grandfather said, "but I notice that you say it anyway."

"Those boys – how did you happen onto them? They'll have to testify at the trial."

"No, they won't," Grandfather said. "They weren't anywhere near this place on Monday. That was just a little scheme we cooked up together. And I owe them a couple of sodas." He fished in his pocket and came up with two quarters. "Here you are, kids," he said. "It was a very good performance, and you earned them, but I hope you won't buy them from that cheapskate Ferguson."

The twins took the quarters, and grinned, and backed away.

"Amazing," the county attorney said. "But how did you figure it out?"

"It didn't take much figuring," Grandfather told him. "Mrs. Hammer is in her forties, which is a dangerous age for a woman. Joe was nearly seventy, and here was a strong, good-looking young fellow living with them, and even if he is kind of dumb he maybe seemed more attractive than an elderly husband. In case you haven't heard, that sort of thing is called a triangle. The big city papers talk about it all the time, and I've even heard it mentioned once or twice right here in Borg County. Now in Detroit, in 1946 –"

Sheriff Pilkins interrupted. "I'd better go and have it out with Stella. That woman's been too smart for her own good."

"She coached Ed pretty good," Grandfather agreed. "The two of them put on a good act Monday. Today, too."

"They did," the sheriff said. "And don't you go around sticking your chest out over this, Rastin. The whole business is your fault."

"How's that?" Grandfather asked.

"You and your predictions. You were telling everyone that Borgville would have a murder this year, and Ed heard you. He told Stella about it, and between them they made a prophet out of you. I expect you're too old to learn to keep your mouth shut, but you might give it a try."

I expected Grandfather to point out that he'd predicted a *Borgville* murder, and the Hammer farm missed that considerably, but he didn't.

He leaned forward, and stuck his jaw out at the sheriff, and prodded the sheriff's chest with one finger. "Now let me tell you something. If you had an ounce of brains – just one ounce, mind you – you wouldn't have needed me to straighten you out on this. Even if you were too stupid to see anything else, that spectacle we staged this afternoon gave it away. Do you mean you *still* haven't caught on? Stella Hammer picked Nat Barlow both times when you and I and everyone else up by the house couldn't tell him from Adam. And Stella's eyes have been bad all her life. She's needed glasses since she was a kid, but she'd never wear them because she thought they'd ruin her looks. Just this afternoon, over at Schmidt's, she couldn't even thread a needle. And yet she picked Nat both times. *Now* have you got it figured out?" The sheriff didn't say anything.

"Ed was sitting down by the barn," Grandfather said. "When Nat ran, he gave her a signal. They cooked it up between them as soon as she got here. He took his hat off and practically waved it, and she could see that. If you'd been paying attention instead of trying to count votes in the next election, you'd have noticed it."

"All right," the sheriff said. "I'll hand it to you. You figured it out. But the whole thing is your fault, and don't you forget it. Statistics, phooey!"

There you have it – an almanac, and a bet on a horse, and a murder. Grandfather says if people have murder in them, they don't need any prompting.

Sheriff Pilkins says there wouldn't have been any murder if Grandfather hadn't started spouting statistics out of that almanac. As for the bet on the horse, I'll let you decide where that came it.

Grandfather wasn't quite finished with Sheriff Pilkins. "Lots of people overlook little things," he said. "So maybe it's natural that you wouldn't notice a triangle with a woman and an elderly husband and a younger man. And maybe it's natural that you'd forget that a tractor motor running doesn't necessarily guarantee that someone is there keeping it company. But you are the only lawman in these fifty states, including Alaska and Hawaii, that ever got a murder case all ready for trial and overlooked the fact *that the principal and only eye-witness couldn't see*."

That was Grandfather having the last word.

THE UNASKED QUESTION

Grandfather Rastin gave up hunting when he passed his sixtieth birthday – not because he thought he was getting too old for it, but because he didn't want to get shot. His attitude toward hunting being what it is, and his attitude toward Sheriff Pilkins being what that is, it isn't surprising that he stormed up to his room and locked the door when Sheriff Pilkins turned up at our house wearing a brand new red hunting jacket and a slick, long-billed, red hunting cap.

The sheriff banged on the front door with one hand while turning the handle of the doorbell with the other. I recognized his mood and got there before he started kicking the door.

I was wrong about his mood. He wasn't mad; he just had troubles. He asked almost politely, "Your Grandfather at home?"

"He's temporarily indisposed," I said. "He says the sight of you makes him sick."

"That's too bad, because I'm about to make him sicker. John Deet's been killed in a hunting accident. Tell your Grandfather I want to talk with him."

I tromped upstairs and told Grandfather through his locked door, and he said, "Tell Pilkins I'm surprised it didn't happen years ago, and I don't want to talk about it."

I went back downstairs and told the sheriff, and he thought it over, still not mad but maybe a little more troubled. "Tell him it's important," he said finally.

"Look," I said. "I wouldn't want you to think I don't have respect for the law, but this could go on all afternoon, and Mom's worried about the stair carpet wearing out. Why don't you go up and tell him?"

He knew that would be a waste of time, so he decided to talk with me. He said, "Johnny, what do you know about Ronnie Mayer's .22 rifle?"

I stared at him. "He hasn't got one! He wouldn't dare! His dad would break his neck."

"Sure. That's what he says, and that's also what his dad says, but the fact is he has one. How well do you know Evelyn Deet?"

"No better than I can help," I said. "She's a brat."

"How'd she get along with her stepfather?"

"It wouldn't surprise me if she's out celebrating right now. She still calls herself 'Anderson,' you know. She won't use the name 'Deet.' "

"Does she date Ronnie Mayer?"

"You'll have to ask the Wiston High kids about that."

The sheriff pushed himself to his feet. "About ten minutes after I leave, your Grandfather will get over being a mule and want to know what happened. Just to save him the trouble of finding out, I'll tell you. John Deet and Jim Tyler were hunting pheasant on the Mayer farm this morning. They were working south from Squaw Road, and they separated to go around a thicket. At the other side, Tyler waited ten, fifteen minutes, afraid he might spoil a shot for John if he stepped out before John was ready. Finally he circled back around the thicket and found John dead. He'd been shot in the head with a .22 rifle."

"What were they hunting with?" I asked.

The sheriff snorted. "Shotguns. Who'd hunt pheasant with a .22? They were both using John's guns. Tyler never hunted before, and John loaned him the shotgun and also an old hunting jacket. He says he'll never hunt again, but that's as it may be. The ground is low, there, and there's a gradual rise to the north and west. The bullet could have come quite a distance, but even if it was an accident I've got to find out who fired that shot. The first question is who in that vicinity owns a .22. The second question is where Evelyn Deet was this morning."

"Why don't you ask her?"

"I did," he said disgustedly. "She won't tell me."

He went out to his car and stood there for a moment, scratching his head and looking back at our house. Finally he drove away.

I sat down and watched the clock. Three minutes and sixteen seconds after the sheriff left, Grandfather's door opened. He came clomping down the stairs and picked up the telephone.

"What are you doing?" I asked him.

"I want to find out what happened."

I told him I knew what happened, and he sat down in his rocking chair to listen. He rocked without saying anything until I mentioned Ronnie Mayer's .22, and that brought him to a dead stop.

"First question – bah!" That surprised me.

"What's wrong with asking who owns a .22?"

"As a question, nothing. But as a *first* question –"

"What difference does it make what order he asks the questions in?" Grandfather got up, not looking happy. "I should go over there and have a look at things. But it's hunting season, drat it!"

As Grandfather tells it, the front lines of either of the World Wars have nothing on the main highway between Borgville and Wiston when the hunters are out. He thought it over for the rest of the day and most of Sunday and didn't make up his mind until late Sunday afternoon when Ed Mayer called to tell him that the sheriff had just arrested Ronnie. Five minutes later we were on our way to Wiston.

Before going out to the Mayer farm we stopped at the Deet house, which is an old place not far from the Wiston business district. Those two houses made quite a contrast. Mrs. Deet already had a black wreath on her front door, and inside Evelyn was playing rock and roll records. There wasn't any wreath at the Mayers' house, but the place was dead.

Doc Hodge was paying a friendly call on Mrs. Deet, and he went to see if she felt like coming down. Grandfather sat down in John Deet's den and started looking through a pile of magazines. One wall of the room was a long gun case with sliding glass doors, and I put my nose against the glass and looked at the guns.

"Isn't that a .22?" I asked.

"It's a .22," Doc Hodge said, returning from upstairs. "John had the only key, and Nancy had company here all morning, and no one could have borrowed it. Sheriff Pilkins checked on that. Believe me, he checked. Nancy will be down in a minute. She's doing as well as can be expected, and Evelyn doesn't need anything but a good paddling, which doesn't require a doctor, so I'll be on my way."

"Do you suppose Nancy would care if I borrowed some of these magazines?" Grandfather asked.

Doc walked over to have a look at them. "Water skiing, archery, boating, hunting, skin diving, camping, nature trails – all that stuff looked good on John Deet, but it's a shade inappropriate for you, isn't it?"

"I like to look at the ads," Grandfather said.

"Ask Nancy. I'm sure it'd be all right as long as you don't turn the pages too recklessly."

He went out laughing, and a moment later Mrs. Deet came in. She was wearing a black dress and she didn't look as pretty as I remembered her, but she also didn't look as though she cared how she looked. Grandfather had just one question for her. It absolutely floored me, and she didn't even blink. "Who were the business people and customers on John's Christmas list last year?"

She said John always looked after that himself, but she gave him a few names she thought were on it. Then we looked in on Evelyn, who was down in the basement thumping her feet in time with the music. She ignored us until the record was finished.

"How'd you make out with the sheriff?" Grandfather asked her.

She made a face at him, which is one thing that girl really has talent for. "He's a nosey old creep," she said. "Wanted to know if I date Ronnie Mayer."

"Do you?" Grandfather asked.

"That goodie-goodie? *Nobody* dates him. His mother won't let him go out with girls. Look here." She stood up and glared at him, hands on hips. She was wearing slacks and a baggy shirt, but for all that she might have been pretty if it hadn't been for making faces. "I won't say I'm sorry John was killed. I never liked him when he was alive, and I'm not going to pretend I did now that he's dead."

"Evelyn –" Mrs. Deet said from the top of the stairs. She sounded as if she were about to cry.

"Never mind, mother. He's just another snoop, like the sheriff. I hated John from the first time he ever came to see mother, when I was only seven, but as I got older I did learn to respect him. In all those years I can't think of a time he wasn't nice to me. I used to want him dead, but I got over that. I've known for a long time that as men go he was a damn good one, but that didn't make me stop hating him. Nothing would, as long as people expected me to call him 'dad.' "

She put on another record and turned the volume up a notch. This may not be a polite way to end a conversation, but it certainly is effective. Grandfather and I went back upstairs, and Grandfather picked up the magazines he was borrowing, and Mrs. Deet saw us to the door. She didn't say anything, and if she had it probably would have embarrassed all three of us.

We found Mr. Mayer pacing in a circle in his parlor. He paced all the time we were there. He looked *beaten – he's* a big man, but his shoulders weren't coping with the weight that had been dumped onto them.

"Guns!" he said. "All Ronnie's life I've told him guns were no good. I wouldn't let him play with guns when he was little. Guns kill. Why would he save his money to buy one and not tell me? He's always been a good boy."

Grandfather found a rocking chair in the corner and went to work in it. "I guess that's why. Sometimes the things a boy isn't allowed to have seem pretty attractive."

Mrs. Mayer had been crying, but she managed to bring in coffee and cake, and a glass of milk for me, and then she went upstairs. Mr. Mayer kept on pacing.

"Why haven't they made a ballistics test?" Grandfather asked. "Even Sheriff Pilkins should be bright enough to know that if Ronnie's gun –"

"That's the problem. Ronnie doesn't have the gun. It was stolen."

Grandfather stopped rocking. "Stolen? When?"

"A couple of weeks ago. Ronnie parked the car in Wiston without locking it, and the gun was stolen. He was afraid to report it."

"That is a problem."

"The sheriff thinks he hid the gun somewhere after he shot John Deet."

"To Pilkins, that would be a logical assumption. Did you get a lawyer for Ronnie?"

"Lawyer!" Mr. Mayer snorted. "If Ronnie is guilty, he'll have to pay the penalty. I don't want no lawyers twisting the law and making deals."

"Ronnie had no more to do with John Deet's death than you did. He should have a lawyer. You don't want him paying the penalty for something he didn't do."

"All right. I'll get him a lawyer."

"This is what comes of Pilkins asking the wrong questions," Grandfather said. "Come on, Johnny. Let's go see some people."

We drove back to Wiston, and Grandfather got out the names from John Deet's Christmas list. At the first two places no one was home. At the third place there was company, and Grandfather wouldn't stop. The fourth name was Jake McFarland, a long-time friend of Grandfather's, and when Grandfather asked him one of those right questions, it was quite a letdown.

"What did John give you for Christmas last year?"

"A wallet," Jake said. "He noticed that mine was worn out. Trouble was, everyone noticed, so I got six. Why?"

"Just curious. I heard he was giving magazine subscriptions for Christmas. Know who got them?"

Jake shook his head.

"Ever go hunting with John?"

"Once, a long time ago. He gave me my Christmas present early that year – a hunting license. Always trying to make hunters out of people, John was. I went out with him once so as not to seem ungrateful. We went to the Mayer farm, too. He hunted there every year. How's Nancy taking it?"

"Pretty well. Did John give out any early Christmas presents this year?"

"Not that I know of. Nancy must be taking it a lot better than John's Partner. Jim Tyler is all broken up – emotionally and financially."

"Why financially?" Grandfather asked.

"When a partner dies, the survivor is in trouble. Bill Elgin was after them a couple of years ago to draw up some kind of legal agreement and take out life insurance to cover this sort of thing. They never did get around to it. Jim thinks he'll have to sell out to satisfy John's estate."

"Nancy will work out something with him. They've always been good friends."

"Friendship bends funny ways under stress," Jake said. "Nancy's already called in a lawyer to advise her. You'd think she could wait until after the funeral."

"That is odd," Grandfather agreed. "It doesn't sound like Nancy."

"You never can tell how a woman will react to anything. Seems to me I've heard *you* say that more than once."

"Men can be pretty unpredictable, too," Grandfather said. "Not to mention sons and stepdaughters."

The conversation died a natural death, and we went back to my jalopy. I said to Grandfather, "Is that the question the sheriff should have asked? 'What did John Deet give you for Christmas?' "

"The most important questions aren't the ones a law enforcement officer asks other people. They're the questions he asks himself. Pilkins doesn't know the difference."

The next name on the list was Ben Carse, who lived in a plush tri-level house in a plush neighborhood of plush tri-level houses. He was a jolly little bald headed man who could have played Santa Clause with no props at all except large amounts of hair in the right places.

"John was like a son to me," he said. "I warned him about that partnership with Tyler – John's a fine salesman, and Tyler is the best TV repair man in Wiston, but neither of them is a businessman. But they seem to have done well."

"I heard you started out with them on Saturday," Grandfather said. "What happened?"

"All I know is that maybe half, three-quarters of an hour after we separated, Tyler came tearing after us like a madman saying John had been shot, so I went back with him and my boy Mike ran up to the Forbes house to telephone for help." He waved a hand. "But John was already past any help we or anyone else could have given him."

There was a magazine rack beside my chair. Remembering Grandfather's question about magazine subscriptions, I pawed through it and turned up two hunting magazines and one nature trails. I held one of them up so Grandfather could see the cover, and he nodded and asked Mr. Carse, "What'd John give you for Christmas last year?"

Carse grinned. "A lovely smoking set, and every piece is engraved, 'THE WISTON APPLIANCE COMPANY.' John had a sense of humor."

Grandfather thanked him very politely. I was ready to go home, but Grandfather said Jim Tyler lived somewhere in the neighborhood and he wanted to see him. Actually it was a couple of plush neighborhoods away in the fanciest part of Wiston, and the house looked the way Mount Vernon would look if it were shrunk a bit and crowded onto a city lot. Mrs. Tyler said Jim was at the store.

"Any idea when he'll be back?" Grandfather asked.

She shook her head. "He's getting things ready for inventory."

"Mind if we wait?"

I think she was glad to have company. She offered food, which Grandfather declined without consulting me, and we sat down in the living room. While she and Grandfather talked, I found another magazine rack to work on. This time I turned up a boating magazine. At the first break in the conversation I decided to help out with Grandfather's detecting. "Did Mr. Deet give this to Mr. Tyler for Christmas?" I asked.

"For his birthday," Mrs. Tyler said. "John gave him subscriptions to four magazines, but that's the only one he liked. He's always been daft about boats. We almost bought a cabin cruiser last summer, but fortunately we decided to wait."

"I hear Jim is worried about the store," Grandfather said.

"The store is ruined," Mrs. Tyler said grimly. "Even if Jim could satisfy John's estate without liquidation, he couldn't make a go of it alone."

"He ought to give it a try."

She shook her head. "You know how they operated. John looked after the front of the store – he was a wonderful salesman. Jim looked after the back. They were getting along wonderfully well. Now – well, we talked it over at dinner. Jim very easily could go broke trying to find someone who could take John's place. The wisest thing is to salvage what we can and go back to our TV repair business. We won't get rich, but it's *safe*, and we've made some very fortunate investments. It's just a shame. John was only forty-two and such a wonderful person. And they were doing so well. Would you like to see the house?"

She gave us the grand tour, from Jim Tyler's electronic gadgets in the basement workshop to the attic, which really was a sort of unfinished upstairs. At the top of the stairway, lying on a big pile of boxes, was a .22 rifle.

Mrs. Tyler saw me staring at it, and she laughed and said if I was going into the detective business I'd have to work faster. "Steve Carling-the deputy sheriff, you know – he was here to look at it yesterday. He didn't bother to wipe the dust off. Something or other won't work, and it hasn't been fired since Jim was a kid."

Jim Tyler turned out to be real tall and thin, and when he finally arrived he looked dead beat and well on his way to being a corpse himself. He didn't seem to mind talking about what happened. "There were four of us," he said. "The Carses and John and I. We separated at the road – the Carses went north on the Forbes farm, and John and I went south."

"It's surprising John didn't get shot years ago," Grandfather said. "He did most of his hunting with beginners he was trying to make sportsmen out of."

"I don't agree. There never was a man more careful with guns. This was the second time I went out with him. The first time I carried an empty gun, and he blew his top whenever I didn't handle it to suit him."

"Too bad someone hasn't invented a careful bullet," Grandfather said.

"I never wanted to go hunting. John kept pestering me, and I finally decided it would be easier to go than to go on being pestered. It's too late now to wish I hadn't."

"He would have taken someone else."

"I suppose so."

That conversation didn't just die out, it collapsed, and Grandfather and I got out of the house as politely as we could. We headed for home, and as we drove through downtown Wiston, Grandfather pointed out the WISTON APPLIANCE COMPANY, which was the store John Deet and Jim Tyler had been partners in. I didn't see much of it, because I was busy staring at a bigger store on the other side of the street – CARSE APPLIANCE COMPANY.

"Carse!" I exclaimed.

"Ben Carse. That's the man we were talking with."

"John Deet went hunting with an enemy?"

"Competitor. Nobody could be an enemy of John Deet. He worked for Carse for ten years. You heard Carse say John was like a son to him."

"Even so, the Carse Appliance Company doesn't have a wreath on the door, and it's business won't suffer if the Wiston Appliance Company is liquidated. Darn – just when I was thinking *nobody* profited from John Deet's death!"

"It all depends on what you mean by 'profit,' " Grandfather said.

"Does Ben Carse own a .22?"

"Now that's an angle for Pilkins! Why don't you suggest it to him?"

"Sure. I'll drive right over to his house and do it now."

"Let's let him have one more night's sleep thinking John Deet was killed accidentally," Grandfather said. "Now stop talking and drive. I want to get home so I can look at these magazines."

On Monday I came home from school expecting to spend the rest of the afternoon and maybe most of the night chauffeuring Grandfather all over Borg County while he looked for the answer to one of his right questions. I found him rocking in his room, and he politely asked me to leave and close the door. Mom told me he'd been on the telephone most of the day, and she supposed he'd found out what he wanted to know.

"What did he talk about?" I asked.

"I wasn't paying any attention. Unlike you two, I have work to do."

"Was it anything about Christmas presents?"

"The idea! Christmas is still weeks away!"

I pestered her until she managed to remember a big argument Grandfather had with Sheriff Pilkins shortly before noon. As a result they probably weren't speaking to each other, but that state of affairs wasn't abnormal or even unusual.

I sat down and tried to do my math assignment. Grandfather's rocking chair was hitting a squeaky floor board on the backswing, which didn't help my concentration. Finally I gave up, told Mom not to wait supper for me, and drove to Wiston.

A certain amount of information was floating about the joints where the high school crowd hangs out. I heard right away that the sheriff hadn't really arrested Ronnie Mayer; he just took him in for questioning. Opinion was pretty evenly divided as to whether Ronnie really owned a .22 and whether he had anything to do with John Deet's death even if he did have one. His parents had been gone, and he claimed he spent the whole morning in his room writing a term paper on the life of the boll weevil. He had the term paper for evidence, but the sheriff didn't seem to think that proved anything.

A girl told me Evelyn Deet was crazy enough about Ronnie to invite him to the Sadie Hawkins Dance, but his mother wouldn't let him go, or maybe he didn't want to go. No one I talked with knew where Evelyn Deet was on Saturday morning.

It added up to a wasted afternoon. I headed for home saturated with ginger ale and with my whole week's allowance shot, and when I pulled up in front of the house I couldn't park in my favorite parking place because someone had absent-mindedly left a State Police car there.

It was Sergeant Reichel, who commands the State Police Post in Wiston. He came down from Grandfather's room while I was eating supper, and when I asked him what he and Grandfather were hatching he said he'd just sworn a solemn oath not to tell anyone.

"Naturally I wouldn't expect an officer of the law to violate his solemn oath," I said. I went up to see Grandfather about that, and he threw a slipper at me for derailing his train of thought. This being a game that two can play, when he came down later and asked me what I'd found out in Wiston, I refused to talk. And the next noon, when Sheriff Pilkins waylaid me at Marty's Rapid Lunch to ask me what Grandfather and the State Police were up to, I could tell him honestly that he knew at least as much about it as I did.

Sheriff Pilkins must have spent that entire day in strenuous thought.

He telephoned me right after school with the brilliant suggestion that I date Evelyn Deet and romance her into confessing where she was Saturday morning, and not even the sheriff could have come up with a notion like that one if his brain hadn't been fatigued. I told him there weren't many things I wouldn't be willing to do to serve the cause of justice, but he'd sure hit on one of them.

Then I got to thinking of what Grandfather once said about the sheriff's knack for putting good ideas in such a stupid way that Almighty God couldn't see the merit in them, and I drove over to the Deets' house in Wiston.

Mrs. Deet seemed surprised to see me. Evelyn didn't. She was in the basement listening to records, and she made a face and said, "Et tu, Brute?"

"Who are you calling a brute?" I asked.

She turned off the record player. "That snoopy sheriff is siccing everyone onto me to find out where I was Saturday."

"I don't care where you were Saturday," I said. "I just stopped to ask you if you'd like to play detective."

"How do you play detective?"

"You try to find out who shot John."

She made a face. "Who cares?"

"I thought maybe you did. You said he was a good man, and his being shot made your mother unhappy."

"How would we find out who did it?"

"I don't know. If it was an accident, it could be almost anyone who has a .22. If it wasn't an accident, then John was murdered, and that's a different sort of problem. Then it'd be someone who had a motive."

"Someone like me?" she suggested.

"Right. You hated him, so you had a motive. That's why the sheriff is bothering you. You're maybe the only person in Borg County who had that particular motive, because everyone else seemed to like John a lot."

"What other motives are there?"

"Money," I suggested.

"John didn't have a lot of money. We always got along all right, but we weren't rich."

"Romance," I said. "If he was in love with some other man's wife, or some other man was in love with your mother –"

"Bosh! Those two have been honeymooning ever since they were married. Sometimes it was embarrassing living in the same house with them. What else?"

"There could be motives no one knows about. There's also the angle that it had to be someone who knew he was going hunting, but half of Wiston could have known."

She snapped her fingers. "If I was going to kill someone, and I knew where he'd be and when, know what I'd do? I'd practice."

"That doesn't narrow the problem very much. Probably quite a few people have been target practicing with a .22 in the last month or two."

"It narrows it a lot," she said. "The murderer will be someone who doesn't have a .22, because if he had one he wouldn't use it because that would point suspicion at him. So we should look for someone who's been target shooting with a .22 who doesn't have one." I raised my eyebrows at her. "He borrowed or stole one," she explained. "Say – Ronnie said his was stolen!"

We stared at each other. "You're a pretty good detective," I said.

"The murderer had to sneak his target practice because he didn't want anyone to know he had a .22," she went on. "He couldn't go where other people practice, and he couldn't go near the Mayer farm because after the murder people around there would be questioned and if they'd seen someone sneaking target practice they'd remember it. The Mayer farm is west of Wiston, so he'd do his target practice somewhere out east."

"Why not north or south?" I asked.

"Don't be silly. If we found out where he practiced, what would we look for?"

".22 cartridge cases," I said.

"Then if – just for example – if it was Mr. Hillburg next door murdering John because of that argument they had two years ago when Mr. Hillburg borrowed our power mower and broke it, and we found he'd been out at his cottage early last week, and we went there and found .22 cartridge cases, that would prove he did it?"

"Not exactly, but it would be a start."

"I like playing detective," she said. "Let's go out to his cottage and look."

"It's getting late," I said. "Don't you think it'd be better if we found out first if he's still mad about the mower and if he actually was at the cottage?"

"I forgot. He broke *our* mower – it wasn't him that was mad, it was John. Anyway, his cottage isn't out east. We want someone who was practicing out east. Go upstairs and get on the extension. I'm going to telephone."

I went upstairs. Mrs. Deet asked me what we were doing, and I told her I'd let her know as soon as I found out. Evelyn called Eddie Longer, whose father is a farmer east of Wiston, and she told him she was tracking down a murderer. "Where is it people go to practice shooting?" she asked.

"Weston's quarry," Eddie said.

"This jerk didn't go there, because he practiced sneaky like."

Eddie pointed out that in that case no one would have seen him. "Of course someone saw him – otherwise we couldn't catch him, could we?"

Eddie said he'd ask around, and I decided I'd had as much of this kind of detecting as I could take far one evening. I went back downstairs and told Evelyn I had to leave, and she said okay, she'd keep making calls, and by the next evening she'd have places for us to go and do same real detecting.

Darned if she didn't. She skipped school and John Deet's funeral, and when I got to her house after school she had a list of names and addresses. We drove east of Wiston and started working our way down the list, and the only fact we were able to detect was that a lot of farmers didn't like hunters. We reached the second name from the bottom before we found any evidence of a suspicious character who'd actually done some target practice.

An old geezer named Gerold Ambeth was renting the farm next to his. Its barn had burned long before, and the rickety old farmhouse was boarded up and overgrown with weeds and shrubs. When Ambeth took his cows down a lane to the pasture, he passed a place where he could see the rear of the farmhouse, and one Sunday morning a couple of weeks before, there'd been a car parked there out of sight of the road and a man standing beside it aiming a gun. Ambeth couldn't remember hearing him shoot. He hadn't been interested enough to pay much attention.

"What sort of a gun was it?" I asked.

"Shotgun," he said.

"We're looking far someone target practicing with a .22," I said.

He scratched his head and decided it could save been a .22. Anyway, there was one of those canvas gun cases lying an the ground, so the guy could have had other guns with him. He showed us the place where he'd seen the man standing, and then he drove away.

"He thinks we're nuts," Evelyn said.

"He may be right. Let's have a look before it gets dark and then head for some food. My stomach has been complaining lately about my irregular meals."

She found a stick of gum in her handbag and divided it with me, and we went to look.

Evelyn got down on her hands and knees and started parting the long grass. I looked the place over and started wondering out loud if a murderer wouldn't have had enough sense to pick up the cartridge cases when he did his sneaky practicing.

"What's that"? she asked suddenly.

It was a .22 cartridge case.

She reached for it, and I slapped her hand. "It should be checked for fingerprints," I said, "and when it is, we don't want them to find yours on it."

"Oh," she said, looking excited but not the least bit scared. "And if it has a fingerprint from Mr. Hillburg, then it means he killed John?"

"Not quite, but I'll tell you this for sure – if it's a real clue, it's nothing for amateurs to be messing around with."

"Let's call your Grandfather."

"He'd feel complimented, but where fingerprints are concerned he's as much an amateur as we are. Anyway, we aren't speaking to each other. At breakfast he asks Mom to ask me to pass the butter. I guess we'd better telephone the sheriff."

We marked the location with a stick and tied Evelyn's handkerchief to it, and then we drove back to the highway where I remembered seeing a gas station. I called the sheriff and told him as plainly as I could that we'd played a long shot and didn't know what we'd hit, but if he didn't have something better to do he might want a look at it.

"Who's we?" he asked.

"Evelyn Deet and I."

He grunted. "Where was she Saturday morning?"

I turned to Evelyn. "He won't come unless you tell him where you were Saturday morning."

She made a face. "The old snoop! I was at Betty Lowell's listening to records."

I told the sheriff, and he grunted again and told me to stay put and he'd get there when he could. It was dark when he and Steve Carling arrived, followed by a car with two more deputies. We led them to the cartridge case, and the deputies picked it up very scientifically and went to work looking for more while the sheriff drove over to talk with Gerold Ambeth. We wished everyone good luck and headed for Wiston.

"What'll they do with it?" Evelyn asked.

"They'll test it for fingerprints, and they'll show Ambeth some photographs to see if he can identify the guy."

"Do you think he can?"

"Nope. He saw him from a long way off and wasn't interested anyway."

"Being a detective isn't as much fun as I expected," she said. "Nothing seems to settle anything."

"It's adding up a lot of little things more than finding one big thing," I told her. "You saw how eager the sheriff was even though I warned him that it probably wouldn't amount to anything. I think maybe I should stop and tell the State Police about it. All you and I are interested in is making sure the guy gets caught. We don't care who catches him. Right?"

"I guess so," she said. "But I sort of wanted to catch him myself."

Coming out the door of the State Police Post were Grandfather and Sergeant Reichel. I drove on by, turned a corner, and made an illegal U-turn.

"Did you see that?" I asked. She nodded. "Grandfather wouldn't come all the way over here just to pass the time of day," I said. "Especially at this time of night. Maybe they're about to close the trap on the murderer. Shall we follow them?"

She bounced up and down and said, "Goody, goody gumdrops," and I resisted the impulse to open the door and push her out. We followed Sergeant Reichel's car for two blocks, and then it turned onto Highway 29 and headed north. The sergeant was just taking Grandfather home. I took Evelyn home, and then I turned onto Highway 29 and headed north.

On Thursday neither Evelyn nor I could think of any detecting that needed doing, so I stayed home. Late in the evening Sheriff Pilkins called. Grandfather answered the phone, and the sheriff asked for me, and the expression on Grandfather's face was worth the time I'd wasted the day before.

"There weren't any fingerprints on that cartridge case," the sheriff said.

"What was that about fingerprints?" I asked, knowing that Grandfather would be straining for every word.

"There weren't any."

"That's very interesting," I said.

"What's interesting about it?"

"Did you try him on photographs?"

"Ambeth? He couldn't pick his own mother out of a lineup."

"That's the way I had it figured," I said.

"So it all adds up to a big zero, except that you did romance Evelyn –"

"Careful!" I yelled.

"Anyway, you found out where she was, and I checked it out, and that's where she was, So thanks. I appreciate it. This other thing – well, we'll keep it in mind, just in case something turns up to go with it."

"Right," I said. "Thanks for telling me."

I hung up. For the rest of the evening Grandfather didn't have a word to say.

Friday afternoon I was jerked out of a history test by an emergency telephone call. It was Evelyn Deet, and I had to talk to her with our high school principal, Mr. Obermeyer, looking on disapprovingly.

"Come on over," she said. "Right away."

"This history test I'm taking can't be made up," I said.

"I know who murdered John! I want to catch him myself! Come on over!" I didn't know who murdered John, but by that time I knew Evelyn Deet pretty well. "I'll come right after school and watch you catch him," I said. And hung up.

For once she wasn't listening to records when I got there. She was waiting for me.

"It's been an awful day," she said. "Mother's upstairs crying. There was a long meeting, mother and Mr. Tyler and the lawyers. Mother and Mr. Tyler are sick about it. The store owes so many bills that they're going to lose everything if they don't raise some cash, and the only way to do that quickly is to sell part of the inventory to Mr. Carse, and he's offering so little it's virtually a holdup. It looks as if we'll lose everything no matter what happens."

I decided right then that I'd avoid men who look like Santa Clause and also that I wouldn't give Ben Carse any excuse for being like a father to me. "That's too bad," I said, "but what's it got to do with murdering John?"

"The only one who's going to make any money out of John being dead is Ben Carse," she said. "He's lost his biggest competitor, and he's also going to make a lot of money by buying our inventory at forced sale. So he's the only one with a motive, right? He was out there hunting that day, so he could have done it, easily. And I telephoned the sheriff and asked him if he'd checked Mr. Carse's .22 rifle, and he said Mr. Carse doesn't have one. That proves it!"

"Just a moment. He doesn't have one, so that proves –"

"Don't you remember? We decided it had to be someone who didn't have a .22. So now all we have to do is prove Mr. Carse does have one. Right?"

"All we have to do is prove –"

"Tonight," she said, "He and his wife are going to a church social. We'll sneak into his house while he's gone and find the .22, and the sheriff can arrest him right at church, which serves him right. Him pretending to be such a good friend of John's!"

"Maybe he's just being a shrewd businessman," I said.

"That's right. He never lets murder stand in the way of a profit. Say – you're not going to chicken out *now*, are you?"

There had to be a lot of things wrong with her logic, but I couldn't think what they were. "If we're caught," I said, "I hope they call the sheriff, because the city police aren't going to believe this. Come to think of it, the sheriff isn't going to believe it, either."

We cleaned up all the cold cuts in the refrigerator, and then we sat around drinking pop until it got dark. She had a route picked out for us, and a place in an alley to park my jalopy, and she led me along a back fence where we wouldn't be seen and right up to the Carses' rear door.

"There," she said, and from that point it was my problem.

I haven't had much burglary experience, but I have been locked out of the house a few times, and it struck me as pretty much the same problem. The lower windows of a tri-level house are just above the ground. The screens had been removed from these, and the storm windows weren't up yet. I tried the first window, it opened, and I climbed in. Then I helped Evelyn in and closed the window.

She handed me her penlight. "Let's start looking."

"If we walk through the house flashing this, the neighbors will have the police here in nothing flat."

"All right, smartie. Then how'll we do it?"

"We'll start with the attic," I said. "That's a good place to hide a .22, and there won't be any windows where the light will show."

She thought that was brilliant, but she changed her mind after we'd been completely through the house without finding an entrance to the attic. I used the penlight very carefully and looked for a ceiling trap in some stupid place like an out-of-the-way corner or a closet, but we couldn't find one. We were about to start over again when I heard a noise. It sounded like a window opening.

I whispered to Evelyn, "Stay here."

I tiptoed back to the middle level and stood looking down the short flight of steps that led to the family room where we'd entered. Beyond the family room was the garage. I didn't remember a door being open, but one was, and enough light came in from a streetlight for me to see someone moving there. He was fumbling around in the far corner.

Then a flashlight stabbed through the family room window, someone shouted, and the guy in the garage came tearing through the family room and up the steps. If I'd had time to think about it I would have let him go. It was pretty obvious that he had no business there, but neither did I.

I didn't have time to think. He hurdled the steps, I stuck out my foot, and he fell with a crash that shook the house, going head first into the wall on the other side of the hallway. I dove on top of him to try to hold him, and he didn't even move.

Then a flashlight beam hit me in the face, and from somewhere close to my right ear Evelyn squealed. Grandfather's voice bellowed, "*What in thunderation are you doing here?*"

"Just staying one jump ahead of you," I said.

Evelyn whispered in my ear, "I was right! It was Mr. Carse!"

Then a state trooper turned ever the guy I'd been sitting on, and it was Jim Tyler. He'd been carrying something in his hand – a thingamagadget such as I'd never seen outside of comic books. It was a tube eight, nine inches long, with one big end and an adjusting screw. It looked like a half-baked inventor's mechanical pea shooter.

"We blew it," Sergeant Reichel's voice said. "Now we'll have to search the house."

"For what?" I asked him.

He pointed at the thingamagadget. "The other one," he said. "Obviously he planted it on Ben Carse, and he was planting this one, too, when we interrupted him."

I was adding up one and one and one and liking the answer. "It's in the garage," I said.

"Sure about that?"

"I'll show you." I led him to the corner where I'd seen Tyler poking around. On a shelf behind boxes of screws and old paint cans was another thingamagadget. Sergeant Reichel started to reach for it, and I slapped his hand. "Use your handkerchief," I said. "It may have fingerprints."

He looked at me very strangely and get out his handkerchief.

"Just tell me one thing," I said. "What is it?"

"An adapter. An insert barrel that converts a shotgun into a .22 rifle."

I didn't need a moving picture to see what that meant. "One of these would be very handy," I said, "if someone wanted to fix himself with an unbreakable alibi for a rifle killing by carrying a shotgun."

"You aren't kidding. How'd you know it was Tyler?"

I smiled modestly. What he and Grandfather didn't knew wouldn't hurt them. "Evelyn Deet and I have been working on the case all week," I said. "We found the place where Tyler did some target practice before he used this gadget for real. A farmer saw him there with a shotgun, but Evelyn and I found a .22 cartridge case."

"The devil you did!" Sergeant Reichel exclaimed.

Grandfather had followed us, and he was listening very quietly. "The sheriff has the cartridge case," I went on. "We figured Tyler wouldn't try a murder without testing the gadget first, so we looked for the place he tested it."

We went back upstairs. The troopers had Tyler handcuffed, but obviously he had a king-sized headache and was too dazed to give them any trouble. They seemed less certain of how to handle Evelyn Deet, who had walked ever to Tyler and was staring up at him.

Suddenly she screamed, "You crud! You murdered my dad!" And burst into tears.

The police seemed to think she was my problem, since I'd brought her, so I hurried her out of there and took her home.

Saturday afternoon, when Grandfather walked ever to Main Street to borrow Mr. Snubbs's morning paper, I telephoned Sergeant Reichel. "Grandfather's so mad about my getting there first that he isn't speaking to me," I told him. "There are a couple of things I'd like to knew."

"As long as you keep it in the family," he said. "That was a good piece of work you did. The farmer couldn't identify Tyler, but we may be able to prove the cartridge case was used in the adapter, and we get a lovely cast that matches one of Tyler's tire treads."

"Tell me this. How'd Grandfather get onto that adapter business?"

"Last summer John Deet loaned him a copy of a gun magazine. It had an article Deet wanted him to read about how safe it is to go hunting. He didn't read the article, but he had a lot of fun looking at the ads, and one of the ads described that adapter. He claims that as soon as he heard about John Deet's death he knew Tyler did it and how, and after that it was only a matter of finding the evidence."

"What was all that fa-de-la about John Deet's Christmas list?"

"Your Grandfather's hunch was that Deet gave Tyler a subscription to the magazine with the ad in it – which he did, though it was a birthday present. The dealer had only one recent order for an adapter from this part of the state, and that turned out to be from Tyler using an assumed name in care of General Delivery in Jackson. He was so eager to get his hands on the gadget that he went up there twice to ask about it before it arrived. The post office clerk didn't have any trouble identifying him."

"How'd the second adapter come into it?" I asked.

"Well we had a good case, but we figured it'd be better if we found out what he did with the adapter after he used it. We had the dealer airmail another one to Jackson, and your Grandfather filed a change of address in Jackson for Tyler's assumed name so the thing would be forwarded in care of James Tyler, Wiston. It arrived yesterday, and Tyler must have flipped his lid trying to figure out how the Jackson post office identified him. We hoped he'd dispose of it where he did the other one – bury it in his back yard or something. We had no notion that he'd planted the first one in Carse's house, and even if we'd had we wouldn't have expected him to go completely off his rocker and take the other one there, too."

"Was he really trying to frame Ben Carse?"

"He was and he lost his nerve, or he was laying the groundwork for it just in case he was suspected himself. Not that it would have mattered. Those adapters are coated with a special oil, and we found traces of it in the pocket of the hunting jacket he borrowed from John Deet. We got a real good case."

"Sure," I said. "Why'd he kill his partner and ruin his business?"

"Because the business was already ruined. Deet looked after the front of the store. Tyler looked after the back, which included the office, and he stole so much that the store was virtually bankrupt. Deet wanted to hire an auditor to go ever the books and tell them why they weren't making money. Tyler knew he'd go to jail, so he stalled Deet off until hunting season and planned a murder. He thought he'd be able to conceal the thefts in the confusion that would follow. When they split up at that thicket, he inserted the adapter, circled around behind Deet, and shot him."

"Sure," I said. "Now tell me again how Grandfather knew Tyler did it as soon as he heard Deet was dead."

He laughed. "I haven't told you that. I've wondered about it myself. Why don't you ask your Grandfather?"

"It wouldn't do any good," I said disgustedly. "He'd just say that he asked himself the right question."

But I did ask him. As soon as he get back from Main Street, I said, "Look – I've got everything else figured out. Just tell me how come you knew right away that John Deet had been murdered and Tyler did it."

"I asked myself the right question," he said.

I started feeling around for something to threw at him, and he chuckled and said, "Law enforcement officers ought to use their eyes and ears. When a man is shot, whether it looks accidental or not, the first question has to be – did anyone in the immediate vicinity have a reason for wanting him dead?"

"And you knew Tyler had a reason?"

"The Tylers have been living well, they have that expensive new house, they have money to invest, and Mrs. Tyler can't say enough about how well the store was doing. The Deets weren't able to afford a new house, and Mrs. Deet knew her husband was worried about the store. The first thing she did after he died was hire a lawyer to see what could be saved. Anyone who knew the two families well had to be aware that something was haywire, because one partner was prospering and the other wasn't."

"I think you've got it wrong," I told him. "It isn't asking the right question that's so important. It's knowing the right answer."

THE FACE IS FAMILIAR

The Borgville Bank was held up in 1937, which was a long time before I was born. If that makes you think I don't remember anything about it, you're wrong. Everyone in Borgville remembers the bank robbery. People have been talking about it ever since, and I could describe it just as well as the old timers who saw it happen.

Until yesterday, that bank robbery was the most important thing that ever happened in our town. Every state trooper in this corner of the state converged on Borgville. Sheriff Pilkins, who then was a brash young sheriff, swore in seventeen deputies, which was only one less than he had yesterday. The village president asked the governor to call out the National Guard. Not only was it an exciting afternoon, but the bank failed a week later because of the robbery, and just about everyone in this part of Borg County lost money. It made an impression on people.

The F.B.I. and the State Police were in and out of Borgville for weeks afterward, and my Grandfather Rastin was one of the star witnesses. The people in the bank didn't see the robber very well, because he kept his hat down and his coat pulled up over his face, but Grandfather saw him driving away, and he got a good look at him. The F.B.I. brought him stacks of pictures to look at, to see if he could identify the robber. He couldn't, and the robber never got caught, and the bank never got its ten thousand dollars back.

It was a nice thing for Grandfather, though. He's always been an independent sort of person, and because Borgville is a solid Republican town, Grandfather naturally became a Democrat and didn't care who knew it. People were a little suspicious of him until he saw the bank robber and got to be such an important person.

To understand what happened in Borgville yesterday, you have to know just how the town felt about that bank robbery. Folks have been talking about it ever since it happened, and ever since 1937 Grandfather has been saying maybe twice a week that he'd recognize the robber if he ever saw him again. Grandfather never forgets a face.

Grandfather left the house at one o'clock yesterday afternoon and walked over to Main Street. He stopped in at Snubbs's Hardware Store and borrowed Mr. Snubb's morning paper, went across the street to the bench in front of Jake Palmer's barber shop and sat down in the sun to read. Except for Grandfather's liking to sit in the sun for awhile of an afternoon, his being past eighty is hardly noticeable. He was a blacksmith when he was a young man, and he's still built like one. He hasn't a gray hair on his head because he hasn't any hair on his head. According to Mom, he's a lot spryer than I am. His eyes are as sharp as they ever were, and he still never forgets a face.

Nat Barlow was sitting there with Grandfather, in front of the barber shop, and when a stranger drove up and parked, Nat nudged Grandfather and asked, "Who's that?"

Grandfather looked over the top of his paper and said, "That's the bank robber," and went on reading.

Nat grabbed Grandfather's arm and shouted, "Are you sure?"

And Grandfather said, "Of course I'm sure. I never forget a face."

Nat jumped up and ran into the barber shop. There were five or six men in there, talking with Jake, and Nat pointed at the stranger and said, "That's the bank robber!"

Those men tore out the back door of the shop, Nat with them, and Jake pulled down the curtain in the front window and hung up the "CLOSED" sign and locked the door. And in ten minutes everyone in Borgville knew that the bank robber had come back.

I was over at the Borgville Pharmacy having a chocolate malted and talking with Mollie Adams. I'd been dating Mollie – I hadn't had a chance, yet, to find out how emotionally unstable she was – and someone called in through the back door that the bank robber was back in town and coming our way.

Mollie and I were still staring at each other when the stranger walked in. I thought it couldn't possibly be the insolent young man I'd heard described so often – and then I remembered that he'd be thirty-six years older, now. He was nattily dressed and trim looking, but there were streaks of gray in his hair, and the bags under his eyes had been there longer than overnight. He looked as if he'd been good looking, once, and he thought he still was. He winked at Mollie and said, "Hi, girlie. Got any cigarettes?"

Mollie had a lemon-meringue pie on the counter that she'd just started to cut, and she picked it up and threw it at the stranger. He was ten feet from her, but it smacked him squarely in the face, and Mollie ran out the back door and stood in the alley screaming.

The stranger grabbed some paper napkins from the counter and started wiping pie off his face and clothing. I'd like to tell you what he said, but we don't hear that kind of language very often in Borgville, and I probably wouldn't get it right.

He cleaned himself off as well as he could, and then he walked out. Next door to the pharmacy is the Borgville Garage, which is an extension of the Borgville Service Station. The service entrance was open, and the stranger saw a cigarette machine near the door. He walked in and started fumbling in his pocket for change.

Bob Adams was there, working on my jalopy, and of course someone had told him that the bank robber was in town. Bob didn't ask questions. He had a wrench in his hand, and he threw it. This wasn't such a good idea, because the wrench was heavy and Bob's hand was greasy. The wrench didn't go anywhere near the stranger. It broke the windshield on Doc Beyers' new Cadillac, and Bob crawled under my jalopy and stayed there until all the excitement was over.

The stranger ducked out of the garage and walked on down the street to the Star Restaurant. Old Mr. Gregory was standing behind the counter at the cash register. The stranger said, "Got any cigarettes?" Mr. Gregory dropped out of sight and crawled away on his hands and knees, and when the stranger walked up and looked over the counter there wasn't anyone there.

Things were happening all over Borgville. Mr. Hanson, the bank president, sent the teller to the basement, and hung the *BANK CLOSED – LEGAL HOLIDAY* sign in the door, and locked it. He locked the time vault and the back door, too. Then he found a stack of money in the teller's cage that he'd forgot to put in the vault. He was running in circles trying to figure out what to do when Fred Dimmit came down the alley to the back door with a bag full of money.

Fred had dumped all of Dimmit's Grocery Store's money into the bag, and he brought it to the bank because the bank's money was insured and his wasn't. He pounded on the back door and shouted, "Let me in! I want to make a deposit!" Mr. Hanson shouted back at him, "The bank is closed!" They were still pounding and shouting at each other when the State Police got there.

Sheriff Pilkins was one of the first to hear about the bank robber coming back, and the sheriff prides himself on being a pretty smart man. He said to himself, "Why try to catch him up town, and destroy a lot of property, and maybe get some people shot? Why not set up a road block and capture him when he tries to leave?"

The sheriff radioed a call to the State Police, and then he collected a lot of guns and swore in as many deputies as he could find and went out to the south end of town to set up a road block.

Karl Schmidt came along in his tractor, pulling a trailer load of corn to the Farm Bureau, and the sheriff stopped him and upset the trailer across the road and blocked off one shoulder with the tractor. Then he stopped Mike Wilkins and told him to put his Model T on the other shoulder. Mike didn't have much in the way of brakes, and the Model T slipped down into the ditch. Mike says his Model T hasn't run the same since then, and he's threatening to sue the sheriff for a new one.

The stranger didn't know anything about this, of course. He came out of the Star Restaurant and hurried back up Main Street toward his car. People were peeking out of windows and doors to watch him, but Grandfather was the only person in sight. He was still sitting on the bench in front of the barber shop, reading the paper. The stranger walked up and started to talk to him.

Just then Mrs. Pobloch, who lives up above the barber shop, stuck her husband's shot gun out the window and pulled the trigger. She said afterward she wasn't trying to hit anything – she just wanted to scare the robber away. She certainly did that. The blast went across the street and broke the window of Snubbs's Hardware Store, and the stranger tore back to his car and drove off. He was all the way to the edge of town before he got out of second.

Unfortunately for Sheriff Pilkins, he drove out of town to the north, so the sheriff's road block didn't do any good. The only thing it accomplished was to make the State Police waste about ten minutes at the south edge of town while they waited for the sheriff to get Karl Schmidt's trailer off the road. The sheriff said later that in the excitement he was thinking North Borgville Road still dead-ended on Manning's pasture. He forgot all about the new super-highway that went through there last year.

As soon as the stranger left, a mob of people hurried out to crowd around Grandfather, which made him plenty mad. He said it was a fine thing when a man couldn't sit in the sun and read the paper without folks standing around staring and asking silly questions. Everyone wanted to know what the stranger had said, and Grandfather told them,

"He asked me if everybody in this town is crazy, and I asked him what he expected from a town full of Republicans."

That was all we could get out of Grandfather. When the State Police finally got there and asked him about the bank robber, Grandfather said, "What bank robber?" They kept asking him questions until he got disgusted and went home.

Things were kind of mixed up after that. People stood around arguing about what kind of car the stranger had, and what color it was, and what he looked like. The only ones who'd got a close look at him, other than Grandfather, were Mollie and I. Mollie was too hysterical to remember anything, and I decided to play dumb. I said that the only time I saw him he had pie on his face, so of course I wouldn't recognize him if I saw him again unless someone had just hit him with a lemon-meringue pie.

The State Police would have agreed with the stranger about everyone in Borgville being crazy if it hadn't been for Mr. Snubbs and Jeff Morgan.

When Mr. Snubbs heard that the bank robber was back, he peeked out the door of his hardware store and wrote down the stranger's license number.

And Jeff Morgan, who sinks just about every penny he gets ahold of into photographic stuff, went up to his sister's apartment above the bank with his camera and one of those telescope things and got half a dozen good shots of the stranger walking down Main Street. He was back in his dark room developing them before the stranger left Borgville.

Most of us didn't know anything about that, and after the State Police left, folks went back to whatever they'd been doing, and by the time the reporters got there, most of Borgville had decided to forget the whole thing. The reporters couldn't find anyone who was willing to answer questions.

I followed Grandfather home and found him sitting on the front porch. He was acting grumpy, but I thought that was because he hadn't got to finish his paper while the sun was right.

"What was all the excitement about?" he asked.

"You should know," I told him. "Ever since 1937 you've been saying you'd recognize that bank robber if you ever saw him again, and naturally people got upset when you said he was back."

"Oh," Grandfather said. "That bank robber."

"What bank robber did you think it was?" I asked.

The only answer I got was a couple of grunts, so I went in the house. Five minutes later Nat Barlow came along. He started shouting when he was still half a block down the street. "Lookee here, Bill Rastin, you know derned well you told me that fellow was the bank robber!"

Grandfather didn't say anything, and Nat stormed up on the porch and stood there with his fists clenched. He's a frail old man, and if Grandfather had uttered a good, loud sneeze it would have knocked him over, but he was mad enough to fight.

"What fellow?" Grandfather asked.

"Why, that fellow –"

Grandfather picked up the paper and opened it up in that lordly way he has when he's riled about something.

"Look," he said. "See that picture? Bank robber, it says. This fellow robbed a bank down in Mississippi, it says. You *can* read, can't you? I was reading the paper. Right here, I was reading, and you said, 'Who's that?' and I said, 'That's the bank robber.' Now take a good look. Isn't it the bank robber? Read it. Doesn't it say he's the bank robber?"

Nat stared at that picture for maybe five minutes, and then he turned around and stomped down the porch steps. He went around the house and out the back gate and sneaked home down the alley.

Grandfather tossed the paper aside and went upstairs to his room, and as soon as his door closed I tore out to the porch to get that paper. I took a good look at the picture of the bank robber, and then I went upstairs to see Grandfather. He was sitting in the rocking chair in the corner of his room. Usually he rocks about sixty per, but this time he was just sitting there.

"There's something funny here," I said. "This paper – it's today's paper, but pages three and four and nine and ten are dated two weeks ago."

Grandfather took the paper and examined it carefully. He looked confused, which for him is definitely not normal. "Just like those city slickers to try to peddle their old papers in Borgville," he said. "Snubbs ought to get his money back."

"I'll tell him about it," I said. I tucked the paper under my arm and started for the door.

"Ah – Johnny," Grandfather said. "I wouldn't bother Snubbs about this. As long as he didn't notice it –"

"Okay," I said. "I won't say anything."

I stood outside his door for a moment, waiting for the rocking chair to start up, but nothing happened.

If you've read today's papers you know how the State Police caught up with that stranger a hundred miles upstate, and how they chased him for miles and finally cornered him at a road block, and how they found he was one Walter Donaldson, wanted by the F.B.I. for a bank robbery over in Illinois last month and quite a few other things. That was quite a confession they got out of him, and of course one of the things he mentioned was that he robbed the Borgville bank back in 1937, when he was just a kid, and he'd gone back to Borgville yesterday to look the place over and see if he could do it again.

The reporters started coming before we were out of bed this morning, and they kept coming. They filled the living room, and I went up half a dozen times to try and get Grandfather down to talk to them. He was still sitting in his rocking chair, looking as if he'd been there all night, and I couldn't make him budge. And when one of the reporters sneaked around to the kitchen door and up the back stairway, Grandfather threw two pairs of shoes at him and chased him back down the stairs.

Quite a few of our neighbors dropped in during the morning, excited about the State Police catching the bank robber and wanting to talk about it, so *they* talked with the reporters and told them how Grandfather had been the only person to get a good look at the bank robber back in 1937, and how he kept saying for thirty-six years that he'd know him if he ever saw him again, and how he'd recognized the stranger the minute he drove up and told Nat Barlow it was the bank robber. Nat was there, too, grinning and nodding his head, and the reporters seemed to think it was a pretty good story. I dug up a snap shot of Grandfather and took the negative over to Jeff Morgan, and he made prints for all the reporters.

When I got home, Mom was sitting in the kitchen, worrying because Grandfather hadn't come down for breakfast. He wouldn't come down to lunch, either, though he ate what I took up to him. And when I took him the afternoon papers to show him the big story and his picture on page one, and how they were saying he might get a reward, he shoved me out of his bedroom and threw the papers out after me.

"What is the matter with him?" I asked Morn. "He ought to be proud of himself. *I'm* proud of him."

Mom looked sad and a little worried. "I think it would be best. If we don't say any more about this," she said. "You see, this man Donaldson was quite young when he robbed the bank. Your Grandfather recognized him as soon as he saw him, yesterday, but when he got a closer look at him he was shocked to see how much older the man looked. Your Grandfather hasn't seemed to notice that the people he sees every day are getting older, and he can't understand how that young bank robber can be a man almost sixty. He doesn't want to admit that it's possible, and it has him worried. He's started thinking about how old he's getting himself."

"All right," I said. "I won't mention it again."

I went out and sat on the porch, and for the first time in my life I felt sorry for Grandfather. I finally understood what he was doing up there in his bedroom, sitting in his rocking chair and not rocking. He was looking in the bureau mirror.

SOURCES

"The Knave of Hearts," first published in this collection, copyright © 2007 by Kenneth Lloyd Biggle and Donna Biggle Emerson

"The Phantom Thief," first published in *Ellery Queen's Mystery Magazine*, May, 1968, as "Grandfather and the Phantom Thief," copyright 1968, by Davis Publications, Inc.

"The Mother Goose Murder," first published in *Ellery Queen's Mystery Magazine*, January, 1972, as "Grandfather and the Little Bone," copyright © 1971, by Lloyd Biggle, Jr.

"A Matter of Friendship," first published in this collection, copyright © 2007 by Kenneth Lloyd Biggle and Donna Biggle Emerson

"The Fabulous Fiddle," first published in *Ellery Queen's Mystery Magazine*, May, 1963, as "Have You a Fortune in Your Attic?" Copyright © 1963, by Davis Publications, Inc.

"The Gentle Swindler," first published in *Ellery Queen's Mystery Magazine*, February, 1960, as "Grandfather and the Gentle Swindler," copyright © 1959, by Davis Publications, Inc.

"The Great Horseshoe Mystery" first published in *Ellery Queen's Mystery Magazine*, April, 1962, copyright © 1962, by Davis Publications, Inc.; included in *Ellery Queen's 1968 Anthology*, edited by Ellery Queen

"The Pair of Knaves," first published in *Ellery Queen's Mystery Magazine*, October, 1965, as "The Labor Day Mystery," copyright © 1965, by Davis Publications, Inc., included in *Best Detective Stories of the Year, 21st Series*, edited by Anthony Boucher

"The Automation Mystery," first published in *Ellery Queen's Mystery Magazine*, August, 1969, as "Grandfather and the Automation Mystery," copyright © 1969, by Davis Publication, Inc.

"A Case of Heredity," first published in *Ellery Queen's Mystery Magazine*, June, 1959, copyright © 1959, by Davis Publications, Inc.

"The Unmurdered Professor," first published in *Ellery Queen's Mystery Magazine*, November, 1964, as "The Great Alma Mater Mystery," copyright © 1964, by Davis Publication, Inc.

"The Lesser Thing," first published in *Ellery Queen's Mystery Magazine*,

August, 1960, as "Grandfather Predicts a Murder," copyright © 1960, by Davis Publications, Inc.

"The Unasked Question," first published in *Ellery Queen's Mystery Magazine*, October, 1971, as "Grandfather and the Right Question," copyright © 1971, by Lloyd Biggle, Jr.

"The Face Is Familiar," first published in *Alfred Hitchcock's Mystery Magazine*, August, 1957, as "The Greatest Robbery on Earth," copyright © 1957, by H.S.D. Publications.

The Grandfather Rastin Mysteries

The Grandfather Rastin Mysteries by Lloyd Biggle, Jr., with an introduction by Kenneth Biggle and Donna Biggle Emerson, is set in Baskerville and printed on 60 pound Natural acid-free paper. The cover illustration is by Barbara Mitchell, and the Lost Classics design is by Deborah Miller. *The Grandfather Rastin Mysteries* was published in March 2007 by Crippen & Landru Publishers, Norfolk, Virginia.

CRIPPEN & LANDRU, PUBLISHERS
P. O. Box 9315, Norfolk, VA 23505
E-mail: info@crippenlandru.com; toll-free 877 622-6656
Web: www.crippenlandru.com

LOST CLASSICS

Crippen & Landru is proud to publish a series of *new* short-story collections by great authors who specialized in traditional mysteries. Each book collects stories from crumbling pages of old pulp, digest, and slick magazines, and most of the stories have been "lost" since their first publication. The following books are in print:

The Newtonian Egg and Other Cases of Rolf le Roux by Peter Godfrey, introduction by Ronald Godfrey. 2002.

Murder, Mystery and Malone by Craig Rice, edited by Jeffrey A. Marks. 2002.

The Sleuth of Baghdad: The Inspector Chafik Stories, by Charles B. Child. 2002.

Hildegarde Withers: Uncollected Riddles by Stuart Palmer, introduction by Mrs. Stuart Palmer. 2002.

The Spotted Cat and Other Mysteries from Inspector Cockrill's Casebook by Christianna Brand, edited by Tony Medawar. 2002.

Marksman and Other Stories by William Campbell Gault, edited by Bill Pronzini; afterword by Shelley Gault. 2003.

Karmesin: The World's Greatest Criminal – Or Most Outrageous Liar by Gerald Kersh, edited by Paul Duncan. 2003.

The Complete Curious Mr. Tarrant by C. Daly King, introduction by Edward D. Hoch. 2003.

The Pleasant Assassin and Other Cases of Dr. Basil Willing by Helen McCloy, introduction by B.A. Pike. 2003.

Murder – All Kinds by William L. DeAndrea, introduction by Jane Haddam. 2003.

The Avenging Chance and Other Mysteries from Roger Sheringham's Casebook by Anthony Berkeley, edited by Tony Medawar and Arthur Robinson. 2004.

Banner Deadlines: The Impossible Files of Senator Brooks U. Banner by

Joseph Commings, edited by Robert Adey; memoir by Edward D. Hoch. 2004.

The Danger Zone and Other Stories by Erle Stanley Gardner, edited by Bill Pronzini. 2004.

Dr. Poggioli: Criminologist by T.S. Stribling, edited by Arthur Vidro. 2004.

The Couple Next Door: Collected Short Mysteries by Margaret Millar, edited by Tom Nolan. 2004.

Sleuth's Alchemy: Cases of Mrs. Bradley and Others by Gladys Mitchell, edited by Nicholas Fuller. 2005.

Who Was Guilty? Two Dime Novels by Philip S. Warne/Howard W. Macy, edited by Marlena E. Bremseth. 2005.

Slot-Machine Kelly: The Collected Private Eye Cases of the One-Armed Bandit by Dennis Lynds writing as Michael Collins, introduction by Robert J. Randisi. 2005.

The Evidence of the Sword by Rafael Sabatini, edited by Jesse Knight. 2006.

The Detections of Francis Quarles by Julian Symons, edited by John Cooper; afterword by Kathleen Symons. 2006.

The Casebook of Sidney Zoom by Erle Stanley Gardner, edited by Bill Pronzini. 2006.

The Trinity Cat and Other Mysteries by Ellis Peters (Edith Pargeter), edited by Martin Edwards and Sue Feder. 2006.

The Grandfather Rastin Mysteries by Lloyd Biggle, Jr., introduction by Kenneth Lloyd Biggle and Donna Biggle Emerson. 2007.

FORTHCOMING LOST CLASSICS

Max Brand, *Masquerade: Ten Crime Stories*, edited by William F. Nolan, Jr.

Hugh Pentecost, *The Battles of Jericho*, introduction by S.T. Karnick.

Mignon G. Eberhart, *Dead Yesterday and Other Mysteries*, edited by Rick Cypert and Kirby McCauley.

Victor Canning, *The Minerva Club, The Department of Patterns and Other Stories*, edited by John Higgins.

Elizabeth Ferrars, *The Casebook of Jonas P. Jonas and Others*, edited by John Cooper.

Anthony Boucher and Denis Green, *The Casebook of Gregory Hood*, edited by Joe R. Christopher.

Philip Wylie, *Ten Thousand Blunt Instruments*, edited by Bill Pronzini.
Erle Stanley Gardner, *The Adventures of Señor Lobo*, edited by Bill Pronzini.

SUBSCRIPTIONS

Crippen & Landru offers discounts to individuals and institutions who place Standing Order Subscriptions for its forthcoming publications, either all the Regular Series or all the Lost Classics or (preferably) both. Collectors can thereby guarantee receiving limited editions, and readers won't miss any favorite stories. Standing Order Subscribers receive a specially commissioned story in a deluxe edition as a gift at the end of the year. Please write or e-mail for more details.